A WEB OF SILK

A Selection of Recent Titles by Fiona Buckley

The Ursula Blanchard mysteries

THE ROBSART MYSTERY
THE DOUBLET AFFAIR
QUEEN'S RANSOM
TO RUIN A QUEEN
QUEEN OF AMBITION
A PAWN FOR THE QUEEN
THE FUGITIVE QUEEN
THE SIREN QUEEN
QUEEN WITHOUT A CROWN *
QUEEN'S BOUNTY *
A RESCUE FOR A QUEEN *
A TRAITOR'S TEARS *
A PERILOUS ALLIANCE *
THE HERETIC'S CREED *
A DEADLY BETROTHAL *
THE RELUCTANT ASSASSIN *
A WEB OF SILK *

* available from Severn House

A WEB OF SILK

An Ursula Blanchard mystery

Fiona Buckley

CRÈME de la CRIME

This first world edition published 2019
in Great Britain and the USA by
Crème de la Crime an imprint of
SEVERN HOUSE PUBLISHERS LTD of
Eardley House, 4 Uxbridge Street, London W8 7SY.
Trade paperback edition first published
in Great Britain and the USA 2019 by
SEVERN HOUSE PUBLISHERS LTD.

British Library Cataloguing in Publication Data
A CIP catalogue record for this title is available from the British Library.

ISBN-13: 978-1-78029-113-0 (cased)
ISBN-13: 978-1-78029-593-0 (trade paper)
ISBN-13: 978-1-4483-0205-5 (e-book)

Typeset by Palimpsest Book Production Ltd.,
Falkirk, Stirlingshire, Scotland.

ONE

The Deceptive Calm

I n Hawkswood village, a mile or so from my home at Hawkswood House in the county of Surrey, stands the parish church, St Mary's. It is a beautiful building. Its stone walls keep it cool in summer and shut out the bitter winds of winter, and it has the serene atmosphere that churches acquire when people have prayed in them for generations.

My late husband Hugh always took an interest in the church, and although neither he nor his father were legally required to pay for repairs and innovations, they very often did. I kept up the custom and in the year 1582, at the request of the current vicar, Dr Joynings, I arranged for a hitching rail outside, to discourage those worshippers who come from a distance from tying their mounts to the vicarage fence. But the hitching rail was not my only innovation that year. I had one of the stained-glass windows replaced, as well.

Its stained-glass windows are one of St Mary's great beauties. They are of a good size but are set higher than in most churches, because the medieval founder wanted wall space below for frescoes. During the fiercely anti-Papist reign of the boy-king Edward, the stained glass escaped harm but the frescoes were condemned and limewashed out. What remains are white inner walls with stained-glass windows looking down from a height. In my opinion, and also that of Dr Joynings, in the case of one of them this was just as well because it was a Judgement Window and it was a remarkably lurid, not to say gruesome, depiction of Doomsday. Even so, people did look up at the windows at times. Indeed some well-meaning parents drew their children's attention to the Judgement Window, and some of the children had been upset by it. So eventually I got rid of it. But how that came about is a grim story.

Grim events have often featured in my life. Those of 1582 are a typical example. Whenever I seemed to have settled into the quiet life I wanted, it always dissolved into catastrophe, usually because of the orders that I now and then received from Queen Elizabeth or her ministers, which were apt to precipitate me into hair-raising situations.

Long ago, when I was a young and almost penniless widow with few advantages beyond some good connections, I had joined Elizabeth's court as one of her ladies, and in order to earn a little extra money I undertook a secret mission. Then another. And another. And so on. Now, in later life and no longer short of money, I would have liked to stop undertaking them. But it didn't work out like that.

For one thing, I had discovered who my father was. Until well into my adult life I simply knew that my mother, who had been one of Queen Anne Boleyn's ladies, had been sent home from court in disgrace when she was found to be with child. Only long after my mother's death did I learn from other sources that my father was King Henry the Eighth. I was Elizabeth's half-sister. And from then on, there was a special bond between us.

Now, when she or her chief counsellors – Sir William Cecil (otherwise Lord Burghley) and Sir Francis Walsingham, her spymaster – asked me to carry out secret tasks for them, I could not bring myself to refuse.

On that lazy August afternoon in 1582, everything seemed calm. Hawkswood House was basking in warm sunshine. In the courtyard, which was also the stable yard, doves were happily pecking up the scattering of oats that one of the grooms had spilled when carrying feed to the horses. My two half-mastiff dogs, Freya and Prince, were snoozing outside their kennels and my tabby cat, Whiskers, was lolling in the sun on the tack-room roof. To the south, in the distance, I could see a range of low hills draped with fields of grass and corn and deep-green woodland. The world was all green and gold, and I could almost believe I could hear it purring.

My household were somewhere about. A thin column of smoke from the kitchen chimney suggested that, although supper time was still far away, my cook, John Hawthorn, and his chief assistant, Ben Flood, were making plans for it, and from an open upper window came the sound of a lute. Master Peter Dickson, the elderly but scholarly man who was now tutor to my ten-year-old son Harry, was a proficient musician and Harry had lately shown quite a talent for music himself. Master Dickson was encouraging him.

Of my closest associates in the house, my manservant Roger Brockley and his wife, Fran Dale, who was my maid, had retired to their own quarters for an afternoon sleep, and my friend and companion Sybil Jester was in the great hall, busy with another of the embroidery designs she was so skilled at creating. I was very fond of Sybil. She was older than me, a widow who for her own good reasons had no wish to remarry. Sybil had an unusual face, a little compressed between brow and chin, so that her eyebrows and mouth were long and her nostrils a little splayed. These features were not unduly marked and in fact were oddly attractive, as were her dark eyes and her plentiful hair, pure white now at the temples but apart from that a warm, dark brown.

I was much less fond of Gladys Morgan, who was my other close associate. Gladys was an aged and sometimes maddening hanger-on of mine, whom I had acquired by mistake when, during a visit to Wales, Brockley and I rescued her from a charge of witchcraft. I thought that, like the Brockleys, she was probably asleep.

I had no idea where the maidservants were, but I wouldn't have been surprised to learn that they were taking a brief afternoon rest as well. I had no objection, there was little for them to do just now and my steward, Adam Wilder, who I knew was in his office, his grey head bent over his ever-meticulous accounts, would rouse them in due course.

As for me, I was sitting by the window of my favourite parlour, trying to read a book of verse. But I was too much at ease and too contented to concentrate, and was gazing at the hills instead.

Then, suddenly, Freya and Prince were awake, up on their feet and barking, and Whiskers was sitting up to see why. Hooves were clattering through the arched gate of the courtyard and there, on a splendid blue roan gelding, with a groom riding on a bay mare behind him, was a tall, familiar figure. Magically, my senior groom, Arthur Watts, appeared to greet him, eagerly pursued by my youngest groom, Eddie, who had seen the blue roan before and thought it was wonderful, and hoped for the honour of unsaddling and grooming it. There, too, came Adam Wilder, also hurrying out to meet the new arrivals, bearing himself with his usual dignity, although I could see that he was hastily wiping ink off his fingers with a handkerchief.

I got to my feet and took myself into the great hall, knowing that Wilder would bring my visitor there first. I found Sybil looking out of the window that faced the courtyard. 'It's the Earl of Leicester!' she said.

The Earl of Leicester – Sir Robert Dudley, the queen's Sweet Robin and her Master of Horse – known to a good many of her jealous and competitive courtiers as 'the Gipsy', because of his dark hair and eyes, his swarthy countenance and his persuasive manners. He had at times been the subject of slanderous gossip, including a rumour that he had murdered his first wife, Amy, in the hope of thereby becoming free to marry Elizabeth herself; and a further rumour that he and Elizabeth were lovers, anyway. I had good reason to know that neither of these rumours was true, but for many years I had nevertheless disliked and distrusted him. He was handsome and highly attractive, but I was aware of these things without being moved by them (it is possible to notice when someone is attractive without actually wanting to respond to it).

Initially, I saw him as a man of too much ambition whose father had been executed for treason and who was too close to the queen emotionally to be good for her. Only lately had I grown to realize that he was her friend, a bulwark against the shifting sands and dangerous tides of her political world, who understood her as few others did, and that she would be broken-hearted if anything were to befall him.

I knew how she felt, because I had much the same relationship with my manservant Roger Brockley. Dear, steady Brockley, with his level blue-grey gaze and his gold-freckled forehead, his silent regret over the unwomanly tasks I undertook, and his amazing adventurousness as soon as we were embarked on them. He had once come near to being my lover, but it didn't actually happen and never would. There was nevertheless a link between us that meant a great deal to both of us. In this sense, I was my sister's echo.

Now, I was quite pleased to welcome Leicester to my home, to call Harry from his lute practice to greet our noble visitor as the man of the house should and then, having sent Harry back to his tutor, to sit beside Leicester on the terrace overlooking the rose garden that had once been my husband's delight and enjoy the late-afternoon sunshine.

'When I arrived here this afternoon,' Leicester remarked, 'I felt as if I had disturbed something that was peacefully drowsing in the sun. I have only seen this house once or twice before, but I liked it from my very first visit, especially the soft colour of that light-grey stone and the dormer windows in the roof. How old is it?'

'It was Hugh's family home,' I said. 'Built several generations ago, though I don't know exactly when. I don't think even Hugh did. He did once say that it had been altered and added to at times, which is why it's a slightly unusual shape.'

'It is indeed.' Leicester turned on his bench to look. 'Not many houses have a great hall opening straight on to the stable yard!'

'It was a smaller house once, I believe,' I said. 'Just a farmhouse to begin with. But as Hugh's family prospered the place was gradually enlarged. Although no one ever did anything about the courtyard also being the stable yard, with the hall door opening straight into it, which is convenient in some ways.'

'And yet, despite being altered and added to, the whole thing is harmonious,' said Leicester. 'It struck me like that from the beginning. Or perhaps it was the atmosphere that you and Hugh created. Despite the interruptions.'

'There were certainly interruptions,' I agreed. Then a sudden twinge of unease made me add: 'You haven't said what brings you here so unexpectedly, and not in your coach but on horseback with just one attendant. Your groom is being looked after by my own grooms, of course. Simon and Netta have probably taken him in charge. Netta's one of my maids, and she'll have made sure that the kitchen can produce something for him to eat.'

'I'm Her Majesty's Master of Horse,' said Leicester, 'and a Master of Horse ought to enjoy horseback travel. I do. I would rather be astride my beautiful Blue Leicester than jolting along in a coach. As for what brings me here, because I am the Master of Horse I went to visit a stud on the far side of Guildford, where there are some colts I am interested in, and as Hawkswood is more or less on my way back – I am based at Hampton Court just now – I thought to call and see if the trotting stallion I recommended you to buy last year is doing well. What did you do about the unsatisfactory one you had before him?'

'He wasn't unsatisfactory as a stallion,' I said. I looked ahead, across the rose garden towards the kitchen garden that lay beyond, and the roof of the stud groom's cottage just visible on the far side of that. I was developing a stud of the popular trotters that were so much in demand as showy and fast-paced harness horses. It was to be part of Harry's future inheritance. Its stable and the chief groom's cottage were separate from those belonging to the house.

'That animal was too temperamental,' I explained. 'Thunder sent him wild with panic, and twice he broke out of his stall and caused havoc. He was a fine high-stepping trotter, so we had him altered and found a buyer who wanted a high-stepper to pull a one-horse carriage. His first and only crop of foals were born this year. I just hope they don't inherit his fear of thunder. Maybe a thunderstorm frightened him when he was a foal! I hoped that altering him would calm him down and I warned his buyer, who said he could deal with it. The replacement you found for me seems to be all he should be. My stud groom is pleased with him.'

'I've glanced round your stable,' Leicester said. 'Where's that handsome black mare of yours, Jewel?'

'Last summer,' I said, 'while we were in Warwick Castle, waiting for that trial to begin . . .'

I stopped, not wanting to remember the previous summer and the trial of the conspirators who had kidnapped Harry and tried, by threatening him, to force me into a most terrible act.

Indeed, 1581 had been one of the most terrifying years of my eventful life.

'Go on,' said Leicester. 'Harry is safe now. Those who were a danger to him are either in prison or dead. The ringleader – that innkeeper, Simeon Wilmot – was hanged. Tell me about Jewel.'

'I bought a new horse, Jaunty, so that Brockley could have a really good mount to ride round the country on when he was searching for Harry. He'd had to leave his Firefly behind and get remounts in order to gallop from Hawkswood to Warwickshire. But when it was all over, we didn't want to sell Jaunty – he's a fine animal. And Jewel is such a beauty I thought I'd like a foal from her. The Earl of Warwick advised me about finding a suitable sire and I had her mated. She's out at grass now, with a delightful filly foal beside her, and she's in foal again.'

'You don't like talking about what happened last year, I can see that,' Leicester said. 'Small blame to you. But it has reminded me of something. Have you met your new neighbour, Giles Frost, yet?'

'Giles Frost? Who is he?'

'Do you know Knoll House, a few miles south of Guildford?'

'I've seen it,' I said. 'It's a striking house, up on that hilltop. I've only seen it from a distance, though. I asked Wilder about it once – he was born in this locality and knows every house for miles. He told me its name, but I don't know who lives there now.'

'Giles Frost has just bought it – from me, actually. It was left to me by a distant cousin. Frost used to live in the Midlands. But he was enquiring about properties in Surrey, and the Council were pleased as it would put him in a handier position. I managed to encourage him into becoming my tenant. I wasn't sure if I'd succeed as Knoll House isn't particularly attractive – it's creaky, ill-lit and draughty. But I offered him appealing terms and he agreed. He's a widower but has daughters, and he said they could sharpen their housekeeping skills on improving the place.'

'Why has talking about last year reminded you of him?' I asked. 'And why do the Council want him to move to Surrey?'

'Last year and Giles Frost are both part of the uneasy world of Catholic against Protestant, with Philip of Spain and Mary Stuart the two most dangerous people in it,' said Leicester. 'Frost is Catholic, though he keeps the law about attending Protestant church services. He's a merchant whose goods are of high quality, and is permitted to show them at court sometimes. But we have learned that he gets paid by Philip of Spain for sending useful snippets of information to him. Walsingham,' said Leicester, stretching his long legs, 'has had an eye on him for some time. Walsingham seems to have eyes and ears everywhere!'

'I know,' I said. I did know. Via his web of agents, Walsingham received reports on all manner of people.

'We put a watch on Frost,' said Leicester, 'and know that he only passes on snippets. He doesn't have the contacts for anything more. He's a minnow, not a shark, and doesn't do much harm. The Council has therefore agreed to leave him in place and see if he can be used to transmit inaccurate information to Spain.'

'I see.' My uneasy feeling had increased. The warm afternoon was still there, wrapping me round with comfort and ease, as if I was in a hammock, a gentle breeze stirring the leaves of the rose bushes. But I was no longer at peace. 'Why do you want to talk about this man Frost?' I asked.

'I thought you might be interested. You're quite likely to come across him socially – now he's settled into Knoll House he'll no doubt want to meet his new neighbours.'

'Oh,' I said.

I found I was twisting my hands together in my lap. I deliberately relaxed them. It was all right. Surely it was all right. For a moment I had imagined that Leicester had dragged the unknown Giles Frost into the conversation on purpose. But no, I didn't think so. Leicester wasn't here to inveigle me into another alarming tour of duty. He was just gossiping.

'It's so pleasant, sitting in the sunshine and exchanging news like this,' I said lightly. 'You're staying the night, of course? You'd only have to put up at an inn if you started off for Hampton Court now, and I can smell something tasty in the kitchen. I mentioned chicken pie to my cook this morning and I think he's taken me at my word.'

'Indeed, I was hoping to stay. What other news have I for you? Have you seen your former ward and her husband, Kate and Christopher Spelton, lately? They may have come across Master Frost since their farm is only three miles or so distant from Knoll House.'

'I haven't heard from them lately, no,' I said.

'Christopher has applied to resume his former duties as a Queen's Messenger and occasional agent,' said Leicester casually. 'Apparently they are having a difficult time. They've probably lost their entire wheat harvest for this year, through wheat rust.'

'Wheat rust? Yes, I've heard of it,' I said. 'It's a disease that can attack a maturing crop. I'm so sorry. I must get in touch with them. They have a little girl and a new baby.'

'Yes. Spelton has responsibilities these days,' said Leicester. He looked up at the sky. 'Time is getting on. Before supper, I would like to visit your stud and see for myself that the stallion I recommended you to buy is in good health and meeting with the approval of his grooms.'

'He's met with the approval of the mares,' I said.

Leicester laughed and got to his feet. It was all right. There was no need for the troubled, sinking feeling down in my stomach. He had only come to see if his recommendation had turned out well and have a harmless gossip. There was nothing in that to worry me.

Yet still, the soft, warm green world around me was not quite as beguiling as it had been a little earlier that afternoon. I knew I was being unreasonable, but I felt as if somehow a shadow had fallen.

TWO
Queen's Messenger

B efore supper, Leicester duly inspected my stud and learned from my stud groom, Laurence Miller, that the new stallion – a good-looking chestnut with a satisfactorily high action, which I hoped he would pass to his progeny – was well cared for and performing as he should. His first crop of foals would be born next year. Then Leicester joined us at supper, and afterwards I played the spinet for him and Harry demonstrated how well he could play the lute. The next day dawned clear and sunny and Leicester, having broken his fast with us in the hall, mounted his Blue Leicester and rode away, attended by his groom, to rejoin the court at Hampton Court.

I stood in the hall doorway to see him out of sight, and when he was gone I put him from my mind, for there were, as ever, numerous things to attend to. I wanted to talk to Peter Dickson about Harry's studies. Harry was not good at figures but if he were ever to be master of Hawkswood he would have to understand accounts. Also, I must speak to the gardeners about getting rid of some sickly rose bushes. Thinking of that reminded me of what Leicester had said about wheat rust and the trouble it had caused my friends the Speltons.

I was concerned. Kate Spelton had once been my ward, and I had once come near to marrying Christopher. I did not like to think of him returning to his former occupation – which was not just that of Queen's Messenger but had at times involved him in the world of the secret agent, which on occasion meant running into danger. And Kate had had enough bad times in her life. Before she became my ward she had been through a catastrophic love affair, and although I had settled her in a happy marriage she had lost her first husband in very distressing circumstances. She had experienced quite enough calamities and I had in the end been glad to see her married to Christopher, just as I was glad to see Christopher safely out of what had been a risky way of life.

Just then, Sybil came to find me, wanting to show me the embroidery pattern she had been working on. She was a better designer than I was but we both enjoyed needlework. Before seeking out Peter Dickson, I sat with her in the hall to discuss ways of using the design and the best colours for it. We became so immersed in this that before we knew it half the morning was gone. I tore myself away with difficulty when I realized that if I didn't stir myself I would never get to see Dickson or the gardener. I said so to Sybil and went off laughing. I had completely forgotten the curious sense of unease that Leicester had brought with him.

And then, as if thinking about the Speltons had conjured one of them into appearing, I heard hooves coming into the courtyard, and Adam Wilder was hurrying in to tell me that Christopher Spelton was here and asking for me.

'Christopher!' I said. 'Well, that's a coincidence. Bring him in. Into the little parlour, I think.' And a moment later I was welcoming my old friend and shouting to Wilder to find us some refreshments.

Christopher sat down on one of the cushioned settles that made the little parlour so comfortable and smiled at me. Dear Christopher, I thought. He looked just the same as ever, a stocky man, a little older than myself, with a balding head and friendly brown eyes and an aura of reliability.

He looked, indeed, very much as he had when I first saw him, for he was wearing the livery of a Queen's Messenger then and so he was now. 'I'm happy to see you,' I said, 'but I've heard news of you that has made me anxious. I heard it from Leicester – he rode this way only yesterday. You've gone back to your old work, because you have had trouble at West Leys.'

'Wheat rust,' said Christopher with a grimace. 'We've lost our entire wheat crop for this year. The livestock are all right, we will have plenty of salted meat for the winter and we have this year's calves and lambs to sell. But we rely on sales of grain as well. It makes the difference between being comfortable and just getting by. West Leys isn't so very big. I've been thinking of leasing another field . . . but that's by the way. For the time being, I had to do something at once. So I applied to the court for my old post and was taken on. Kate is upset because it could mean getting into danger again. I was never *just* a messenger, as you know – and being willing to undertake, shall we say, other duties was the main reason why I was welcomed back so easily and offered such a good rate of pay.'

'I'm so sorry,' I said inadequately.

Wilder arrived with the refreshments, and conversation paused while he served wine to us and we helped ourselves to almond pastries and handfuls of nuts and raisins.

'I came by way of the village and met your vicar, Dr Joynings, in the street,' said Christopher once Wilder had gone. 'He insisted on talking to me about the church, and even got me to dismount and go inside to see with my own eyes what he was talking about.'

'Oh dear!' I said.

Dr Joynings had been the vicar of St Mary's in Hawkswood village for not quite two years. He was a short, rotund, jolly kind of man and, as I had already realized, he was very keen on making improvements. But I was beginning to cringe inwardly when he thought of further ideas – although they were always good ones – because he did it so often.

'He's saying,' said Christopher, 'that there aren't enough benches and he dislikes the Judgement Window.'

'Yes. He's mentioned those things to me,' I said ruefully. 'He really detests that window, and he says there are always a few people who need to sit but can't because there aren't enough seats to go round.'

'I don't like to see old people leaning on walking sticks, and young wives with child and near their time, or with babies in their arms, having to stand,' Dr Joynings had said to me. 'I feel I must keep my homilies short, but how can I teach my flock about the teachings of Christianity if I haven't enough time to explain things to them? And as for that Judgement Window, there's too much blood and horror and it sometimes frightens young children . . .'

I agreed with him, but at the time I had had other things

on my mind and murmured something about having to think it over.

'In fact,' I said now to Christopher, 'I've been thinking about the benches and I do intend to do something about them. There's a good carpenter in the village. That window is a different matter, though. Replacing it would be very costly. Also, some of the villagers do like it, even if some of the little ones don't and the vicar doesn't and nor do I. But surely, Christopher, you didn't come to talk to me about Dr Joynings and the church? What did bring you here today?' A depressing thought came into my mind. 'Are you here as a Queen's Messenger? Have you brought me word from the court? I know the queen is back from her summer Progress, but I am not due to take a turn at attending on her for another two months.'

'I do bring a message from court,' said Christopher, 'but it's not from the queen. It's from Walsingham.'

'Oh, no!'

'I'm afraid so. He wishes you to pay him a visit. The court is about to move to Greenwich, will you please attend on him there. Not instantly – not until the move is complete. He wishes you to come next Tuesday. It's Wednesday now, so you have nearly a week to prepare.' He reached into the capacious leather pouch that he carried at his belt and produced a sealed letter. 'Here it is, in writing.'

'What can he want?' I said, exasperatedly.

'That I wouldn't know,' said Christopher carefully, 'I daresay he has some task he wishes you to undertake.'

'I'm sure he does!'

Probably, Leicester had known about this, though he had not attempted to speak of it to me until Walsingham had done so.

I had not imagined the curious sense of unease that Leicester had brought with him. The shadow I feared was not a figment of my imagination. It was going to fall.

THREE
The Shadow Falls

Christopher stayed to dine but then took his leave, wanting to ride back to West Leys without further delay. I saw him off with affectionate messages for Kate. From what he had said, I had realized she must be worrying, both about the disaster to their wheat crop and the tasks that would confront Christopher from now on.

'We shall come through,' Christopher said, when I spoke of this. 'I am not living away from West Leys. I am on a part-time contract – I spend a month at court and a month at home, alternately. Even so, the pay is quite good and I am home quite often enough to be an attentive farmer and an equally attentive husband. I shall take care of myself and take care of Kate. I have told her so, and now I am telling you. Don't fret about us. I hope that whatever Walsingham wants this time isn't anything perilous.'

'So do I,' I said. But the sun was shining, the world seemed calm and bright, and I was inclined to be optimistic and did not want to think about shadows. 'Good journey,' I said and turned back into the house to deal, at last, with the importance of teaching Harry double-entry book-keeping. Then I would step into the garden to discuss the rose bushes.

After that, I had to acquaint my household with the news that I had been summoned to see Sir Francis Walsingham. As I expected, they all expressed candid and vocal disapproval except for Brockley, who just stood by shaking his head in regret.

'It always means trouble, when that man Walsingham wants you to do things,' old Gladys grumbled. And my maid, who was really Mistress Brockley but whom I generally called by her maiden name of Dale, said: 'You'll want me and Roger with you. Please can we use the coach? I just can't abide sitting on a horse, these days!'

Sybil Jester, my companion, was usually a calm woman (though just once or twice I had known her explode into unexpected passion). Now she was still calm, but she looked concerned. She said, very gravely: 'I will look after the house while you're gone, but I wish you wouldn't go. Gladys is right. A summons like this always leads to trouble.'

'It can't be helped,' I told her. I thought of Christopher returning to work as a Queen's Messenger, and probably at times as a secret agent, for the sake of the pay. Well, money was always useful. 'I'll be paid,' I said.

'Let's hope it'll not be with your life. It's come near enough to that once or twice, look you,' said Gladys.

I gazed at her with exasperation, mixed with a reluctant affection. She was a most unprepossessing old woman, bent now and lame, with a withered brown face and a marked body odour, while her few remaining teeth resembled brown fangs – and her habit of hurling lurid curses at people who had displeased her had brought more charges of witchcraft against her than the one from which Brockley and I had saved her long ago. But another factor that had aroused suspicions of witchcraft was her undoubted skill with medicinal potions, which infuriated professional physicians when they chanced to hear of it, especially when – and it *had* happened – her potions worked better than theirs.

I had several times been glad of that skill, which had often been a blessing. It was Brockley, not me, who now told her not to keep on croaking like a raven.

'The mistress will do her duty as she always does, and there's an end to it!' he snapped.

'Thank you, Brockley,' I said. 'I am expected next Tuesday, so we shall need to set off on Monday. We'll have to use the coach anyway, as the letter that Master Spelton brought says I can have accommodation for only two horses. Besides, there will be a great deal of baggage. Court dresses become more elaborate every year. You will drive, while Dale and I will travel in the coach with the luggage. Dale, please look out the clothes I shall need to take with me. Suitable things for travelling and for wearing at court, as usual.'

With that, our conference was over. The day was still fair

and sunlit. I kept my spirits up and hoped that Christopher's good wishes would be justified and I would not be confronted with a task that would be worrying. Or dangerous.

The next morning, Roger Brockley came to me and said: 'Madam, could I have the morning free today? I have some private business to see to before we leave for Greenwich.'

I looked at him with understanding. 'Yes, by all means,' I said.

We were talking, as it were, in code.

When Brockley asked for time off to see to private business, he always meant the same thing: that he was going to see his son, Philip.

Philip Sandley was his lawful son, but because he had been reared by foster parents called Sandley he bore their name. Brockley had learned of his existence the year before when Philip applied for the post of tutor for Harry, only to discover later that he was one of the conspirators who tried to use Harry to force me into committing a terrible act. That had been agony for Brockley. We had protected Philip from the law, but there was no question of his remaining at Hawkswood. I would not, could not, permit him ever to set foot in my home again and did not want to see him ever again. But for Brockley he still represented a wondrous revelation – he was the son my good manservant had not known he had.

If Brockley still wanted to be in touch with him, I could not object, provided that if and when they met it was somewhere else. Brockley respected that and avoided even mentioning Philip's name to me. But when Brockley talked of private business he meant Philip, and I understood. So did Dale. Fran Dale wholeheartedly shared my opinion of Philip. She stood beside me at the door of the hall as we watched Brockley mount his handsome dark-chestnut gelding, Firefly, and ride away.

'It was a sad day when that young man Sandley came to this house,' Dale said, arms akimbo. 'I couldn't abide him from the start. Nothing's been the same since. I understand how Roger feels. But young Philip always did make my hackles rise and when we found he was mixed up with a pack of conspirators, well, it didn't surprise me. I wish I'd been able to have a son. Maybe then Roger wouldn't be so besotted with *that* one. I suppose Dr Joynings would say it was the will of God. The will of the other party's more likely!'

'He'll be back in the afternoon,' I said. 'I gather that Philip is now a tutor in Guildford. A place called Reddings House. I gave him a respectable reference – he was a good enough teacher, I must say. Try not to mind that Roger still sees him, Dale. He won't be gone long. He never is.'

'I wish Philip's new family joy of him,' said Dale with a sniff, meaning the Reddings House employers. 'I just hope he doesn't teach their children how to lay plots and doesn't kidnap any of them!'

The morning passed quietly. Then just before dinner time, when I was in the hall with Sybil, once more discussing her new embroidery pattern, we heard the clatter of hooves arriving at a gallop. We looked at each other, startled.

'That can't be Brockley,' Sybil said. 'He'd never bring a horse home headlong, like that! But who . . .?'

Together, we made for the door into the courtyard.

The rider *was* Brockley. We reached the door in time to see him pull Firefly to a halt and throw himself out of the saddle. The horse's dark-chestnut coat was black with sweat. Young Eddie ran out of the tack-room to take the bridle, because Brockley had simply left his mount standing and was running towards me and Sybil. We stared at him in alarm, for his face was white, dead white. I could not recall ever having seen him look like that before.

I said: 'Brockley!' and he stopped, gasping, catching at the doorpost. 'What is it?' I caught his arm and drew him inside. The other grooms were appearing in the courtyard behind him and staring.

'It's Philip!' Brockley gulped and I pushed him down onto a settle. 'What *is* it, Brockley? What's wrong?'

'I got to Guildford. They said he wasn't there. They didn't know why he wasn't there – he ought to have been. I started for home. I was less than a quarter of a mile away from here. The track goes through a spinney – you know the place, ash trees and elms and there's a rookery in the elms . . .'

'Yes, I know the place. Go on.'

'The rooks were making such a to-do, cawing and wheeling!

And Firefly's hoofbeats disturbed some that must have been pecking at something on the ground, among the trees. They flew up, cawing enough to deafen you. I pulled Firefly round and went to see . . . oh God, oh God . . .!'

He half rose, clutching at me as if for comfort. He said: 'It was Philip. Lying there. In a little glade just off the road. Only a couple of yards to the side. He was dead. He had a crossbow bolt through his chest.'

Quietly, I said to Sybil: 'Find Dale,' and she slipped away.

'I can't think why he was so near here,' Brockley said. 'Was he coming to Hawkswood? I didn't meet him on my way to Guildford. I suppose I came later and rode right past his body, not knowing it was there. But he wouldn't come here! He knew . . .'

'He knew that I wouldn't welcome him,' I said steadily. 'But if there was some emergency, he might have wanted to see you so badly that he decided to come anyway. But . . .'

Brockley was rubbing his forehead in bewilderment. 'If he wasn't coming here, then where was he making for? He was lying by the track that leads straight here! There were hoof-marks about. I expect he came on his horse – but if so, it had run away or been stolen. I can't understand this. There haven't been any reports of footpads or robbers of any kind hereabouts, not for a long time. He . . . Fran!'

Dale was arriving, at a run. 'Roger, what is it? Roger?' She had seen the whiteness of his face and her own was full of alarm. She put a hand on his arm. 'What's the matter?'

He began to explain all over again. I said to Sybil: 'We shall have to inform Sir Edward Heron, the county sheriff. Better him than the constable in Woking. This is obviously murder – and there's a connection to my house, and unfortunately I am who I am.'

I was the queen's sister. It made a difference, in this case the difference between the Woking constable and the county sheriff. What touched me might – could – touch the queen. 'Oh, damn!' I said.

There was a heavy weight in the pit of my stomach. I had sensed a hovering shadow – was this it? I was afraid, though I did not know what it was that I feared.

And yes, we *would* have to tell Sir Edward Heron. And that

would not be reassuring, for he did not like me, nor I him.

Well, I had no need to take the message to him myself. A lady in my social position would naturally delegate such a task to someone else. Just as well, since the sight of me in person would certainly stiffen his back. Sir Edward Heron didn't approve of women like me. In his view, women should concentrate on their households, their children, their still-rooms and their embroidery. He had no idea how much I would have preferred to do just that. Also, he had once had me up on a charge of witchcraft and had been very disappointed when I turned out to be innocent. No, Edward Heron didn't like me at all and he didn't like Brockley either, simply because Brockley was so very much my friend. But my steward was of course the appropriate person. I said to Sybil: 'Where is Wilder?'

'Cleaning silver in the pantry, I believe,' said Sybil. 'You want him to take word to Sir Edward?'

'Yes. Would you call him, please. I'll be in the study, writing the message he is to take.'

Within fifteen minutes, Adam Wilder was getting into the saddle of his preferred mount, a piebald weight carrier called Magpie. Wilder was a heavy man.

'Make all the haste you can,' said Brockley. He and Sybil were standing beside me to see Wilder set off. 'This is a very serious business.'

As soon as Wilder had gone, Brockley turned to me. 'Philip can't be left out there,' he said. 'Those rooks . . . I know Heron will say his men ought to see Philip where he . . . where he died, but he *can't* be left there, he can't. I'm going to take two of the grooms with me and a placid horse – Rusty will do – and fetch him home.'

'We shouldn't,' I said feebly.

'I know, madam, but we're going to, all the same.' There were times when Brockley could be implacable. He turned away. Over his shoulder, he said: 'Now.'

Diffidently, Sybil said: 'I can understand how he feels.'

'I know. So can I,' I said. 'I shan't try to forbid him. We'll argue with Heron's men later on. Meanwhile, I have to let Harry know. After all, Philip was once his tutor.'

*   *   *

Philip had left my household because, although he was Harry's tutor and should have considered Harry's safety and well-being as part of his duty, he had been involved in a conspiracy that brought my son into great danger. But everyone in my household did not know that. I had been careful, because after all we had been sheltering a criminal from the law. By rights, Philip should have been in the Tower; might possibly have been hanged. For Brockley's sake I had protected him – and Sir Edward Heron would have had something to say about that, had he known.

I had therefore made sure that the truth was known to as few people as possible. I knew, the Brockleys knew, Sybil knew, and so of course did Harry. Gladys did as well, though not because anyone had told her. Gladys always knew everything that was going on, though I never found out how she did it. Sometimes I wondered if she was in fact a witch!

Those who did not know, however, included Wilder, my grooms, my maidservants and my cooks. They all believed that Philip had left because I was not satisfied with the standard of his teaching and Harry did not like him. They only knew that I had had words with him and had said that he was never to enter my house again, and they just assumed that the words had been extremely offensive.

Well, he would have to enter my house now.

He came back, wrapped in a blanket and lying across the withers of Rusty, one of the most placid animals in my stable. Brockley rode on one side and Arthur Watts rode on the other, leading Rusty. Simon, my second groom, brought up the rear. They came into the courtyard at a slow walk and the three of them lifted Philip down and carried him, still enswathed in his blanket, with the crossbow bolt still in place, making a pyramid beneath it, into the house and up the stairs to one of the attics, where there was a spare bed. On this, they laid him.

Brockley said, as they passed me, going through the hall: 'Don't look at his face, madam. And keep Fran away. The rooks . . .'

'I know,' I said. 'I know what they can do.'

I hated the thought of it, just as Brockley did. Enough time had gone by for my first furious anger against Philip to subside so that now I could see him clearly. He had been foolish, passionately patriotic in the wrong kind of way. He had believed he was serving the queen; he had also believed he was helping a man who was his foster brother. He had not recognized what a thoroughly undesirable character that foster brother, Simeon Wilmot, was. He had shown little understanding of the suffering he had caused to me and to Harry. Had not seemed to understand the horrible fate that might have befallen Harry, and had not absorbed the fact that he was betraying a boy who had been confided to his care.

He had been naïve, had lacked imagination. But I did not think he was wicked. Brockley's son couldn't be wicked, surely?

Now he was lying cold and dead on a bed in my attic, and once more I had to be careful of every word I said so as to keep his perfidy secret, above all from Sir Edward Heron.

Whose men, at that point, were arriving.

Heron hadn't come himself but he had sent two of his men. One was a powerfully built young man, probably there solely for the sake of his muscles as he would clearly be useful in dealing with obstreperous captives, although he had nothing to say. Indeed, while in my presence he never spoke a single word. The other was a stocky, dark man with a brusque manner and round eyes of the coldest blue I had ever seen. He did not approve of the fact that we had moved the body.

'Sergeant Thomas Robson at your service. Do I understand aright? That the body of the dead man has been brought here instead of being left where it was for me to examine in situ?'

'It was necessary,' I said coldly. 'There were rooks. Probably carrion crows as well. And there could also have been foxes. Or weasels.'

'I have seen worse things,' said Sergeant Robson dismissively, as though my concern had been for him. 'You did wrong. Things should have been left as they were. I would have expected you to know better, considering your station in life, madam.'

I didn't reply, just looked at him steadily and waited for him to continue. 'He was my son,' said Brockley.

'I daresay!' Robson evidently dismissed matters of kinship as well. I wondered if he were married, if he had children of his own. 'Well, I had better see the place and then I will see the body. Will someone kindly show me where it happened?'

'I will show you,' said Brockley, his voice just as cold as mine.

They rode off to look at the place. They returned in due course and Brockley showed the sergeant up to the attic. This time I followed them, impelled by a feeling of responsibility. Brockley had recommended me not to look, but I felt that I should know.

It wasn't a pleasant sight. However, showing some trace of human feeling for once, Sergeant Robson covered the face up after we had had a quick glance, and instead lifted the blanket off the crossbow bolt and revealed Philip's chest. The bolt had gone deep into the body. There wasn't very much blood, only a stain round the point of entry. Scored with the beaks of the rooks though it was, I had still seen that Philip's young face bore a look of surprise.

'He died quickly,' Robson said. 'Probably didn't feel much, if that's any help.'

I was glad of that. That face had upset me badly, and not only because of the pecking. He had such a resemblance to Brockley. I felt as if I was looking at Brockley himself made young and mutilated, but Brockley all the same. Tears stung my eyes. Brockley, standing at my side, said: 'I had hoped, in time, to have grandchildren.' I heard the sob in his throat.

'Ambushed, I should think,' the sergeant was saying. 'There were traces of trampling among the trees close to the glade where he was found. And quite a lot of hoof tracks – not just one horse – leading back through the woods, going towards the glade but not from this direction. We think there were two horses, one bigger than the other. One was probably his, but there was another rider . . . Someone was waiting for him, that's my theory. I'm going to send my men to ask questions at cottages and in villages along the track, and try to trace the paths of those two horses. I'd like to know the exact direction that the assailant came from. Where was the victim coming from?'

'A place called Reddings House,' I said. 'In Guildford.'

'Thank you,' said Robson. He added: 'There will have to be an inquest. You will, I trust, be on hand for it.'

'I have to visit the court,' I said. 'I have been summoned by Sir Francis Walsingham.' I used Walsingham's full name on purpose. It seemed somehow to lend weight to the summons. I would have to go, whether Heron and his sergeant liked it or not. 'I am leaving next Monday,' I said. 'This is Friday. I shall therefore be here for two more days. I don't expect to be absent long, however. At least, I hope not.'

'You could come back for the occasion,' said Robson. 'You wouldn't have that far to come. How do we reach you if necessary?'

'I shall be at Greenwich. There are the usual White Stave officials who know where visitors are housed.'

'Very well.' Robson looked down at the crossbow bolt and then pulled the blanket back over it. 'I shall report to Sir Edward. This man lived in Guildford, did he not? The coroner for Guildford must see the body but I think he will give permission for a funeral. He can be fetched tomorrow morning – he lives this side of Guildford. The inquest will be formal because there's not much doubt about the cause of death. No need to wait long, and better not to in this warm weather. We will let you know before Monday whether the body can be buried.'

'You will want to be at the burial,' I said to Brockley, after the coroner, a stoutly built and resolute gentleman of middle age and obvious experience, had come, examined Philip's body, given consent to a funeral forthwith, declined refreshment and departed. 'I will speak with Philip's employers, and if they agree it can be held here, so your son can be buried at Hawkswood, if you wish. We'll see if Dr Joynings can be ready on Monday morning. Then we can set off for Greenwich afterwards and still be there the same day.'

Brockley said: 'Will you attend the funeral, madam?'

I sighed. 'If you would like me to be there . . . yes. I will.'

FOUR
Misinformation

On Monday, the warm weather which had seemed so kindly suddenly became unpleasantly hot. Philip's body had been removed to the church, so he was no longer under my roof, and everyone was relieved to think that his burial was not to be delayed. Not many of the villagers had really known him so the church wasn't crowded during the service, but it was still stifling. I had ordered the benches that Joynings wanted but they hadn't yet been delivered, so I stood there, sweltering inside my black gown, alongside the Brockleys and the rest of my household, plus Master Samuel Hartley, Philip's employer in Guildford, the two Hartley sons, aged twelve and ten, who had been his pupils, and a handful of villagers.

On the way to the church, we had fallen in with Dr Joynings, who had promptly seized the chance to ask me about the benches and to grumble again about the objectionable Judgement Window.

'The benches should be ready by next week,' I said patiently, 'and I *may* later be able to consider replacing that window.' There was a chance that whatever Walsingham wished me to do for him would – for once – prove to be not dangerous and yet still well paid, which might let me think about the window. Now, as I stood there in the heat while Dr Joynings besought us all to remember our mortality and be prepared to face our creator whenever he should choose to call us, I found myself unable to stop looking at the window that was irritating our good vicar so much.

I didn't look at it often. Just appreciated the swathes of colour that it threw across the flagstoned floor and the rood screen, which was also beautifully painted and which I had had refurbished only the year before. But for some reason, my eyes were now being constantly drawn to the window. The demons who were dragging the damned towards a cavern entrance spouting flames had horrible faces and even more horrible pitchforks, and the damned were bleeding from pitchfork wounds, their faces distorted with terror and pain. While the virtuous, who were being led up a pearl-coloured stairway into Paradise, had such smug expressions that – in view of my sometimes unconventional past – I found myself wishing to throw things at them.

No wonder small children were upset by it, I thought. I should have done something about it long ago. I had always disliked it, but I had also taken it for granted as part of the Hawkswood to which Hugh had brought me. Until Dr Joynings' predecessor retired and Joynings arrived, took one look at it and began so vigorously to complain.

No arrangements had been made for any kind of gathering after the burial. Master Hartley and his boys came back to the house with us, but my coach was already standing in the courtyard with our luggage aboard, ready to leave for Greenwich. I gave the Hartleys a few refreshments before they set out for home, and that was all.

Hartley senior was a fussy, voluble man. While consuming the refreshments, he talked a good deal about what an excellent teacher Philip had been and how much his boys would miss him, and the boys themselves politely echoed him. 'My wife would have liked to attend but she is expecting to lie in any day now and we have had a number of disappointments since my younger boy was born . . . We pray that all will go well this time. By the way, Philip's horse came wandering home to my stable. What do you want me to do with it? I suppose it would be yours now, Master Brockley?'

Brockley looked at me. 'Send it over some time,' I said. 'We will decide what to do with it when we return from Greenwich.'

Eventually, to our relief, the Hartleys took their leave, and at that point I suddenly became conscience stricken about Brockley.

'Are you sure you don't mind coming to Greenwich?' I asked him. 'This has been a dreadful time for you. I should have thought about that. Would you rather stay here – to be quiet, to remember Philip, perhaps visit the grave privately? And decide what you want to do with Philip's mare. Dale can stay too. Sybil can come with me – we'll look after each other – and I'll take Simon as driver.'

But Brockley shook his head. 'No, madam, thank you. If I felt like that, I would say so. But I don't. I would rather travel to Greenwich with you and distract my mind.'

'Very well. Then have the horses put to. We can dine on the way.'

It was always a pleasure to visit Greenwich Palace. It was not as elegant and graceful as Richmond, but it was still beautiful, with its red-brick walls aglow in the evening sunshine. Much of it was only two-storey, except for the gatehouse and a few gables and the buttress towers dotted along its extensive river frontage. Its mullioned windows gave it a friendly look. Unlike buildings such as Windsor Castle, it was not designed to withstand a siege. It was immense, a statement of power, and yet it was a home and not a fortress. I could even appreciate it when perspiring and dusty after travelling for hours in hot weather.

The rooms we were given were comfortable though not spacious. Dale fetched jugs of warm water so that we could wash the grime of the journey away, and we were able to take a late supper before we retired to sleep, with windows open and bed-hangings looped back. In the morning, we breakfasted together in a wide hall, along with numerous other people, including the entourages of a couple of visiting ambassadors and a trade delegation from Norway. The crowd of guests explained why I had only been offered stabling for two horses.

We were sharing our table with a master glassmaker from the City, a man who said his name was Taverner. He told us that he had been asked to the court to show the queen a range of glass tableware, for which he was apparently famous. The queen had seen some of his products in Sir William Cecil's house, and had been impressed.

He was quite young and not tall, with light brown hair and eyes of the same colour, beneath thin, arched eyebrows, matching a thin nose with high-arched nostrils. He was well dressed, too, all mulberry velvet and cream silk slashings. He also had an unusually confident way of speaking; an air of being mature beyond his years. The mention of glassware reminded me of the Judgement Window and I asked if he worked in stained-glass but he said no, that was a separate skill. His business concerned good quality tableware and ornaments.

He knew how to sell his wares. Before breakfast was over, I had arranged to view his goods myself and when I did so, later on, I liked them so much that when we got home, our luggage included a blue glass ewer and six blue drinking goblets, wrapped in lambswool.

I didn't have to seek Walsingham out, because after breakfast a page arrived to collect me. The Brockleys came with me, but as usual on such occasions they were asked to stay in Walsingham's anteroom while I went alone into his presence.

Sir Francis Walsingham had offices in all the palaces, and all the offices were much alike. Since they were in palaces, they all had pleasingly patterned leading in their windows and their walls were panelled, some of them in the charming linenfold style. Walsingham, however, was interested in the Puritan movement that was gradually gaining so much ground. He always wore black and, since he was himself dark of hair and eye and so swarthy of skin that Elizabeth had nicknamed him her Old Moor, it made him look alarmingly sinister.

I sometimes wondered if attractively patterned window leading and linenfold panelling offended something in his austere nature and was the real reason why his shelves and cupboards – all full of books and files and document boxes – and the maps on which he followed the movement of world events and the blackboard on which he chalked diagrams and instructions for his agents obscured so much of their beauty, even cutting down the daylight.

His office at Greenwich was no exception, and when I entered I found that as usual it was as dim as a dungeon, with candles to augment the limited sunshine.

It was also stifling because all his windows were shut. The day was already growing over-warm and on the way through the palace I had inhaled, without pleasure, the usual smell of a royal residence in a heatwave – by which I mean the odour of so many perspiring bodies overlaid with the perfumes, flowery, exotic or sickly, that people use to conceal their own smells. The ornate court clothes were quite unsuitable for warm weather, being so heavy with brocade and velvet.

I was myself wearing a satin creation in peach and silver, with an open ruff and a foundation of stays and a wide farthingale, and knitted stockings. I longed to be at home in a loose informal gown, with no corsetry, ruff or farthingale, and bare feet pushed into slippers.

Always polite, Walsingham rose from his seat as the page brought me in, nodded dismissal to the lad, and graciously offered me a chair. I curtsied and accepted.

'You sent for me?' I said.

'Yes. I have something for you to do.'

He paused, gazing at me with an air of slight exasperation. Like Edward Heron, Walsingham didn't consider that women should be involved in state affairs. I suspected that at heart he wished he could serve a king instead of a queen – though his opinions on such things might have been less jaundiced if Elizabeth had liked him. (She didn't, to the point that sometimes she lost her temper with him and threw things at him.)

I took a deep breath of stuffy air, laden with the smells of paper, dust and ink, and said: 'Yes, Sir Francis?'

'It won't be dangerous. But it will mean spending some time – probably three months – away from home, though you won't have to go far. Do you know of a place called Knoll House, just south of Guildford?'

'The Earl of Leicester mentioned it to me once,' I said. 'Hasn't it just been leased by someone called Giles Frost? I have seen the place but only from the outside. I pass that way when I visit Kate and Christopher Spelton at West Leys. It's a tall, narrow house set at the top of a small hill. The nearest village is Brentvale – about a mile further south.'

'Yes, you have it right. Giles Frost has leased it from Leicester and means to move from the Midlands to live there. There's a small home farm, but he gets most of his income from something else.'

I said: 'The Earl of Leicester told me that this man Frost is suspected of passing information to Spain, but that the Council hope to use him to mislead the Spanish, which is why he hasn't been arrested. Is that so? How does he contact them?'

Walsingham had resumed his seat, behind his desk. He rested his elbows on the desktop and steepled his fingers. 'He has a brother,' he said, 'who lives in London and is a merchant. This man exports leather goods and ironware to Mediterranean countries and brings back silk and spices, and the like. He doesn't do the travelling himself. Giles Frost does it for him. Frost is an experienced seaman. He's been a ship's captain in the past. Between them the brothers own a small trading vessel, and Giles captains that. He has been at sea recently but is back in England and is now in London, handing over his latest purchases to his brother. He will then arrange the move to Knoll House.'

There was another pause. I thought: *I was right to feel misgivings after Leicester called on me. He was preparing the ground, trying not to alarm me but to plant things in my mind – things like the existence of this man Frost and his activities – so that when this moment came it wouldn't be a complete surprise.*

'When Frost travels to the Mediterranean,' said Walsingham, 'he seems to have a regular rendezvous with a Spanish fishing vessel. People such as merchants, travelling players, even some chapmen, who regularly travel to France or to the Mediterranean countries, interest me greatly. I like to keep watch on them. I therefore pay retainers to a number of men who, when opportunity permits, get themselves into the employment of such people or taken on as crew members in their ships. They do the watching.'

Walsingham sometimes made me shiver. I sometimes thought of him as a spider, waiting at the centre of a vast web. Waiting to pounce whenever an unwary fly . . . traitor . . . fell foul of its sticky threads.

'We are particularly interested in such men as Giles Frost,' he said, 'because he not only travels regularly to the Mediterranean, ostensibly to visit Venice and other mercantile centres where goods from the East may be found, he is also a Catholic. Oh, he keeps the law and attends Anglican services from time to time. He also has a personal chaplain, who we suspect says Mass for him in private. I myself would like to have both of them arrested but, as they have never tried to convert anyone, I have no ground for so doing.'

He paused, looking irritable. The queen's insistence that she did not want windows into men's souls, and that if they kept the letter of the law she would not hound them, really annoyed Walsingham.

After a moment, he resumed. 'However,' he said, 'we – Sir William Cecil and I, that is – learned, quite soon, that when Frost is near the Spanish coast he regularly encounters a Spanish fisherman. Always, according to reports turned in by a man who is now an established member of his ship's crew, the same one. On two occasions this so-called fisherman came aboard Frost's vessel, and once my agent succeeded in over-hearing some of the conversation between him and Frost. There is no doubt that Frost is passing information to the Spanish. Mostly he hasn't been able to tell them very much, but some-thing serious did happen after the meeting that our agent overheard. One of our agents in Spain was nearly arrested. He was warned in time and escaped, but it was a near thing. We have taken great care since then to make sure that Frost doesn't learn of anything important. But we have left him alone because,' said Walsingham, with a saturnine grin, 'Sir William thinks – and he has managed to convince me – that Frost could be useful. He sometimes goes with his brother on autumn trips to Continental fairs, and it's likely that he meets contacts there as well.'

I felt as though I too were at sea. I couldn't think how I came into this. But no doubt Walsingham was about to tell me. I waited.

'Giles Frost is a family man,' said Walsingham. 'He married late and was unfortunate enough to lose his wife after only a few years – there was an outbreak of plague – but she left him with twin daughters, now aged seventeen. Their names are Joyce and Jane. He wishes them to learn skilled embroi-dery, including gold and silver work, and apparently they want this, too. The governess they used to have, who died recently, did her best but she wasn't a particularly skilled needlewoman and couldn't teach them gold and silver work at all. You, I know, are quite gifted in such matters and Mistress Jester who lives with you is, I believe, excellent at designing patterns.'

'That is so,' I said. 'Do I understand that you wish me to give these two girls a course of instruction, helped by Mistress Jester? But to what end?'

'Master Frost,' said Walsingham, 'knows of you by sight, as he has occasionally seen you at court, and by reputation as well. He does not approve of you. He does not approve of women being involved in affairs of state. Any more than I do, but I do recognize the value of the services you have given to Her Majesty. Well, Master Frost has heard – I believe it was from Leicester, some time ago – that you have womanly skills as well, including embroidery. It also seems that Leicester mentioned your companion, Mistress Jester, and her gift for design, which is another skill that the Frost girls would like to learn.'

'I still don't see . . . .?'

'Let me finish. When he began to look for teachers, he enquired about you personally. And about Mistress Jester. On my instructions, Leicester has told him where to find you both. You and Mistress Jester will probably receive an invitation. Since he also knows of your confidential work, he may well, while you are in his household, try to get information from you. You are to oblige.'

'Er . . . what am I to tell him?'

Unexpectedly, in fact, so very unexpectedly that I jumped halfway out of my seat before sinking back into it with my mouth open, Walsingham clasped his hands, raised them in front of him and then crashed them down on to his desk, making a stack of papers leap up and spill and causing an inkpot to lurch and send a trail of ink across the desktop. 'That bloody woman!' Walsingham shouted.

I had never heard him swear before and had heard that he never did so in the presence of a female. Presumably he was no longer counting me as one. I wasn't even sure which woman he meant. He saw the trail of ink on his desk, groped in a drawer, produced a napkin and mopped it up. Then he wiped his hands on a clean part of the napkin, thrust it back into its drawer, and with slightly shaking hands shuffled the dislodged papers back into a roughly tidy pile.

He looked at me grimly. 'I am talking about Mary of Scotland. Mary the serpent of discord, Mary who was thrown *out* of Scotland after she married the man who in all probability murdered her husband Lord Darnley, Mary who has been in England ever since, as Elizabeth's guest and prisoner combined, and who if she ever has the chance will conspire with Philip of Spain to bring an army to her aid, either to put her back on the Scottish throne or to kill Elizabeth and put herself on *our* throne instead. She would do it for her own self-aggrandisement but would claim she was doing it for God and the Catholic faith. She makes my stomach churn. I have long wanted Elizabeth to have her head off. But the queen fears that if she did, *that* in itself might bring Philip's army upon us in revenge. Mary is a menace, alive or dead. She makes me sick!'

I sat still. For the moment I had forgotten the physical discomfort of this sweltering office and my own too-heavy garments. I had never seen Walsingham like this before. He shook his head violently, as if trying to disperse a swarm of flies.

'We have kept Philip of Spain's shipping busy,' said Walsingham, 'by allowing our privateers to harass it. That is the queen's wish. We've intercepted and seized some shiploads of treasure, bound for Spain from the New World, and done the queen's Treasury a favour. I have not been in favour of this policy; I fear it will provoke Philip of Spain rather than distract him. There is reason to fear that it has done just that already – and if he and Mary establish contact, I wouldn't like to think of the consequences. We are doing all we can to make sure nothing of that kind happens, but we can't isolate her completely. She has a household. We can't shut them totally away from the outside world and, though they can be searched every time they go out, there is no means of looking inside their heads for messages carried in their memories.'

He sighed. 'In my opinion, what we need to do is give Philip good reason to feel that attacking England might be a mistake. To do that we need to feed inaccurate information to him, though that isn't as easy as it sounds. Frost, for instance, is not a fool. He is wary, and clever. He is good at knowing how to check on information casually fed to him. And who to talk to, oh so guilelessly.'

'Won't he check up on me?' I asked.

'We intend to make sure that the information you pass to him will be repeated to him if he tries to verify it. I fear,' said Walsingham, with another demonic grin, 'that to make what you tell him seem truly convincing, you will need to make yourself appear light-minded and gossipy. Let things out as though you have no idea of their importance.'

'But what is this inaccurate information that I am to pass?'

'Philip of Spain is a danger to England,' said Walsingham. 'A very serious danger. We do not, we cannot, know for sure if he really is planning to attack us but we have reason to think that the possibility is there. We do know that preparations for such an attack are not in progress yet. He clearly doesn't plan to make war on us this year. But our agents have picked up rumours that he is considering plans for the future, next year or the year after. He seems to have been trying to find out what kind of backing he might find within England; how much support there is for the Catholic cause and therefore for Mary's. There isn't much – but that alone might encourage him to sail against us. Because he would certainly like to replace Elizabeth, whom he detests, with Mary, and he will eventually grasp – if he hasn't already done so – that it couldn't be done *without* his aid. The one thing above all others that might hold him off is the belief that our navy outnumbers his. His, according to the agents who have courted appalling dangers to find out, consists of somewhere between a hundred and thirty and a hundred and fifty ships of varying sizes. Our warship fleet contains only sixty vessels.'

I looked at him in horror. 'If it came to war, we would be outnumbered! Spain has a fleet more than twice the size of ours . . .'

'We've increased our navy a lot since Elizabeth came to the throne,' said Walsingham. 'There were only thirty-nine warships then. More ships are being built, but completing them

will take time. They are mostly in shipyards on the Thames
and the Medway. All here in the south. It will be for you to
let fall that new shipyards have been opened in the north and
that eighty vessels are at present under construction, forty of
which will be complete within two months while the rest will
be ready in stages before Christmas. If that were true – if
only! – by Christmas we would have a navy roughly the same
size as the Spanish one.

'Well, as I said, we are sure that Philip can't start an
invasion before next year. He has not yet begun to make
preparations; such preparations take time, and he couldn't do
it now before the weather turns. Information must reach him
that by the time he can be ready to make an attack our navy
will be more than capable of taking on his. Frost won't sail
through Spanish waters again this year but he may go to France
and may well meet a contact there. I fancy he will see that
news of such import gets through. Will you do it? It won't be
dangerous,' he repeated dryly. 'You won't need to wear those
open-fronted gowns with a pouch sewn inside so you can carry
picklocks and a dagger.'

'I didn't know you knew about that,' I said.

'You might be surprised to learn how many things I know,'
said Walsingham. 'I make a point of knowing things. Well?'

There was no question of saying no. There never was with
Walsingham. Or Cecil. Because all my assignments, no matter
which one of them instructed me, were essentially for Elizabeth.
And she was my sister as well as my queen, my kin as well
as the representative of my country.

'When must I go to Knoll House?' I asked.

'As soon as you hear from Frost. You will await his
invitation. You are clear about what we want you to do? Have
you any questions?'

'I don't think so.' It didn't sound dangerous, I said to myself.
I had only to behave like a gossipy woman. Wait, though! I
would have to be careful about that. If Frost really knew of
my reputation, then he would know quite well that I wasn't
that type of woman at all. Perhaps I could put on a show of
being very discreet but then appear to let my tongue off the

leash under the influence of wine. Or perhaps I could get Sybil
to be the one who talked unwisely . . .

I was rising to my feet, about to take my leave, when
Walsingham said: 'There is one more thing.'

Oh, there would be! Of course there would, there always
was!

'Yes?' I said, sitting down again.

'It may be as well for you to be away from home, under
someone else's roof, for a while. Warn your household not to
tell others where you are. Let it be thought that you are visiting
your daughter in Buckinghamshire.'

'I see . . . At least, I don't see. If I am to go officially to
instruct the Frost girls in embroidery . . .'

'Simeon Wilmot, who led last year's wicked attempt on you
and your son, was duly executed,' said Walsingham. 'He died
cursing you. No doubt you remember him all too well.'

'Yes, I do,' I said, recalling with a shudder the man who
had threatened Harry in order to force me to agree to be used
as a means of assassinating Mary Stuart. I remembered his
cold eyes, his authoritative voice, the unnaturally long fingers
that could do card tricks, flicking through the pack as though
it were made of water. I was glad he was dead.

'I spoke with him myself once,' said Walsingham.
'Questioned him personally. A dangerous man, I think. He
had a mind like a sprained ankle.'

'A . . .?' Such a flight of fancy was unlike Walsingham.

But his face was serious. He nodded. 'Hot and hard, and
absolutely rigid. The kind of mind that can't shift its position
or adapt in any way, because it's too stiff to move and trying
would actually hurt. Well, he is dead. But we have learned
that he has a half-brother, a man apparently called Anthony
Hunt. We have tried to find him but without success. However,
I have eyes and ears in many places, including taverns and
markets and so on where people gather and meet and talk.'
*Another part of his spider's web. All in black, with long arms
and legs . . . sometimes I thought he even looked like a spider.*
'I have heard that this man Hunt has made threats against you.
He apparently wants to avenge his brother. I know, and so do
you, that the plot Wilmot and his friends hatched was foolish

and ramshackle, but it was dangerous just the same. This threat may be dangerous, too. Especially if Hunt's mentality is the same as Wilmot's. You should take care until such time as we lay hands on him. Which we no doubt will do before too long.'

'Thank you, Sir Francis,' I said grimly.

'I knew it,' said Dale when I told her what had transpired. Brockley just shook his head and sighed.

'I knew it, too,' I said. 'I'm not so very surprised. Some things never seem to be quite finished. It's happened before, when something we all thought was past and over has risen up like an unfriendly spectre to haunt me.'

'I suspect,' said Brockley, 'that what is needed is for that woman Mary of Scotland to be quite finished! She has been at the bottom of so many of our troubles.'

'Walsingham thinks the same,' I said. 'But the queen is against beheading her cousin, not least because this cousin is a queen, as she is herself. It would be a kind of impiety to behead an anointed queen and would reduce her own sanctity, which is some sort of protection for her. I understand that.'

'What now, madam?' Brockley asked. 'Are you to have an audience with Her Majesty?'

'I think not,' I said. 'Before I left Walsingham I asked if I should seek an audience with her, but she is apparently so busy dealing with ambassadors and delegations that I might have to wait a week or more. I have decided to go home at once. We'll dine and then leave. Get out my travelling dress, Dale. We'll sleep at Hawkswood tonight.'

I was glad to change out of my burdensome court dress and to start on our journey, though Walsingham's warning was working in my mind like yeast in bread dough and I was glad that Brockley, as usual, had his sword with him. The roads we used had all been properly tended, with trees cut back further than a bowshot – or musket range – to discourage footpads, but I still felt that Brockley, up in the driving seat, was exposed. However, nothing happened. The journey was pleasant, as the weather had turned cooler, and by nightfall we were safely back at Hawkswood.

'Well, here we are,' I said as Sybil and Wilder came out of

the house to greet us. 'With plenty of news, and a task not only for me but for you as well. And we have little choice but to accept it. I'll tell you all about it when we are indoors.'

'Dr Joynings was here earlier,' said Sybil. 'He is anxious to see you about something. He asked to be told when you returned.'

'Send young Eddie to tell him, in the morning,' I said.

FIVE
Broken Glass

There was no need to send a message to Dr Joynings the next morning, for he arrived in person and highly agitated while I was still eating breakfast in the great hall along with the Brockleys and Sybil, Gladys, my son Harry and his tutor. The weather was no longer hot but had suddenly turned wet and chilly, with a sharp wind, a first harbinger of the autumn to come. I had ordered a fire to be lit for us. Our short, rotund vicar had a stout cloak wrapped over his black cassock. He bounced in on Wilder's heels like a clerical tennis ball, wiping his nose as he came. His round face, always rubicund, had been scoured by the cold wind to a deeper shade of red, and his somewhat childlike blue eyes were watering.

He was so close behind Wilder that there was little point in announcing him, though my steward, being very correct, nevertheless stopped just inside the door to declare in formal style that Dr Joynings from St Mary's had arrived. Ignoring him, our guest stepped past him and made straight for the hearth, clearly in need of its warmth, and gasped out that he was sorry to interrupt our meal.

'I am sorry to have come so early, but oh, Mistress Stannard, I am thankful that you are home. Such a business! I have never in all my life encountered such a thing. I could not believe my eyes, indeed I could not! I am ashamed that such a thing could happen in a church that is in my care. I have always been a friend to my parishioners, wherever I have served, and I could never have believed . . .'

At this point, he realized from the bewildered faces turned to him from where we sat round our breakfast board that none of us had the slightest idea what he was talking about.

'Wilder,' I said, 'take the good doctor's cloak and mull some red wine for him and call someone to bring him some food.

Dr Joynings, do please be calm. Take a seat. Come to the table – if you sit on the bench nearest the fire, you will be quite warm. And then tell us what all this is about. Start at the beginning.'

'The beginning!' Joynings left the hearth as requested and came to the table. Wilder, having shouted some orders from the door, had pushed a poker into the fire to get hot and was now stooping with his head in the sideboard cupboard, reaching for the wine. My youngest maidservant, Margery, appeared in haste with bread and cold meat, which Joynings accepted, though absently, as if hardly aware of them. Through a mouthful of veal, he said jerkily: 'It happened yesterday. In the afternoon. The village was quiet. I was in the church. The carpenter had just delivered the new benches and we were arranging them.'

He looked at me very straightly. 'I was in the church with the carpenter, Rob Dodd. I was not alone.'

'I don't understand,' I said.

'We heard a crash,' said Joynings. 'And then another. We turned round, and there were two big stones lying on the floor amid a great strewing of broken glass. Stained glass. Someone had thrown those stones through the Judgement Window.'

'I see,' I said.

'I don't like that window and nor do you, Mistress Stannard, and some of the villagers don't, either. But neither I nor you would actually attack it, and I find it hard to believe that anyone in Hawkswood village would. But it *has* happened. We stood there gaping for a moment and then rushed out – but though we heard feet running away, there's that belt of trees behind the church and whoever it was got away through that. I can't run fast, and nor can Rob Dodd. He's got a limp, ever since he had an accident with an axe, and I'm fifty-eight.' I nodded sympathetically. There was a hiss as Wilder applied the hot poker to a jug of wine.

'I don't believe,' said Joynings wretchedly, 'that *anyone* among my parishioners would do such a thing. There are some lively boys among them, but I can't believe it of them. Their fathers would be outraged! Mistress Stannard, what's to be done?'

'We must try to find out who was responsible,' I said, 'and make them pay for a replacement. Which need not be exactly

like the one it's replacing! That one was no doubt the sort of
thing that they liked in medieval times, but it didn't suit the
world of today. Perhaps in a way this is a good thing.'

I thought for a moment, while Wilder filled a goblet and
brought it to Joynings, who sipped it.

Brockley said: 'But *who* did this? Whatever we think of
that Judgement Window, it was a destructive act. First there
was Philip . . .' His voice faded for a moment and shook. 'The
inquest hasn't yet been held,' he said, steadying himself. 'And
now this. I don't like it!'

Neither did I. Nor did any of us. Notification of the inquest
arrived that morning. It was to be held in Guildford on the
twenty-first of August, the day after tomorrow. Meanwhile, I
sent Brockley, Adam Wilder and also Laurence Miller, who
was the principal groom at my stud of trotters, to Hawkswood
village to make some enquiries. The lean, unsmiling Miller
was not only a competent stud groom but was also in the
employ of Lord Burghley – otherwise Sir William Cecil – who,
because I was the queen's sister and also a queen's agent,
liked to have someone near me who would report to him on
my welfare. Miller was good at enquiries.

There is no need to go into detail about their visit to the
village. It produced nothing.

The village itself wasn't big. It lay to the east of my land
and consisted of one straggling street of thatched cottages
with the church at the southern end, and at the north end a
forge, the carpenter's shop, a bakery and a tavern called the
Sign of the Roebuck. The carpenter was Rob Dodd, who lived
with his family over their shop. Rob's brother Luke and their
father, Harry, were the village thatchers. They lived halfway
along the street and were already beginning to train Luke's
two little sons, small as they were, to be thatchers as well.

The Dodds were, to me, an interesting family, because some
years before I married Hugh and came to Hawkswood I had
encountered a couple of brothers called Dodd who were in
the service of William Cecil. I was intrigued to find a Dodd
family in Hawkswood village, and thought it a pleasant coincidence when I learned that they were in fact cousins – third

cousins, I think – of the Dodds who served Cecil. Our Dodds were all thoroughly capable craftsmen, though somewhat inclined to be talkative.

In addition, the village boasted a potter and a saddler, who had workshops behind their homes, on the patch of land that went with every cottage. Other villagers used their patch for fruit trees or vegetables or to grow a little corn. Or to keep livestock: chickens, a pig or two, goats for milk, a donkey or a pony for transport. The whole community was pervaded by a warm farmyard smell, and in wet weather the track that formed the single street was deep in mud.

My late husband, Hugh Stannard, had thought about having the track cobbled, but died before he got round to it. I had never done so, either. It was one of those costly projects, like replacing a large stained-glass window, that one kept on thinking about and then put off for another day.

Hugh had been a good landlord, as had his father before him, and the villagers were usually well-conducted. There would be the occasional fight over a girl, or a squabble in the tavern over a game of darts. But rarely anything worse.

The darts game was popular. In the days of the last King Henry, someone had invented it as a way by which archers could sharpen up their marksmanship even in bad weather, as it was played indoors. Players threw small arrows at a target. At the Sign of the Roebuck, they used a circular section of a tree trunk. Colourful circles were painted on it and points awarded for hitting the little centre circle, with diminishing points for the outer ones. There were occasional disputes when a dart landed on the very edge of a circle. And that was virtually the limit of bad behaviour in Hawkswood. The villagers were not at all pleased to be questioned about anything so outrageous as throwing stones through church windows.

'I spent most of the day going round our land, talking to the men working on it, and come the evening I went into the Roebuck,' said Brockley, returning home late and cross. 'Some of the men in there I'd questioned already and the rest had already heard about it, and none of them were glad to see me. I got a dart in the chest!'

It had been thrown from a distance and not very hard, since

it had lost impetus before it arrived, whereupon it had stuck in Brockley's doublet and then fallen to the floor. It had been a gesture rather than an attack. But it was an indication of just how offended the villagers were.

Wilder and Miller had returned earlier, having gone from house to house to talk to the women. They had taken one side of the street each. Most of the women had been shocked, and sympathetic towards Dr Joynings, but had sprung to the defence of their young. The mere suggestion that any of the village boys could have been responsible had them bristling like indignant hedgehogs.

'And I thought that old biddy in the last cottage, the widow Marge Reed, meant to assault me!' said Miller with feeling, talkative for once. 'She lives squashed in that place along with her ancient father – who's got the joint evil in his knees and sits in a chair all day with a rug over them, grousing all the time and demanding to be waited on – and her son and daughter-in-law, and six grandsons between twelve and twenty. I don't know where they all sleep—'

'Some of them are apprentices in Woking. The others sleep in an attic under the thatch,' Wilder said helpfully.

'There's two sets of twins among them,' said Miller, unheeding. 'And the eldest grandson's now married, and his wife, Bridget, is breeding. And when she and Marge heard what I was there about, well, Bridget stood there in the kitchen with her hands on her hips, and her stomach full of another pair of twins, judging by the size of the bulge, and said her husband had gone to Guildford with their donkey cart to buy flour and cloth and a new hammer for his work at the carpentry place, where he's an assistant, it seems. And she said that when he came back he'd use the hammer to knock my head off for talking insults about their boys, what are all well behaved. Three of them are apprentices in Woking – like you said, Wilder – and two go most days to a school there, and the married one works in the Roebuck. Throwing stones at windows, church or otherwise, she said, is what they wouldn't do. And how did I *dare* come to the house saying they had? Then Marge – my God, that woman has arms like legs of mutton and great big feet in sloppy slippers and shoulders fit for an ox – well, she upped with a meat cleaver.

'And at that point,' said Miller, with what I realized was a kind of grim humour, 'I left.'

There was, evidently, nothing to be learned in the village. However, I thought, we had at least got rid of that unpleasant window. And soon there was a prospect of getting a new one made promptly. Julius Stagg arrived the next morning.

It was another grey morning, with spatters of rain now and then and the wind still cold. It was a Sunday, and when the unexpected visitor rode in I and most of my household had just returned from church. I was in the small parlour with Sybil, starting to embroider the pair of sleeves that were to be decorated with Sybil's new design. They were for a new gown I was making for myself, of a tawny wool cloth, and the design of buttercup flowers on slender, curling green-silk stems would go well with tawny.

At the sound of hooves, I looked up and glanced through the window. The newcomer was just drawing rein in the courtyard. I observed that his horse was a businesslike bay cob with hairy fetlocks and a Roman nose. And also that it was well fed and glossy with grooming, and the rider was well fed and glossy too.

Dismounting, he tossed back a black cloak to reveal a spruce narrow ruff and a brown doublet and hose of good plain wool set off with yellow slashings that had the gleam of silk. His high-crowned black hat had a silver brooch in front, and his riding boots were polished. He was still fairly young, perhaps in his late twenties, but he had a mature and self-possessed air as he stood there pulling off a pair of leather gauntlets and declaring his business to Wilder, who had gone out to meet him. In fact, he had Prosperous Tradesman written all over him.

A moment later, Wilder was bringing him in and announcing that this was Master Julius Stagg from Guildford, a designer and creator of stained glass with a workshop and a staff of skilled craftsmen.

'Stagg?' I said. 'There's a firm on the far side of Guildford that creates stained glass, but the proprietor's name is John Hines.'

'Master Stagg has come to Guildford only lately,' said Wilder, 'and you may not have noticed his signboard yet. He previously had a business in Taunton, in Somerset. He decided that he wanted to be nearer to London. I understand that he is already doing well – to the annoyance of Master Hines, I daresay! Stagg's workshop is on our side of Guildford, closer to us than the Hines one, and he has heard that we may have need of his services.'

'Indeed,' I said. I put my stitchwork aside. 'You are welcome, Master Stagg. Please be seated. It is true that we have had trouble here. Someone has damaged a window in our village church. How did you chance to hear about it?'

'I rode out yesterday morning to see how work was progressing for one of my customers, and met a man coming the other way in a donkey cart.'

He had sat down opposite to me, nursing his hat on his knees. He was in his thirties, I thought, with thick dark hair and alert brown eyes. He was straight of back, I noticed, and had shapely, elegant hands, the hands of an artist. Sybil, who was also artistic, had hands that were similar, though smaller. They were a complete contrast to Dr Joynings' stubby paws, in which the knuckles and the fan of bones at the back were lost in thick flesh.

He said: 'I knew the fellow with the donkey cart. His name is Ned Reed and he comes from Hawkswood village. I have met him in a Guildford tavern now and then. He buys various supplies in the town.'

'Ah,' I said, remembering Laurence Miller's unfortunate encounter with Bridget Reed and the redoubtable Marge on the previous day.

'We stopped to say good day to each other,' said Master Stagg. 'And he told me about it. I came through the village on the way here and saw the damage for myself. A shocking business, if I may say so. But you will need to get the window replaced as soon as possible, I expect. I will be happy to quote.'

Sybil had continued with her needlework. 'I will go on with

this if you wish, Mistress Stannard. Do you mean to go back to the village and show Master Stagg the window at once?'

'Yes, I will,' I said. 'Sunday or no Sunday. Dr Joynings will have finished his morning services by now. We can call on him and ask him to let Master Stagg go into the church. The thing is, Master Stagg, that I don't want to replace the damaged window by a new one of the same pattern, but wish the replacement to have a completely different design. The original one was not well liked. It was a Judgement Window and too grim for my taste or that of the vicar. Would you be able to create a completely new picture for us? And get the work done at reasonable speed?'

Master Stagg looked a little affronted. 'I served a long apprenticeship to my trade, Mistress Stannard, and can create new designs. Indeed, I have often created new window themes for churches – and also for the chapels and great halls of important men. Did you have anything particular in mind?'

'I have an idea or two, but we must talk this over with Dr Joynings. I will call for some refreshments and over them we can discuss possibilities. Then we will go to the village.'

'This is most opportune, most opportune,' said Dr Joynings as we stood in the single aisle of the little church, looking up at the shattered window. A chilly draught blew in on us. 'How fortunate that we have the offer of help so quickly. As it is, rain has been getting in and the wind makes the church so cold.'

'I know,' I said. 'I noticed that earlier this morning!'

Stagg, however, was surveying the scene with great interest. 'It's a fair-sized window. There's space for an interesting design,' he said. 'Though it won't be cheap.'

'I wouldn't expect that,' I said. 'I simply want a new theme.' Joynings nodded vigorously. 'The original one,' I said, 'was far too full of cruelty and condemnation.'

I had done well that spring, with the sale of several young trotters bred at my stud and trained by Laurence Miller and his staff of grooms. In addition, the previous year I had received a generous payment for my part in bringing to justice the conspirators who had endangered my son Harry. Their scheming had also, in Walsingham's mind at least, threatened the security of the realm. The queen had not altogether agreed with him, but she hadn't objected to the payment. This would certainly be a costly project but the window had to be replaced and, after thinking about it, I had decided that if we couldn't find the perpetrator and charge him with the bill then I could afford to take care of it myself. I would have to. Joynings certainly couldn't.

Joynings said: 'There is a hard side to Christianity. It can't be altogether ignored, of course. I think we should keep the theme of Judgement Day, but in a different way. The old window overdid it. After all, our God is a God of love. But that hard side is there and shouldn't be discounted. The last window showed Christ welcoming the righteous into Paradise, while demons drove sinners into the mouth of Hell. I would like the accent to be on the happy righteous, but we have to admit the other side. The other face of God's coin, as it were. It will be a challenge!'

Stagg nodded thoughtfully. 'Yes, I understand. The world can be a very terrible place and men can be terrible too, and we must not pretend otherwise. But there is no need to wallow in it. I can make some drawings for you to consider.'

With the swift unexpectedness of a conjuror, from a pouch attached to his belt, Master Stagg produced a slate, a stylus and a coil of thin leather which, when he shook it out, proved to be marked in inches. 'I need to take some measurements. If I do that now, then I can prepare the drawings in my workshop. It will not take me long. It will be useful for my apprentices – I have two – to watch the process, and perhaps themselves suggest a detail or two. I shall need a ladder if I am to measure the window.'

'I can provide that,' said Joynings.

'I will do the drawings in full colour,' said Master Stagg, 'and can bring them to you in a few days' time, if that will suit. Or perhaps you would like to visit my workshop and see for yourself how the work is done?'

'I would very much like that,' I said.

Master Stagg beamed. 'By all means. Say next week, on Friday. That should give me time enough.'

SIX
Gold and Silver Embroidery

The inquest on poor Philip took place the next day, at the Guildhall in Guildford. His employer, Master Samuel Hartley, had taken on the responsibility of seeing that the business was properly arranged.

This had been done in an orderly fashion which showed respect for Philip, and I sensed that Brockley approved. Every member of the jury looked like a man of substance. Indeed, I recognized several faces, as I had a wide local acquaintance. One of them was the landlord of the Tun Inn, opposite the Guildhall, which was where I had left our coach and pair. We had used the coach because Dale and Sybil wished to attend and neither liked riding, even pillion. It made them stiff.

As far as I could tell, all of the jurors were Guildford men, but among those in the crowd who had come to hear the proceedings I saw my friend Christopher Spelton, whose home at West Leys was several miles away.

I also noticed a man who interested me because he looked as if he had some importance. He was very well dressed and dignified, discreet in dark blue, but his doublet was quilted and its material was surely satin, and his pristine ruff was edged with elegant blackwork. He was in his middle years and I felt sure that if he were a Surrey man, as he must be, it was odd that I had never met him. He was striking to look at because, though no longer young, he wasn't ancient, either, yet he had a thick head of completely white hair and his bushy eyebrows and his moustache were completely white too. The effect was odd: he looked as if he had been left out in a snowstorm. Very often, white-haired people still have brown eyebrows, and the men are likely to have some brown still remaining in their beards and moustaches. This man had not a single brown hair, as far as I could see, although he was not an albino, for his complexion was slightly olive and his eyes, which I could see from where I sat, were bright blue.

The proceedings weren't lengthy. Philip had been found slain by a crossbow. The bolt was still in his body, but it was of a commonplace pattern and offered no clue as to its origin. No one had made threats against him; he was not known to have any enemies, and the body had not been robbed. A purse containing quite a good sum of money had been attached to his belt. I was seated with the Brockleys and Sybil, and we all kept very still when Master Hartley bore witness to the fact that he knew of no one who could wish Philip Sandley ill – for my son Harry probably did! And although I had not actually wished to harm young Philip, I certainly had had a great deal against him and hadn't wanted him under my roof, either. It was only for Brockley's sake that I hadn't reported his perfidy to the authorities.

Brockley was called next. Standing stiffly and speaking in a very calm, very inexpressive voice, he testified that yes, he was Philip's father. Yes, Philip had for a while worked at Hawkswood.

'He had an opportunity, though, for a better paid post with Master Hartley and decided to take it,' said Brockley, not altogether mendaciously, for he really had been more highly paid at Reddings House.

In the end, the jury returned a verdict of murder by a person or persons unknown, and that was that. Sir Edward Heron's men would continue to ask questions, but unless they found anything to point to the killer's identity the whole thing would eventually fade out.

One of the jurors – not one I knew – did suggest that Philip's death might have been an accident. 'He was found among trees, so we've been told. Some irresponsible youth fooling about with a crossbow may have mistaken a movement among the trees for a deer and shot Master Sandley by mistake.'

This, however, was quashed by a weatherbeaten man in a sleeveless leather jerkin, seated near me, who promptly rose to his feet to say that he was a local farmer, knew everyone who lived within a few miles of his land and did not know of any irresponsible youths – or greybeards either – who were likely to be wandering about in the district and shooting wildly with a crossbow, even at deer, though it wouldn't do any harm if they did shoot some deer, considering the damage they could do to a man's cornfields.'

He would have enlarged, except that the coroner, who certainly did have a firm grip on his task, stopped him. We were not there, he said, to discuss the depredations of deer.

When it was all over, Christopher came to speak to me and left with us. We stepped out of the Guildhall into the warm sunlight that had now succeeded the unseasonable spell of wet and chilly weather and we were just crossing the cobbled thoroughfare to the Tun Inn, where we had left our coach and Christopher had stabled his horse, when from behind us a voice called 'Mistress Stannard!' We stopped and turned to see the man with white hair hastening after us.

'It *is* Mistress Stannard, is it not?' he said breathlessly, catching up. I noticed that he had a couple of menservants hastening after him. Yes, he was a man of substance. 'Mistress Stannard of Hawkswood? I guessed at who you were since you were seated with Master Brockley, the poor victim's father, and when I asked Master Spelton there, whom I know slightly, he said that yes, I had guessed aright. Did you not, Master Spelton?'

'So I did,' said Christopher.

'I have never chanced to see you at court, Mistress Stannard, though I attend there sometimes . . . I am Master Giles Frost. I have just returned from London. Since the beginning of August I have been at court with my brother. We are merchants, bringing in luxury goods from abroad, and we are granted opportunities to display them to the queen's officers – even to the queen, on occasion. Sir Francis Walsingham may have mentioned me to you, he said he would do so.'

'Oh . . . yes,' I said, thinking what a splendidly suitable surname Frost was for a man with all that white hair. 'He did.'

'I have been meaning to visit you. But this is such a good opportunity. Perhaps, if we could all go to a tavern . . .'

'We are going to the Tun inn anyway,' I said. 'We have left a coach and some horses there. We can take some refreshment together if you wish.'

The inn was a busy place, with sawdust strewn over a cobbled floor that made the scattering of tables and benches wobble. We gave orders for ale and presented Sybil and Dale to Master Frost. Frost observed that Christopher evidently knew me well, and Christopher explained that his wife had once been my ward. 'Kate is sorry she couldn't come today, but our little daughter Christina is not well and she can't leave her. Poor little thing! Christina is only two months old.'

'How is your stepdaughter?' I asked.

Susanna Lake, Kate's daughter by her first husband, had had her first birthday the previous January. She was a beautiful child, with the golden hair and bright-blue eyes that her father had inherited from Norwegian ancestors. Christopher, who had become quite as fond of her as he was of his own daughter, beamed and said: 'She is enchanting, and promises to be such a beauty that I hope to get her well married without having to spend a fortune on her dowry. Her looks will probably be a dowry on their own.'

Everyone laughed and Master Frost said that Susanna sounded delightful. It was a joy to have daughters, he said. He asked Dale and then Sybil if they had any. Dale shook her head and Sybil told him about her girl, Ambrosia, who was living in Edinburgh with her second husband. He then turned to me and remarked that he had heard I had a daughter, too. Also grown up and married, was she not? I smiled and said yes. I could guess why he wished to talk to me. Although Walsingham had said that he didn't approve of me, he was being affable enough now.

He turned back to Sybil. 'So you are Mistress Jester, and companion to Mistress Stannard. I believe you are skilled not only in embroidery, but in the design of new patterns. So Sir Francis Walsingham told me.'

'I have a modest skill,' Sybil said quietly.

'And Mistress Stannard is gifted at the art of embroidery and can even work with gold and silver thread – which is an art in its own right, so I have heard,' said Frost.

'I understand the method,' I agreed. 'It is more difficult than ordinary embroidery. For one thing, the threads are more fragile. And more expensive! They consist of silken threads wrapped in thin gold or silver, and the finished work won't stand up to much washing or brushing. It has to be treated with great care.'

I spoke mildly, as one who is interested in the subject under discussion, but without too much emphasis. Walsingham wanted me to enter the Frost household, but I hadn't as yet actually been asked. Frost was a fish on my line and I needed to play him with caution. He might still break away.

'Sir Francis,' said Frost, 'chancing to hear that my two daughters, Joyce and Jane, are anxious to learn embroidering skills, and perhaps learn gold and silver work as well, suggested that I ask if you would give them some instruction. Their previous governess contracted a chill not long ago and died quite suddenly. She was not all that skilled with the art in any case, and not always very patient, either. Because a girl is slow to grasp a particular stitch is no reason for hitting her knuckles with a ruler. Sir Francis did not think I would encounter such problems in you, Mistress Stannard.'

He looked at me steadily for a moment and then said: 'I have heard of your reputation as . . . shall we say an agent for the queen. I commend your courage, although I cannot approve of the idea of a woman being engaged in such tasks. In my view, it is not fitting. But that's no reason for rejecting your skills with a needle, for that is of all things most appropriate for a lady.' He was now favouring me with a charming smile. 'I welcomed Sir Francis's advice,' Frost continued. 'He suggested that it might be best if I invited you to make a stay in my house. He also remarked that you had heavy responsibilities both at court and at home, but thought you might welcome a break from them. I believe you have a reliable steward?'

'Two,' I said. 'I have a second house, in Sussex. In fact, from time to time I move most of my household there for a while so that Hawkswood can be thoroughly cleaned and its cesspool drained. I leave a small staff behind to attend to the cleaning and hire engineers to drain the cesspool. I have formed the habit of doing that at the end of the summer, each year. And then I have the same work done at my Sussex property, Withysham. The small permanent staff I keep there stay put and help the engineers.'

'Would a stay at my home, Knoll House, have an appeal
for you instead? We can make you very comfortable and my
girls would be pleased to welcome you. You will find them
willing pupils.'

I hoped so. I had once before, during an assignment in the
distant past, acted as embroidery teacher to someone's daughters and had lurid memories of one clumsy-fingered girl whose
work regularly ended up stained with blood from her pricked
fingers. She was in fact a lovable girl in other ways, but I
would no more have tried to instruct her in gold and silver
embroidery than I would have tried to instruct a baboon.

'I am not averse to the idea,' I said carefully. 'Sir Francis
has mentioned it to me.' The landlord of the Tun Inn, now
released from his duties as a juror, had returned to the inn
while we were talking and now came bustling towards us with
a tray of tankards. They were distributed to us and Frost,
waving down any offers to pay for them, produced his purse
and saw to it himself.

'I don't ask you to come instantly,' he said. 'I am going
back to London for two weeks to go on helping my brother
with marketing the merchandise I have lately brought back
from the Mediterranean countries. I was lucky. A very fine
consignment of silks was being auctioned in Florence. We
sold some of it at court and hope to find buyers for the rest
in London.'

He smiled broadly, displaying teeth as white as his hair.
'The Italian city states have become skilled producers of silk.
Such goods no longer have to travel by camel train from
Cathay, under heavy guard and the trains still lucky if they
arrive unmolested. Times have changed. I was able to bring
back a fine variety. There are plain silks, dyed and undyed,
embroidered silks, brocaded fabrics, silk velvets in various
weights. My brother is pleased. But I have now managed to
move my household from the Midlands to Knoll House, here
in Surrey. I mean to return there by the seventh of September.
If I were to send word to you then, Mistress Stannard . . .?'

'You will want Mistress Jester too?' I asked.

'Oh yes, most certainly.'

I inclined my head, a lady considering a pleasant invitation.

Not – oh, of course not! – one of Walsingham's stealthy army of agents, sliding a foot through the door of a suspect's house in order to feed him with lies for transmission to the king of Spain, to discourage that gentleman from any plans he might have about making war on England. To discourage him from any romantic notions of being Mary of Scotland's chivalrous champion. To protect my homeland from the Inquisition.

And, of course, Frost must never know it. To him I must be the obliging Mistress Stannard of Hawkswood, happy to impart the ladylike skill of embroidery to two harmless young girls.

'I would like to consider your invitation and see how I can organize my household in accordance with it,' I said. 'If you will give me your direction in London, I can then send word to you, perhaps in a few days' time, to say whether I will be coming or not.'

I let myself give him a smile in return for his. 'I must say,' I told him, 'I feel that very likely the answer will be yes.'

SEVEN
Bridal Chest

Near the end of the following week, I received word from Master Stagg that if Dr Joynings and I wished to visit his premises to see how far the new designs had progressed, they were now ready for our inspection. If we preferred, he would of course bring them to us, but as I had shown an interest in seeing his workshop, he had pleasure in offering me and Dr Joynings a most cordial invitation. I consulted with Joynings and we agreed to go to Guildford on the Friday.

'I like to see how things are done,' Joynings said. 'And when one is using a workman for the first time, it's always a good idea to look at his premises.'

We didn't need the coach this time, but set off on horseback, enjoying the chance of a ride, with me on my bay gelding, known as Jaunty because of his proud head carriage and lofty tail, and the vicar happily astride his skewbald cob – which he had named Ireland, not because the horse was Irish but because the chestnut patch on his offside flank was, according to a map in Dr Joynings' study, much the same shape as Ireland. Brockley came too, saying that if we needed to leave the horses anywhere for any length of time, he could look after them. I knew, though, that he would enjoy the ride to Guildford on his handsome Firefly and guessed that he, too, would like to see a workshop where stained glass was created.

When we got to Guildford, I said amiably that the Tun Inn, where we once more proposed to leave the horses, wasn't far from the workshop and they would be perfectly all right there, so Brockley could come along to Stagg's premises with Joynings and me.

The premises were only a short walk from the inn. I had passed them before without noticing them, for they weren't remarkable. Just a plain shop front with diamond-pane windows, a halved door, with the top half usually open so that callers could look inside before entering, and a sign above displaying a painting of a stained-glass window. This morning, a cart stood outside with a thickset brown horse in the shafts enjoying a nosebag.

'Deliveries of raw materials?' said Brockley.

I leaned over the half door and called. A voice from within replied: 'Come in! Just push the lower door open!' We stepped inside to find ourselves in a big room with a table on the left, where there was a pile of folders, a writing set and an abacus, while on the right a grey-haired man with a hooked nose and eyeglasses that seemed to be sliding down it stood before an easel that held a very large sheet of paper. He was using a fine brush to draw an outline round an oddly shaped piece of wood, and copying from a much smaller drawing on a work-bench beside him. Also on the bench was a row of little glass pots – paints, judging by the smears on their sides – an inkstand, a holder full of brushes of various sizes and a whole lot of aids to draughtsmanship such as compasses, rulers of varying lengths and more of the curious wooden shapes. Beside the hook-nosed draughtsman, a tired-looking man seated in a chair with wheels, with a blanket over his knees, was watching the work with curiosity.

Master Stagg himself was at the other table, with the folders and the abacus. He got to his feet at once. 'Mistress Stannard! Dr Joynings! And Brockley. How prompt you are. Come in, come in. Ah, I see that you are looking at Dirk Clarke's work. Would you like to see it more closely?'

He left his desk and led us across the room to the draughtsman. Master Clarke set his brush down as we approached and looked round at us, but continued to hold his piece of shaped wood in place. The man in the wheeled chair turned as we reached him, and Stagg said: 'This is my brother-in-law, Daniel Johns. He is paying us a visit. Daniel, these are my clients from Hawkswood: Dr Joynings, vicar of St Mary's in the village there, Mistress Ursula Stannard, and her manservant Roger Brockley.'

'Forgive me for not rising in the presence of a lady,' said

Johns. 'I have the joint evil in my knees and I can only just stand using two sticks.'

'Daniel used to be in my line of work,' said Stagg, 'but fortunately his father, who was likewise, did well enough to invest in some land. That is Daniel's support now.'

'I'm luckier than some,' said Johns. 'I find going round my farms in a horse and cart and waving my stick at fencing that needs repair or crops that need drainage quite as enjoyable as toiling with geometric patterns and paints. And I enjoy the fresh air, too.'

He had the same problem as Marge Reed's old father, back in Hawkswood village. But this man wasn't old, probably not yet fifty. He was putting a good face on it, but Nature had been unkind to him.

There was a further flurry of sociable conversation and then Master Stagg got down to explaining what the grey-haired man with the hooked nose and eyeglasses was doing.

'Dirk is making a full-size painting of a window. Not yours, though. This one is a window for a big house, to go over the front door. As you see, he has a sketch in front of him showing the shapes of the panes, marked with their dimensions and notes about their colour. The painting that Dirk is preparing will have the correct measurements and will be finished in the right colours. Then it will be ready to be shown to the client, for approval. Or not, as the case may be.'

We nodded, impressed.

'It takes time,' said Master Clarke. There was a trace of impatience in his voice, as if he wished we would all go away and let him get on with it.

'Quite,' said Master Stagg repressively. 'Well, that's how it's done in my workshop. Every Master in the trade has his own system. My own is as thorough as I can make it, and as economical. But sometimes, with complex designs, we need further intermediate stages.'

'This one's simple enough,' Master Clarke said. He had a gravelly voice and a jerky manner of speech, as though he didn't talk overmuch. 'Not a picture. Round window. Just a geometric pattern made of stained-glass panes. Different colours. Straightforward.'

Interested, Brockley looked more closely at the wooden shape that Master Clarke was still holding in place. It was an elongated triangular shape marked in inches along its edges, varnished and polished meticulously as if it was to be used as a piece of decorative furniture. I glanced at the workbench where I had noticed several others and saw that they too were polished. The shapes and sizes were very varied.

'Those are standard shapes and dimensions, frequently used,' said Stagg. He added: 'I like even our tools to look elegant. It keeps the purpose of our trade in mind. Our windows must be beautiful.'

'How long have you worked here, Dirk?' enquired Dr Joynings.

'All my life. Started at ten,' said Master Clarke. His eyeglasses slipped further and he pushed them back up his nose. 'Started off sweeping up glass dust.' Which probably accounted for the gravelly voice. 'Then I learned to varnish these here shapes and mix paints. And then progressed to this. I'm turned sixty-seven now.'

'He was first taken on in my grandfather's day,' said Stagg. 'There's nothing about the work that he doesn't know.'

'Can't draw well freehand,' Dirk said regretfully.

'No one can do it all,' said Stagg. 'You go on with what you're doing, Dirk, while I take our visitors through to the back.'

We were already aware of activity somewhere in the rear of the building; sounds of grinding and knocking. We said good day to Clarke and Johns, and followed Stagg through a rear door into another spacious room. This was a busy place, with a noticeable smell of dust and paint.

'Why is Master Clarke out in the front office and not in here?' Dr Joynings asked, surprised.

Stagg smiled. 'One could call it a demonstration. When customers come in, they don't just see a man doing accounts at a desk; they see some actual work being carried out. They see a craftsman with his tools and materials, and can smell the ink and the paints. It creates an impression.'

'An atmosphere,' said Joynings, understanding. He added: 'I do the same in my church. I cannot agree with the modern fad for making things plain. When worshippers enter the house of their Creator, it should have an atmosphere that induces reverence, awe, wonder. I'm no Papist, but I see no harm in a few candles in beautiful holders. And I very much wish for beautiful stained-glass windows.'

Stagg paused, casting a benign eye over his workforce, and then said: 'Let me show you how everything is done. You have taken the trouble to visit me, and I must make it worth your while. Then we can look at the drawings I have made for you.'

His enthusiasm was almost childlike. He swept us along. We had come to see how our order was progressing and how the workshop was arranged, but Master Stagg went into far more detail than we had bargained for. He was voluble, and relentless. Brockley, aware of it, winked at me once or twice.

'First,' Stagg said, leading us to a table where there was a basket full of folders like the ones we had seen on his desk, 'there are rough drawings of the designs, with suggestions for the colours of the panes and outlines of the pictures and of the leading that defines each pane of glass. I do most of that.'

He lifted a folder from the basket and took a drawing out, laying it before us so that we could see it closely. It was clearly freehand, but very skilled and detailed all the same.

'Next,' our guide said, 'come the precise drawings with notes and measurements. You have just seen Dirk Clarke working from one, translating from a line drawing to a complete painted facsimile of a window.'

He put the drawing back in its folder, replaced the folder tenderly in the basket, and marched us to a workbench and easel and a sloping desk where an artist was working with the same concentrated air as Dirk Clarke. He was younger than Dirk, though this man too had eyeglasses.

The easel held a full-size painting of a window depicting a haloed saint. On the desk was a sheet of glass. With ruler and compass, another wooden shape, and a brush laden with lime-wash, the artist was copying the outline of just one pane very carefully on to the glass. Master Stagg signalled to us not to disturb him, and pointed to a pile of completed panes on the workbench.

'This stage has to be exact for it must all eventually fit together,' Stagg said quietly, drawing us backwards. 'When he has assembled all the panes for this window, he will cut them out in rough with a special implement, a dividing iron. Let me show you.'

We inspected the dividing iron, moving softly, as Master Stagg was doing, so as not to disturb the artist.

We were led on further, to where another craftsman, also quite young, with fair hair and a round face, and a scarf round his nose and mouth, was working with immense care on a roughly cut pane. Guided by the limewash outline, he was chipping its edges to make them smooth and perfect. A pile of more roughly cut panes awaited his attention. He too was concentrating hard and did not even glance at us. There was a dusty smell, of ground glass presumably. I had to seize hold of my nose to prevent myself from sneezing, and Brockley actually did sneeze. No wonder the craftsman wore protection over his nose and mouth.

I noticed that on each pane, in one corner, there was a small painted number and in a quiet voice, I asked Stagg why.

'That shows both the colour of the pane and its place in the pattern,' said Stagg in a near whisper.

The painting took place at the next table, which was presided over by a stern-looking fellow who was showing two youths how to mix paints and apply them.

'It's another window for the client that Dirk is working for,' said Stagg. 'The number of each pane is carefully preserved at every stage. This stage is complex.'

I noticed that the process of mixing the pigments seemed to be complex, too. From a tall earthenware jug, something other than pigment was being added. Whatever it was had a strong smell that made me and my two companions wrinkle our noses. 'Is that urine?' asked Brockley in astonishment.

'It helps to bond the paint to the glass,' said Master Stagg with amusement. 'Some people use wine or vinegar, but this works just as well – and at least one thing in my workroom comes free! Bonding to the glass is very important. There is powdered glass in the paints, too, which helps because we fire the painted panes in a kiln – over here – and that almost completes the bonding. There is still one final stage. We have nothing ready for it at the moment, but on these shelves . . .' (he pushed past an empty workbench to point to the said

shelves) '. . . are the constituents for it. The very last stage is
to add a thin layer of what we call vitreous paint to each pane.
It is made of powdered glass mixed with metallic pigments,
such as iron, copper and cobalt, according to the colour
required. Once that is on, nothing will bleach or wash the
pigment out of the glass. Some details – the exact quantities
and proportions, for instance – are a trade secret.'

He smiled at me as if he suspected I had come to steal his
trade secrets and was pleased at having defeated me.

'And now,' he said, with a complete change of tone, 'let us
look at the drawings I have prepared for your church.'

Beside the kiln was another door, which led into a small room,
evidently a study or studio of some kind. Here again was a
table with paint pots and brushes and supplies of paper. On
the floor, to the left of the door, just inside it, there was a
wooden chest. At the sight of it, Stagg stopped short, so that
I almost bumped into him.

'Well, really! Whatever is that doing here? It should have
been put away in the cupboard over there. These boys have no
sense! I wanted it brought downstairs this morning but my
servants were busy just then and I asked my two apprentices
to carry it down. Fancy leaving it here – where it could be
kicked or fallen over, or even damaged! It's of value! Master
Brockley, would you help me to put it away? I can't lift it by
myself. It's too heavy.'

'It's beautiful,' I remarked.

And it was. It was made of a timber I had not seen before
– a deep, warm red, with a lovely grain – and was elaborately
carved. It was about three feet long by just over two feet from
back to front and roughly two and a half feet deep, including
the dome of its lid, and it was polished to a satin finish. Sprays
of silver leaves were inlaid on each of its sides, and a complex
pattern like a twisted silver rope ran round the edges of the
lid. It was secured by a padlock. Master Stagg smiled, produced
a key and said: 'Ah, but you should see what's in it!' And
with that, he undid the lock and threw back the lid.

'The timber is called rosewood,' he said. 'It comes from
the Far East. The chest alone is valuable. But look at this.'

He lifted out a large object which was wrapped and padded in soft cloths. This he set down on a nearby table, before unwrapping it to reveal a magnificent silver salt, square in shape, nearly two feet high and elaborately chased, with numerous little drawers for pepper and other spices. The lid of the salt compartment and the handles of the little drawers were each set with amethysts. He stroked the gleaming thing gently, his sensitive, artistic fingers clearly savouring its beauty.

'This is the bridal gift I have put together for my niece, Eleanor. It's my contribution to her dowry. My wife died some years ago and we had no children; I look on Eleanor as a substitute daughter. She is my sister's child – well, my half-sister's, our mother having married twice – and she has no parents now. Her father died when she was a baby, then my half-sister married again and, after losing two children in baby-hood, lost her own life trying to have another. Eleanor is now in the care of her stepfather, Daniel Johns, whom you have just met. He is a decent man and has taken good care of her, but in the last few years his own health has become poor. He wishes to do his duty by Eleanor, but it is difficult for him. However, she will have her own home soon. She is to be married shortly before Christmas.'

'What a splendid wedding gift!' Brockley exclaimed.

'I have enjoyed preparing it,' said Master Stagg. 'Her bridegroom is well off, he is a master craftsman in the city of London and a man of position. The wedding will be in December. She will have turned eighteen by then – Johns didn't want her to marry too young. I felt that my gift should be in accordance with her bridegroom's position. Because of his limitations, Master Johns asked if I would undertake the business of finding a husband for her. I took care over the matter. They were betrothed four years ago, just before she had her fourteenth birthday, although we haven't yet held a formal betrothal party. That will take place shortly before the wedding itself. Her husband-to-be will expect her to be well dowered, and I and Johns have made sure that she is. I have been saving up for years to do my part, and Johns is going to give her a sum of money and some jewellery. Her father left her something, too.'

'But are you keeping this here?' Brockley asked, frowning.
'Surely, it ought to be locked away somewhere?'

'I live upstairs and have been keeping it in my chamber,' said
Master Stagg. 'I have had it brought down because I am about
to give this to my niece and wished to have it to hand. Why
my careless apprentices left it on the floor and almost in a
doorway, instead of putting it away as I told them, I can't think.
I shall speak to them. Eleanor knows about the salt, though her
stepfather doesn't, as yet. She and I have decided that I should
present it to her formally when we hold the betrothal party.
Daniel Johns will have a surprise!'

He beamed. 'At the same party, Daniel will tell her the
details of the dowry her father left for her. It includes a small
farm, which will bring in useful rents. It should be a most
happy family occasion. I only wish my late wife could be here
to share it.' He wrapped the salt up again and laid it tenderly
back in the chest.

'Master Brockley, as I said, if you would lend a hand, we
can put this out of sight and then I shall bring out the drawings I have prepared for St Mary's window. I say drawings,
plural. I have given you a choice.'

With the chest safely hidden in a cupboard, Stagg returned
to the table and pulled out a drawer from under the top. It
was a big drawer and so were the sheets of paper he lifted
out of it. 'Here we are,' he said. 'They represent the detailed
stage on which you saw Dirk Clarke working. Dirk and I took
great care with these. It is not every day that I carry out a
commission for a relative of the queen.'

He pushed the things on the table aside and spread out the
drawings. 'I was particular over choosing the colours,' he said.
'In fact, I rode to Hawkswood village the other day to look
at the church again, to get an idea of how the light falls and
what colours have been used in the other windows. I saw, Dr
Joynings, that you have had the damaged window secured
with wooden boards. It makes part of the church very shadowy.
I must say, the sooner the new window is in place, the better!
Now, what do you think?'

We all studied the examples before us, and there was no
doubt that Master Stagg was a gifted craftsman. There were

six alternative designs. For me, however, one stood out; and I was pleased when Joynings pointed to the same picture and said 'That one!' and Brockley said 'I think so, too.'

I nodded. It was conventional enough in some ways, but there was a sensible restraint. The demons who were leading the damned to hell were not too monstrous, and the damned were depicted as a flock of goats. They had human faces, but their expressions were sad rather than terror-stricken.

I smiled in approval. 'Master Stagg, you can go ahead at once. I have to be away soon, probably during September. I shall be staying at Knoll House, in the household of Master Frost, quite likely for two or three months, but it isn't far and I can return at any time to see the new window put in—'

'Master Giles Frost?' Stagg looked surprised. 'I have met him! When he first came to Surrey to look at Knoll House, he approached me to do some work there. It has a little private chapel and one of the stained-glass windows had two cracked panes, which I replaced for him. So you would like me to go straight ahead and get the window made and installed?'

It was agreed.

As we were walking back to the Tun Inn, Brockley said: 'He strikes me as a very good craftsman, who loves his trade. Though, dear heaven, how he can talk!'

We were on our horses and had started the ride home when I felt the first sense of uncertainty. It formed a curious picture in my imagination. I saw it as a smooth, slender, silvery snake gliding through my mind. I couldn't understand where it came from or what it portended.

It was simply there, a feeling that something was not right, that something in the meeting we had just had with Master Stagg had been false, contrived. I could not identify it, but the feeling was strong and unpleasant. And there was nothing I could do about it, not until its meaning became clear.

But it was a long time before that happened – and understanding came too late.

EIGHT
Unwanted Assignment

'We shall need the coach,' I said, as I helped Dale fold dresses and pack them into a big basketwork hamper. 'You and Sybil can travel in it with the luggage. Brockley and I will ride. We'll want our horses during our stay at Knoll House, since we'll be living there for some time. Eddie can drive the coach.'

'I don't understand why you can't just visit two or three times a week, ma'am, if it's to give lessons in embroidery. It isn't that far.'

'No, it's only about nine miles,' I agreed. 'In fact, I expect to do it the other way about and visit Hawkswood two or three times a week. I'm staying at Knoll House because Walsingham wishes me to be part of the household. You know why.'

I had not told my entire household about the assignment that Walsingham had given me, but I had mentioned it to my close associates. I usually did. The Brockleys, Sybil and Wilder could all be trusted. I didn't always tell Gladys but she invariably found out, and I gathered that this was one of the times when she knew all about it without a single word from me.

'What sort of a household is it? We don't really know, do we?' Dale grumbled. 'Will you want court fashions there?' She held up an elaborate brocade gown. 'Should I pack this? And do you want those big open ruffs and the best jewellery – your long rope of pearls and the gold earrings and all?'

'Better pack them,' I said. 'And my other brocade gown. And some warm clothing – shawls and woollen shifts. I've never seen such changeable weather. One minute we're sweltering, the next we're shivering.' I looked at the window, at the spatter of rain on the glass and the low grey sky beyond it. This was another unseasonably damp and chilly day. 'I want to be prepared for anything . . . yes, Wilder?'

My steward had appeared in the doorway of my chamber. 'Madam, Master Stagg is here and he has a young lady with him. He seems put out and is asking to see you. He doesn't want to tell me why.'

'He's brought a young lady?' I was puzzled. If Julius Stagg had come to report a problem with the new window, he would hardly have fetched a girl along as well. 'Where are they, Wilder?'

'In the great hall, madam.'

'Take them into the East Parlour, and tell Phoebe to put a taper to the fire in there. It's laid. I'll join them in a moment.'

I waited long enough to give Dale a few more instructions about what to pack for Knoll House, and then went downstairs to the big parlour at the eastern end of the house. It was more formal than my favourite small parlour, but more domestic and would be more welcoming than the hall if a young woman was to be entertained.

When I entered the room, my senior maid, Phoebe, was on her knees by the fire, coaxing it, and Gladys was also there – out of curiosity, of course, but armed with a tray of snacks and wine glasses. She was trying to offer refreshments to my guests, but wasn't getting any custom. Master Stagg was pacing restlessly about, and as I came in he turned sharply with a swish of his damp riding cloak and showed me an unsmiling, anxious face. The young lady was over by the window, just standing there.

I signalled to Gladys and Phoebe to leave us. Phoebe went at once, without displaying curiosity, but Gladys departed with visible reluctance as my two visitors came towards me, the girl hesitantly, lingering a little way behind Master Stagg. She was dressed for the weather in a long hooded cloak of pale blue. She had put the hood back, revealing light-brown hair gathered in a net at the back of her head, and I could see that she wore a narrow ruff. She had no farthingale, and her cloak hung straight.

She was certainly young, seventeen or eighteen, by my estimate. She looked taller than she really was, because she was so slender and held herself so well. She had big grey eyes and her skin was fair, with a soft flush of health over her cheekbones and no spots or pockmarks. She was holding the cloak closed with her left hand and I saw that the hand was slim and fine, and that she was wearing a heavy sapphire-and-diamond ring on the third finger. She seemed very nervous.

'My dear Mistress Stannard,' Stagg said, 'I must apologize for descending on you like this, and with such a strange request. It is nothing to do with the commission for the church window, all that is going as it should. But . . . I am so upset, I'm forgetting how to do things properly. I must first introduce you. This is my niece, Eleanor Liversedge. She is shortly to be married, as I think I told you. Eleanor, my dear, this is Mistress Ursula Stannard. I hope – I hope so much – that she can help us.'

Eleanor curtsied and I said: 'When I know what kind of help you need, I will of course do my best. Meanwhile, Eleanor, do please take your cloak off. This room is already becoming pleasantly warm.'

I looked round and, as I expected, saw that Wilder was waiting attentively in the passage behind me. Phoebe had now joined him. 'Phoebe, take my guests' cloaks. Wilder, I have just sent Gladys away with the tray of refreshments. Please send her back.'

I turned back to the newcomers. 'Let us all be seated, and then, Master Stagg, perhaps you will explain. All this seems so mysterious.'

They surrendered their cloaks and took seats. The East Parlour was well supplied with settles and stools. They looked at me and I looked at them. Stagg cleared his throat. Eventually, he said: 'It is so difficult. I now wonder if I should have thought of you at all, Mistress Stannard. It is only that you have a . . . a certain reputation . . . and by sheer, magical chance, you are I believe about to make a stay at Knoll House, with Master Giles Frost and his daughters.'

'As you have made the effort to come to Hawkswood,' I said, 'the least I can do is make the effort to listen to what you have to say. So please say it. I take it that Mistress Liversedge here is concerned in some way?'

For the first time, Eleanor spoke. 'It's about my dowry chest,' she said.

I was startled and probably looked it, since I couldn't imagine any way in which Eleanor's dowry chest could concern me. Stagg said: 'You saw it when you visited my workshop. I expect you remember.'

'Yes, of course I do. But . . .'

I broke off, because Gladys had reappeared with her tray. She was grumbling. 'First you say go away, then Wilder says bring it back . . .'

'Just hand the things round, Gladys,' I said, as patiently as possible. It wasn't Gladys's job to carry refreshment trays about – not least because nowadays she limped on account of the rheumatics and was all too liable to spill things. But she sometimes volunteered all the same because of her incurable desire to know everything that was going on. Not witchcraft, just curiosity and determination. I didn't really mind. Gladys had sometimes been helpful in unexpected ways.

'Master Stagg, you were saying?'

Before Stagg could reply, Eleanor said: 'The dowry chest has been stolen. We've come to ask you to help us get it back.'

'Stolen? But . . . what has that to do with Knoll House?'

'We think,' said Stagg, 'that Giles Frost may have stolen it.' I stared at him in astonishment.

This time, Stagg and Eleanor accepted wine from Gladys and allowed her to put a platter of small meat pies and saffron cakes in front of them. In an undertone, I told her to sit down in a corner and stay quiet. Then I said: 'I don't understand. That is a very serious accusation. You will have to explain more clearly.'

'I think I told you, did I not, that I recently did a small repair to the windows of the private chapel at Knoll House?' said Stagg.

'Yes, you did. But . . .'

'In the eyes of Master Frost, I am not of the level of society that he would invite to dinner,' said Stagg. 'Though he might well receive Eleanor's affianced. It's a strange world! However, he did most graciously accept a casual suggestion from me that he might call in on the formal betrothal party that we held for Eleanor two days ago. It took place at my home in Guildford – I live above my workshop, as you know. Although Eleanor has been betrothed since she was thirteen, with the wedding imminent an official betrothal party seemed appropriate. Eleanor was to take the bridal chest and various other gifts home with her after the party. Well, Master Frost called in briefly, as promised, to drink the couple's health.'

At this point, he stopped, looking awkward. 'And?' I asked.

'When I was at Knoll House, I was once or twice called into the house itself, to discuss details or to be paid. I was taken into their great hall for these things. I noticed that there were many ornaments and utensils of silver on display, and Master Frost told me that he has a great admiration for silver goods and collects them. He even admitted to being obsessive about it. And after the betrothal party . . .'

'It would have been easy enough,' said Eleanor.

She had a clear voice, with curiously little expression. She didn't sound angry, or distressed or bewildered. She just said the words she wished to say and showed no hint of her feelings. 'I came in my stepfather's wagon, which has a cover to provide protection from the weather, and after the party I was to take the gifts home in the wagon. There were quite a lot of presents and during the party we put them out on display, including the dowry chest that my uncle wanted to give me.'

'People had given her jewellery and a set of bronze tableware and rolls of linen and silk . . . all sorts of things,' Stagg added.

'Master Frost was on horseback,' said Eleanor, 'but he also had a cart with him. He said that since he needed to come to Guildford to call in at my party, he was taking the opportunity to collect some goods he'd ordered in the town . . .' Her voice trailed away and she looked to her uncle to continue.

'Yes,' Stagg said. 'He told me that he had collected some gowns for himself and his daughters, and some furniture for Knoll House, and it was all in his cart. At the end of the party, my servants were going back and forth, taking Eleanor's things to her stepfather's wagon, and Master Frost's groom – the one who was driving the cart – was helping them.'

'They were all going back and forth,' Eleanor said. 'Master Frost had only to pick a moment when the groom happened to be collecting things from upstairs and the other servants were outside packing things into the wagon. He had only to say to him "Oh, that chest is mine, bring it down and put it in my cart." It was heavy, but the groom was young and strong, and could manage. The man probably thought nothing of it, just did it because his master told him to.' Eleanor's tone did have a trace of expression this time. It was acid.

'When I got home and everything was brought into my stepfather's house, the dowry chest my uncle had given me wasn't there. The chest itself had silver decorations and there was a silver salt inside and . . . And Master Frost admits to being a passionate collector.'

'But you can't be sure—' I began, and was cut short.

'Can't be sure that Frost was the thief?' said Stagg. 'That's just it. We can. As soon as I heard that Eleanor's chest was missing, I started asking questions of people who had been at the gathering, and a neighbour of mine who'd been a guest said he had seen a chest being loaded into Master Frost's cart. I was horrified. I didn't want to start scandalous gossip, so I said that was all right, it was something I'd collected for him and been looking after until he could fetch it. But I was lying. It *has* to have been my niece's bridal silver.'

'I see,' I said. 'But . . . er . . . I don't see how I can help. I will if I can, naturally, but . . .'

'You do have a certain reputation,' said Stagg. 'And you are going to stay at Knoll House. You will have opportunities to search the place. I doubt if he will put his loot out on display yetawhile. He would expect me to report it stolen, and perhaps have the news cried in public and the lost goods described. He would keep it out of sight for the time being, unless he is a fool.'

'He sounds as if he is!' I said with asperity. 'To have the chest taken out of your house by his own groom on a public occasion, with witnesses everywhere, would have been very foolish indeed.'

'But it happened,' said Stagg. He added: 'I know little of Frost. Does he have the reputation of an honest man?'

'I don't know,' I said, although Walsingham's comments about Frost's contacts with Spain wriggled wormlike through my mind. I added: 'Surely, you yourself could . . .'

Stagg cut me short. 'I have no entrée to Knoll House. I was there as a tradesman, working in the chapel and saw little of the interior of the house. Master Frost called in at Eleanor's party to drink her health, and to see and admire the gifts, as a gracious courtesy to an inferior.'

'Or so we thought,' Eleanor put in.

'I see. Well,' I said, 'if I find it, what then? I inform you, I suppose, and then you will inform the local constable, or perhaps the sheriff, Sir Edward Heron. Then there can be an official search of the premises and . . .'

Eleanor exclaimed: '*No!*'

I looked at her in amazement. 'But why ever not? Isn't that the natural course of events?'

'Not this time! Please!' Eleanor's voice did now sound extremely expressive. In fact, it sounded urgent. Again, she looked appealingly at her uncle.

'Her husband-to-be,' said Stagg, 'is a very serious and upright man, careful of his reputation and utterly repelled by the thought of any scandal in his family or household – or his bride. He . . .'

'There is nothing scandalous about being the victim of a robbery,' I pointed out. 'It's a misfortune, requiring sympathy!'

'Martin doesn't think in that way,' Eleanor said. She was actually trembling. 'The idea of the preparations for our wedding being mingled with constables and perhaps a trial, at which my uncle would have to give evidence and so perhaps might I, would horrify him. He might be questioned himself since he was at the gathering! And maybe my stepfather would be questioned – he was there too. It would be dreadful: there would be so much talk and gossip, and people *saying* things to each other and even sniggering across dinner tables or after church. You know what I mean – how people talk and find other people's disasters comical and try to make something of it . . .'

Her voice trailed away, but I found myself nodding my head. I did know. There are people like that. Plenty of them. However, I said: 'But your betrothed is a Londoner, is he not? You will be going to live in London, and Guildford gossip won't mean much there. Anyway, gossip dies away after a while, and this gossip can't really harm you. You are the victim.'

'But we might still have to go through being questioned,' said Eleanor miserably, 'and perhaps attend a trial.'

'She means,' said Stagg, patiently, as though he were addressing an idiot, 'that her future husband would feel such distaste for the whole matter that he might withdraw from the betrothal. Betrothals are no longer legally binding, you know. I doubt if he could be compelled to honour it.'

Eleanor's head came up, proudly. 'And I wouldn't want to marry a man who didn't want to marry me!'

'So,' I said, 'if I find the chest, what *does* happen next?'

'It would be best,' said Stagg, 'if it could be quietly returned to Eleanor, or to me, without any fuss and without anyone but ourselves knowing it was ever stolen.'

'You mean,' I said, thinking it out, 'that if I find the chest, you would come to Knoll House and quietly request Master Frost to return it? I suppose that might work.'

'You don't sound sure,' said Master Stagg. 'Nor am I. The chances are that Frost would just have me thrown out, and if I then went to the authorities he would make sure the chest was moved and safely hidden where it wouldn't be found. He would protect his good name. And again, if the authorities became involved, then Eleanor's betrothed might hear of it, and well, he wouldn't like it.'

I was beginning to feel that if Eleanor's betrothed, Martin whoever he was, were to call the marriage off, Eleanor would be well out of it. He didn't sound at all a pleasant or reasonable man.

'So just what do you want me to do?' I asked.

'Well, if you find the chest . . .' Master Stagg hesitated and then plunged. 'You will be taking your own servants with you, I believe?'

'One or two,' I said.

'Well, could you, between you, just quietly steal it back and bring it to me in secret? After all, I – and Eleanor – are its lawful owners.'

'I am sorry,' I said. 'But I think you are quite . . . quite . . .'

'Quite out of my mind?' Stagg smiled. Eleanor looked at

me pleadingly. 'I can offer an inducement,' he said. 'I can cut
the price of your new church window by half. And after all,
what would you be doing that is wrong? I repeat, Eleanor and
I *are* the legal owners of that chest and its contents! We have
witnesses to that. And I don't expect you to run any risk at
all. I wouldn't expect you to touch the chest unless you were
quite sure you could do it safely.'

'I can't possibly agree to this,' I said. 'I'll look for the chest.
I suppose there is nothing against that. But if I find it, I will
simply inform you and then it will be for you to act, or not,
as the case may be. I will *not* attempt to steal the wretched
thing back.'

'Oh, please!' said Eleanor. And with that, the big grey eyes
filled with imploring tears.

'I don't think you should go to Knoll House at all,'
Christopher Spelton said. It was the next day. He had called
on me while on the way to deliver a message in Guildford,
found me pensive, and asked why. As it happened, Gladys
was in the room when he arrived and burst into speech at
once, doing the explaining before I did. I had only to say,
yes, Gladys has it right. She was there.

'I suppose there's no harm in giving embroidery lessons,'
Christopher said. 'Or in dropping a few political lies into a
conversation. Even if they're recognized as untruths, I suppose
you can always take refuge in being a foolish female who gets
things wrong, but . . .'

'Thank you!' I said.

'I know you're not,' said Christopher comfortingly. 'But
the idea of searching for stolen goods in the house of one's
host . . . that does strike me as foolish.'

'It doesn't amount to anything much,' I said. 'Just keeping
my eyes open, and little more than that. I wouldn't be *doing*
anything.'

'I can't quite explain,' said Christopher, 'but this business
gives me a bad feeling. It's so extraordinary. It makes me feel
that there might be some hidden purpose behind it, though I
can't imagine what. I really do think it would be better if you
didn't go to Knoll House at all.'

'That's what I say,' grumbled Gladys.

'Walsingham's orders,' I said.

Christopher gave me a wry grin. 'Yes, Walsingham's orders. One always feels that they have to be obeyed. But be careful, Ursula. I know Knoll House, by the way. I called there once – a long time ago, well before this man Frost took over. Carrying a message, of course. It's a gloomy sort of place.'

'I can hardly refuse Walsingham because Knoll House is gloomy!'

Christopher sighed. He thought for a moment and then said: 'Are you going to tell Laurence Miller about this . . . er . . . unwanted assignment? It's the sort of thing he will want to know.'

'So that he can report to Sir William Cecil? No, I don't think I should. That would almost amount to pointing a finger of suspicion at Master Frost in a public way, and Eleanor would object to that. She is so anxious to keep it all a secret from the man she's betrothed to. She wouldn't want it bruited about, even to Cecil. Even to Walsingham, discreet though they are. Anyway,' I added, perhaps pettishly, 'I have always disliked the idea that I have someone watching me and sending reports of me to William Cecil. It's supposed to be for my protection but I still don't like it. No, I shan't tell Miller. After all, as I keep telling you, I'm not going to *do* anything, other than look about me when I'm at Knoll House. If I find the chest, I'll tell Master Stagg and leave the rest to him.'

'You didn't agree, madam!' Brockley said it as a statement and a question both at the same time. 'You're not going to try to steal the chest back, surely! Even if the lass did behave like an overflowing river!'

'No, no, *no!*' I said, with exasperation. Christopher had gone, and I had gathered my close associates round me in the East Parlour: the Brockleys, Sybil and Gladys. I had placed myself on the broad window seat, while the others had disposed themselves around the room, the Brockleys side by side on a padded settle and Sybil on another, her face composed and her skirts spread tidily round her, while Gladys, with her mottled brown complexion and hooked nose and the curved back that the years had inflicted on her, was crouched on a low stool close to the empty hearth. The variable weather had varied once again, and the day was too warm for a fire.

'I keep saying it,' I declared. 'I said it to Eleanor and Stagg, and I said it to Christopher Spelton when he came here this morning! I told him I was prepared to look for the chest, but wouldn't attempt to spirit it away. Master Spelton would be against me going to Knoll House at all, were it not on Walsingham's orders.'

'Why?' asked Brockley bluntly. 'I mean, why is Master Spelton so opposed to it?'

'He says he has a bad feeling about my visit. You can't call that a reason! And I repeat, all I will do is look for the chest.'

'Wild geese!' said Brockley in exasperated tones, and everyone laughed.

They all knew the story. Years before, on a journey to Cambridge in the company of an old friend, Rob Henderson, dead now for three years, I had heard a flight of wild geese calling as they flew overhead and said that I liked the sound they made, that it was full of salt winds and empty spaces, and Rob had said I had revealed something in my nature, something untamed. There was some truth in that, as I realized at the time. Without it, I would never have eloped with my first husband by climbing out of my bedchamber window and sliding down the sloping roof of a single-storey room jutting out below.

Nor, I suspected, would I ever have become involved in the adventures that had befallen me over the years. I had always thought of myself as undertaking my various assignments out of loyalty to the queen, but I knew that I wouldn't have been asked to undertake them in the first place if that strange wild streak in me hadn't been there. But all the same . . .

'I have always,' I said with dignity, 'done my best to behave like a lady. I just haven't always been treated as one.'

'Who rode through the night as one of a party who meant to assault a house, because she thought her son might be imprisoned there?' enquired Brockley. 'Who once crouched on the floor of a warehouse in Antwerp in the middle of the night, helping to take up floorboards in search of missing treasure? Who . . .?'

'I *had* to try to rescue Harry. And I was in that warehouse because Dale's life was in danger and I needed that treasure to buy her safety. Anyway, you weren't there. You didn't actually see me pulling up floorboards.'

'No, madam. But you did tell me about it,' Brockley said mildly.

And suddenly, for a moment as brief as a flash of lightning, it was there – the curious rapport that Brockley and I had, which once had made Dale violently jealous and still occasionally made her unhappy, so that we tried never to let her be aware of it. This time it was our joint remembrance of more than one dangerous adventure in which Brockley and I had taken part. There was a silence.

'All right,' Brockley said at last. 'But please, madam, *please* take care. Be sure that you do no more than look around you to see if your glance lights on the chest. No one's life is in danger, no one has been kidnapped, and neither the queen nor Cecil nor Walsingham have asked you to do it. Personally, I wish they hadn't asked you to do anything. I don't like the idea of you – our – actually staying in the house of a questionable fellow, which is what this Giles Frost seems to be.'

'I know,' I said. 'I agree with you. But we're going, all the same. Moreover, I'll be paid,' I added brightly, 'by Walsingham. And if I instruct the Frost girls well, I might even be paid by Master Frost!'

They laughed, but then Brockley said soberly: 'Ah well, there's one thing. It may be as well for you to be away from home for a while, madam, in view of the threats which, according to Walsingham, have been made against you by the brother of Simeon Wilmot.'

'Walsingham himself said as much,' I told him.

'He may well be right,' Sybil chimed in. 'When poor Philip was killed I even wondered if it had something to do with this brother. What were you told his name was, Ursula?'

'Hunt. Anthony Hunt. I wondered too,' I said. 'But nothing more has come of it. It's still a mystery.' I looked at Brockley. 'Perhaps you will find it helpful to be away from here for a while, it may distract your mind. Philip must be very much in your thoughts.'

'He is,' said Brockley. 'My poor boy. Murdered by someone unknown, and since then nothing. He has been wiped out. It's as if he had never existed at all.'

Again there was a silence, and again one of those curious flashes between us. I knew, of course, that it had been wonderful for Brockley when he found that he had a son, and I knew what a bitter disappointment it had been for him when Philip became involved in a foolish plot. And I knew too that he had grieved like any other father when Philip died. Only, I hadn't realized until this moment just how deeply Brockley had felt about all those things. He had not expressed his feelings very openly.

He never did. He always put his duties first. I had left it to Dale to comfort him and I knew that she had tried. I had stepped back, as it were, and not intruded on them. Now I wondered if I should have been more openly sympathetic – except that Dale might not have liked that.

These things could be very complicated. I smiled round at my servants, my companions, my friends, and said: 'Remember, if any outsider wants to know where we are going, we are bound for Buckinghamshire to visit Meg.'

Whereupon, Gladys pulled a face that made her nutcracker countenance look even less pleasing than usual and said: 'Let's hope, indeed, that this man Anthony Hunt don't get on your scent. Reckon he's likely to try, do you?'

'It's possible,' I said.

Gladys snorted. 'And let's hope there ain't nothing dangerous in this place Knoll House, seeing that it's that Walsingham that's sending you there, and the kind of trouble you mostly land in when he gives you a task.'

'Gladys,' I said, 'once again you are croaking like a raven. It's depressing.'

It was. And unfortunately, with Gladys, her croakings all too often came true.

NINE
Knoll House

Knoll House was a little to the north of the town of
Leatherhead. I had seen it from a distance often enough.
It crowned its hill, a tall house, built of dark-red bricks.
Standing there outlined against the sky, it had a forbidding
air. All the more so on the day we arrived, because the sky
was overcast.

I noticed, as we made our way up the long sloping track
to the gate, that the house had some modern mullioned
windows, but there were others with the narrow, upright lancehead shapes of the previous century, when it was probably
built. There was a gatehouse and a porter complete with errand
boy, who escorted us for the last part of the track and hushed
the noisy greeting given by a pair of enormous mastiffs, which
came bounding to meet us.

As we drew near I saw that, as Master Stagg had said, the
house possessed a chapel. It was an extension, built out to the
right, a miniature church with a squat tower rising from its
outer end. To our left was a wall with an archway through
which grooms came hastening to meet us. Eddie leapt down
from the driving seat of the coach and Brockley, dismounting
from Firefly, began to explain that the coach needed to be
unloaded as soon as possible and asked that both Eddie and
the coach horses should be fed and watered. After that, Eddie
would drive the coach back to Hawkswood. I dismounted as
well and Dale helped Sybil out of the coach. Brockley then
disappeared into the stable yard, leading Firefly and Jaunty.
Brockley always preferred to care for our horses himself when
they were housed in unfamiliar stables.

The front door of the house was a massive oak affair sunk
in a deep porch. Our young escort pulled a chain attached to
a big iron bell that clanged with a mournful noise, as though

it were tolling for a death, but caused the door to be opened by a stern-faced black-gowned figure with a gold chain of office, who declared that he was the steward and that he was glad to welcome us, we were expected, and please to enter.

Sybil said something about our luggage but the steward said we need not concern ourselves, it would be brought up to our bedchambers shortly. All was in readiness for us. With a wave of his hand he dismissed the boy, who ran off, back to his master in the gatehouse, and then he closed the door.

My first impression was that this was a horrible house.

We were standing in what seemed to be a small-scale version of a great hall. The walls were panelled in dark wood and decorated with numerous pairs of antlers, and to our right a staircase slanted upwards. To the left was a closed door and beside it a cupboard standing on legs and doubling as a table, with two tall silver candlesticks on it. Beneath our feet there was a chessboard pattern of large black and white paving stones, while above our heads were dark beams and a plaster ceiling decorated with paintings, but the place was too shadowy to see what they depicted.

There were several tall candle stands placed along the walls, though none of the candles were lit. Some daylight did come in through an archway at the far end. Beyond it, I had the impression of a window and thought I could see the foot of another stair (as a faint smell of cooking drifted from that direction, I supposed that the kitchen quarters lay there). But apart from that, the only illumination came through the stained-glass fanlight over the door behind us. This was sizeable and might have shed a good light except that most of the stained glass was deep crimson. Such light as entered through it lay on the black-and-white floor like a stain of blood and drenched the candlesticks with red.

'Please to follow me,' said the steward. 'I am Hamble,' he added, confusing me (and Dale and Sybil as well, as they later told me) because it sounded as though he were saying that he was humble, and anyone less humble would be hard to imagine. He led us through a door on the right, into what was evidently the real great hall. There was dark panelling here as well, but the windows were mullioned and a respectable amount of daylight came in. A door beside the big hearth had an ecclesiastic air, with a pointed arch, and probably led to the chapel. I also noticed another door at the rear of the room, which I thought might lead out to the grounds. Logs were laid in the hearth, though they were not lit.

In the middle of the room was a long table with high-backed benches along each side and a chair with carved arms at one end. There were also three hefty sideboards, on which dishes and goblets, ornaments and candlesticks were displayed, all of them silver. So was the casing of the ornate clock which hung on one wall. Frost certainly did seem to like silver.

'If you will wait here,' said the steward, 'I will fetch the young ladies. Master Frost is out on the home farm. We did not know what time you would arrive.'

'Thank you,' I said.

A young maidservant appeared in the doorway, with Brockley behind her. She stepped aside to let him pass and he said: 'I am happy with the grooms here, madam. They are rubbing down our horses for us, with Eddie to help them and keep an eye on them. They have promised, once they've finished with the horses, to take Eddie to the kitchen for a meal and a glass of ale before he starts for home. One of the grooms showed me the way in through the kitchen, and young Bessie here said you would have been shown into the great hall.'

'I thought it best to bring Master Brockley here, Hamble,' said the maidservant, obligingly clarifying Hamble's name for us.

'Quite correct, Bessie. Off with you now,' said the steward. He turned to me. 'Your names, if you will, so that I know I have them right. Yours, of course, is Mistress Ursula Stannard. But the others . . .?'

I introduced Sybil and the Brockleys. Hamble gave us a brief bow, and then left. We heard his feet retreating up the staircase from the entrance hall. The stairs creaked, as though their timbers were old and tired of being trodden on. Presently we heard footsteps coming down again, and a moment later he was opening the door for two young girls and making the necessary introductions. Then he withdrew and we were left with our hostesses-cum-pupils.

I had somehow assumed that since the girls were twins they
would be identical, but they were not. They were dressed alike,
though, in peach-coloured gowns with matching caps, moderate
farthingales and small ruffs. Joyce was a good two inches taller
than her sister, with hair of a dark-brown shade that edged
towards auburn, whereas Jane was slight, not much above five
feet tall, and her hair was much lighter. Their eyes however
were the same greenish hazel – lighter in shade than my own
– and they both had clear complexions unmarked by any pocks.

Both were smiling but Joyce took the lead, coming forward
to take my hands. 'Mistress Stannard! We are so happy to
welcome you and so sorry that Father is out. He will not be
long. There was some trouble with our bullocks – they got
out of their field and would have been in the corn if not
promptly chased back to their proper place. And this is Mistress
Jester?' She turned to Sybil, and now Jane came forward and
very sweetly kissed Sybil in greeting.

'And this is Fran Dale, my maid and my friend,' I said,
establishing relationships firmly. I never allowed the Brockleys
to be regarded as mere servants to be kept in the background,
but insisted that they should be treated as guests like myself
and Sybil. 'And her husband, my manservant and also my
friend, Roger Brockley.'

'You must take off your riding cloaks and come up to
our parlour,' said Joyce. 'Hamble is already bespeaking
refreshments for us all. Will you come now?'

We followed the two of them out of the hall and up the
staircase, which was long and just as ill-lit as the entrance
hall. It led up to a wide passage with slender lancehead
windows at each end. I could see that at the far end there was
another staircase, probably a continuation of the one I had
reckoned led up from the kitchen quarters. It went on up to
the floor above, but the front staircase which we had just
ascended apparently did not continue.

As a means of letting in daylight the lancehead windows
were hopelessly inadequate, and this too was a place of
shadows. But Joyce threw open a door on our left and we
went into what, to our relief, was a comfortable parlour with
more mullioned windows.

'Here we are,' said Joyce, waving us to an array of cushioned settles and stools. 'Jane and I embroidered some of those cushions – you can see which ones by all the mistakes. With your help, we hope to improve. Do please be seated. Jane, will you go and see why Hamble is taking so long? He should be here with his tray by now.'

'I am here,' said a voice behind us, and we moved hastily to let the steward through. His tray held a wine jug, goblets (silver, what else?) and several dishes of small eatables – raisins, nuts, some little pies. 'These pies are chicken, and these have plum preserve in them,' Hamble said, setting the tray down on a small table and pointing.

Joyce dismissed him. She was the dignified twin, I thought, and usually the foremost one, while Jane was sweeter, less commanding and more impulsive. We all sat down to partake of the refreshments. Joyce asked what kind of journey we had had; Jane told us that when our lessons began they would take place in the same parlour, if that should be agreeable to us, as the light was good. 'It isn't good everywhere in this house,' she said and then, with candour, added: 'We don't like this house very much. The one we had in the Midlands was much pleasanter.'

'We shall have to make the best of it,' Joyce said austerely, and then changed the subject by telling us that she had been looking out of the window when we arrived and had caught sight of our horses. She very much liked the look of the dark chestnut.

'That is my Firefly,' said Brockley, and she began to tell him about her dappled mare, Patches, who was the greediest animal on earth. 'One has to stop her from trying to snatch a mouthful from every bush we pass. If I relax for an instant, down goes her head and she starts to graze! And we do feed our horses properly, believe me.'

We were deep in friendly conversation when the door opened to admit Master Frost, who came in hastily, with an apologetic air.

'I am sorry I was not here when you arrived. Welcome, Mistress Stannard. And Mistress Jester, and the Brockleys! I hope you had easy travelling. Is there any wine left in that jug? I have been with the men, chivvying bullocks away from my cornfield. I am exhausted and parched, and I still have to see the bailiff about the bullocks' field. It wants new fencing and better drainage.'

We all greeted him politely. Joyce poured him some wine and offered him the various dishes. He looked as much as ever as if he had just been out in a blizzard and I kept half-expecting him to call for a towel to wipe the snow off his hair, eyebrows and moustache.

After a while, he said: 'Joyce, my dear, when I came in I saw the baggage being brought upstairs. I think it is time that you showed our guests where they are to sleep. I must go to my study. The bailiff should be there by now, waiting to see me.'

He left the room, and Joyce said: 'The guest rooms are upstairs. Come, we'll show you.'

The twins led the way and we followed. 'Most of the rooms on this floor are bedchambers,' Joyce said. 'But they are all occupied.' She pointed to a door opposite. 'That's Father's room, in the front of the house, and his study leads out of it. That other door leads straight into the study. Next to the study are the two rooms that the Hambles use. Mrs Hamble – they like the modern fashion of address – is our housekeeper. Their son is the porter's boy. Beyond those, in the corner by the back stairs, is quite a nice chamber that our chaplain, Dr Andrew Lambert, uses – you'll meet him at supper. In the other corner there's a music room. Our bedchamber is next door to this parlour, and beyond that is where Susie sleeps – she's our maid, we share her. The rest of the women servants have a dormitory on the floor above, opposite the guest chambers, and the men are up another flight of stairs, in the attic along with the lumber rooms.'

'Father likes Susie to be near us,' said Jane. 'She's very pretty,' she added.

I wondered if that was really a *non sequitur*, but saw the reproving glance that Joyce shot at her twin and decided it wasn't. For a moment, I felt that something secret and question-able had slid into the atmosphere.

No, I thought. I didn't like this house any more than the

twins did, though probably for quite different reasons. I said: 'Shall we go upstairs, then?'

Brockley said: 'I must go to the stables, or the kitchen, and find Eddie. He had better start for home soon.'

The rest of us followed the twins to the staircase at the far end and went up. This flight was tiresomely shadowy, like so much else in this house, and it creaked as well.

The next floor was similar to the one below except that only the back stairs continued to it. Here, too, was a wide passage, or elongated vestibule, running from the back of the house to the front with rooms on either side. We had been allocated two rooms, one for Sybil and myself, the other for the Brockleys. Sybil's and mine was the bigger of the two, but both, I was glad to see, were reasonably well lit and comfortable.

Both rooms had four-poster beds, corner cupboards and good-sized clothes presses, and the deep window seats lifted up to reveal ample storage space beneath. Each room also had a washstand and several floor rugs, and a prie-dieu with a little statuette of the Virgin and Child. There was no pretence that this was not a Catholic household. Dale, who had once, in Catholic France, been charged with heresy, drew her breath in with a disapproving hiss.

'The rooms are very pleasant,' I said loudly, and hoped the twins hadn't heard the hiss.

I asked a few artless questions about the layout of the house. If I was going to search it for Eleanor's stolen chest, and I supposed I had better at least try, then knowing my way round would be useful.

'Oh, the women's dormitory is behind that door opposite? And there's a spare bedchamber on the other side of the one for the Brockleys, and a little one at the back of the house next to the dormitory? And those are the stairs up to the attic floor? It's quite a big house, isn't it!'

'It seems odd having the guest rooms on the same floor as one of the servants' rooms,' said Joyce apologetically, 'but we had to arrange things to fit our household. Well, we will leave you. We will have some hot water sent up, and there are towels

in your corner cupboards. Do come down to the hall when
you are ready. We shall be there with Father and Dr Lambert.'

I asked another artless question. 'What's the room to the
left as one comes through the front door? Opposite the door
to the great hall, I mean.'

'Oh, that's the ballroom,' said Jane. 'We hope to do some
entertaining once we are properly settled in. We'll show you
when you come downstairs.'

When we presently descended, they duly met us in the
entrance hall. Jane, with the air of a showman, led us at once
to the door opposite the great hall and flung it open, revealing
a wide and empty room, with a wooden floor, numerous lamp
stands and at least a dozen multi-branched (silver) candelabra,
which would certainly be needed when the ballroom was in
use because this was yet another shadowy place. I looked to
the right and saw that in the corner there was a low, unobtrusive door. Like the one I had noticed at the rear of the great
hall, it presumably led outside. Much more noticeable was the
dais beside it, with a clavichord standing on it alongside a
table on which lay a sackbut.

'When minstrels come, they have their own instruments, of
course,' Joyce said, 'but sometimes they find we have something they haven't got and are happy to use it. We have a harp
in that little music room upstairs and our lutes are there, too.
We practise regularly. Father often likes us to make music
after dinner.'

'I shall look forward to hearing you play,' I said politely.
One comprehensive glance had shown me that wherever Master
Frost had stowed the purloined chest – *if* he had purloined it
at all – it wasn't in this empty and public place.

It was not yet dusk but the sky was beginning to dim, so
that inside Knoll House the shadows were deepening more
than ever. As we left the ballroom, Brockley reappeared from
the stables and kitchen quarters to say that Eddie had left over
an hour ago and should be well on his way home by now. 'He
should be there before it's fully dark, madam.'

I said 'Good,' and we all started towards the door of the great
hall. As we did so, a tall woman appeared from the direction
of the kitchen, carrying a lit taper. She began to light candles.

Light sprang up, glinting on the silver candlesticks and the ivory-coloured points of the antler decorations, though there were still shadows in plenty, stretching this way and that, elongating and shrinking, racing ahead of us as we crossed the chessboard floor.

'This is Mrs Hamble, our housekeeper,' said Joyce. 'Mrs Hamble, here are our guests. This is Mistress Stannard . . . Mistress Jester . . . Master Roger Brockley and his wife Frances . . .'

'Welcome to Knoll House,' said the housekeeper, turning to us. She was lean as well as tall, and dressed in businesslike fashion in a plain black woollen gown. The dark material was relieved by a small white ruff and a white cap. Between ruff and cap, her face was a long, pale oval with little expression. Her words expressed welcome, but there was no accompanying smile.

We all murmured that we were happy to make her acquaintance and then we followed her and her taper into the great hall, where she set about lighting yet more candles, and we saw that the table was set for supper. An ornate salt had been set out in the middle of the table. It was bigger and even more costly, I thought, than the one that Stagg wanted to give to Eleanor. Why on earth, I thought, should Giles Frost wish to steal it, when he already had this?

The twins led us towards the hearth, where a fire had now been lit and where a thin man in the dark gown and cap of a cleric was seated. He rose to greet us. He had been telling the beads of a rosary, which he was now putting away in a belt pouch. 'This is Dr Lambert, our chaplain,' Joyce said. 'Dr Lambert, this is . . .'

She got no further with the introductions, because Master Frost suddenly appeared and took them smoothly over. Lambert greeted us in a most amiable fashion, but I realized at once that he was going to be a permanent source of irritation, for he had a maddeningly affected ecclesiastical voice which sounded as though he were intoning through his nose. We heard more of it during supper, which was served almost at once, as Lambert said grace and thereafter did a good deal of talking – on numerous topics, including the fencing and drainage of the bullocks' field, how much he approved of young ladies learning the skill of embroidery, and the tiresomeness of winter for Master Frost when seagoing trade was almost at a standstill.

Frost himself said little, though he made some small talk with me and Sybil. The Brockleys were at the table as well – because during an exchange of letters before our arrival I had made it clear that I wished this to be so – but Master Frost didn't choose to talk to them.

I wondered when and how I would get a chance to feed untruthful remarks about the size of Elizabeth's navy into the conversation, and decided that it must not be too soon. I needed to absorb atmosphere, learn the way people talked to each other in this house, make haste slowly.

And search the house for an errant dowry chest as well. But how on earth I was going to manage that, with creaking staircases and the twins and various servants coming and going all the time, I couldn't think.

Well, I would find a way, no doubt. Meanwhile, I had to admit that the cooking in this house was excellent.

TEN
The Search Begins

That night I had a bad dream. I was searching Knoll House. In the dream it was even gloomier than it was in reality. I groped my way about and bumped into pieces of furniture that I couldn't see. Tall black figures came and went. One of them thrust a pale oval face into mine and laughed, before vanishing; another came at me with a knife. I woke sweating, thankful to find myself safe in a four-poster bed with Sybil fast asleep beside me, but wondering what the source of the dream could be. It suggested that in this house there was something to fear, and somewhere deep in my mind I knew what it was. But if so, it was too deeply buried to be found. I did not know what it could be.

In the morning, Dale came to help us dress and, when she had done so, said: 'Roger would like to see you, ma'am – well both of you – before we all go downstairs. Shall I call him?'

'Of course,' I said.

He must have been waiting just outside, because Dale merely put her head out of the door and spoke his name and there he was. Shaved, and dressed for the day in a serviceable brown doublet and hose, looking both anxious and tired.

'I've been awake half the night,' he said. 'Thinking.'

'And I've been dreaming,' I told him. 'I had a nightmare last night. I don't like this house, though I couldn't really tell you why. But I remember feeling like this once before. Do you remember Stonemoor House, in Yorkshire? I had an unreasonable feeling there that something was wrong, only it turned out to be not so unreasonable after all. I have the same feeling now. What is it that is worrying you, Brockley? Do sit down, you do indeed look tired.'

With an air of thankfulness, he seated himself on a stool. 'There are too many mysteries – too many strange things –

crowding in on us, madam. There was Sir Francis Walsingham, giving you orders to come here and give false information. And warning you against Simeon Wilmot's brother. Then there was Philip's death. Well, who did attack him? And *why* did they attack him? The coroner just dismissed it as "murder by someone unknown". Philip let us down, he betrayed us, I know that, madam, but he *was* my son, the son I didn't know I had until he suddenly appeared and then . . .'

His voice shook. Quietly, I said: 'I know. I really do know. Last year I feared I had lost my own son.' Dale went to him and laid a hand on his shoulder, and after a moment, he recovered himself.

'Then there was the broken window in the church,' he said. 'And after that, Julius Stagg asked you, since you were coming here, to look for the stolen bridal chest. When we visited his workshop, he brought that chest to your attention almost like a conjuror forcing a card on someone, playing one of those tricks that Wilmot used to do when he was pretending to be an entertainer. He . . .'

'That was it!' I said, suddenly enlightened. 'After that visit I had a feeling that there had been something wrong, a false note. That was it. We were *made* to look at that chest, to admire it, to be told what it was for!'

'Yes, madam. It's all too much. So many things. I keep feeling that they must be part – facets – of just one thing, one hidden thing, but I can't imagine what it is. But last night it all came together in my head and kept me awake. I'm afraid for you, though I can't guess where or what the danger is.'

'I think you are very likely right.' Sybil spoke briskly. 'But we are here now, with tasks to carry out. All we can do is carry them out and keep our eyes and ears open. I've been thinking too. If we're really going to look for this wretched chest, well, it won't be easy to search this house. There will be so many people about.'

'Yes. Very true,' Brockley said. 'Last night I did some prowling. We all retired at the same time, but after that I put my dressing robe on and went down to the kitchen. Everyone was still very much awake there. The chief cook – he's a jolly sort of fellow, nearly the size of an elephant and a great contrast to the Hambles – was overseeing the arrangements for tomorrow's breakfast . . .'

'Making bread dough and counting out chops?' asked Sybil, amused.

'Not him. He was sitting in a chair in the middle of the room shouting orders to three scuttling minions – two young fellows and that young Bessie. And Mrs Hamble was there too, lecturing another young maid about pans not scoured to her satisfaction. I asked her if I could have some mulled wine because my wife thought she had a chill.'

'That black clad beanpole!' said Dale. 'She makes me feel creepy.'

'She was quite human when I spoke to her,' Brockley said. 'She said certainly, she would prepare it herself while I waited, and I could call in every evening if I liked and collect mulled wine for two. Guests are to be made comfortable, she said. And while I was there, the steward came in through a door I hadn't noticed, carrying a tray with several flagons of wine on it. I took a look through the door, and there were steps leading downwards. This house has cellars. We shall need to search those too. Probably on tiptoe in the middle of the night, which won't be easy.'

'We're facing problems,' I said.

But for the moment, we had other things to do. We went to breakfast and afterwards Brockley, who had told the grooms that he wished to groom and exercise Jaunty and Firefly himself, departed to the stables to attend to them. I asked the twins if we could now go to the parlour to begin the embroidery lessons, and sent Dale to our room to fetch the necessary materials. Dale brought them to the parlour and then left us, saying that she wished to press the pleats in my ruffs and would also walk through the house 'so as to get used to it'. She gave me – not a wink, exactly, but a briefly drooping eyelid which amounted to the same thing. The search was beginning, in a cautious way.

The day was overcast and I asked for candles. Then we settled down. Sybil and I had worked out a rough programme. First of all, we needed to find out whether the twins knew all the basic stitches, and if not, fill in the gaps. Once that was done, I had brought some cushion covers from Hawkswood made of a beige cloth. On the front of each, Sybil had drawn a quite simple geometrical pattern in the centre and round the edges a slightly more complex pattern of bluebells and daisies with thin curved stalks and leaves. These would require a variety of stitches, varying shades of green and blue, a choice of yellows for the centres of the daisies, and white or pale cream for their petals.

'This way they can get some practice both in stitchwork and in choosing colours,' Sybil had said.

I said moodily that when I taught embroidery once before I had a pupil who bled all over things, and hoped history wouldn't repeat itself!

It soon emerged that this was not the case. Within the first quarter of an hour, we established that both of the twins knew the basic stitches. Of the two, Jane was the more deft, handling her needle with real skill. Joyce was slower and sometimes made mistakes, but she wasn't clumsy. And neither of them were at all likely to smear their work with blood.

We worked for nearly two hours. Once they'd started on the cushion covers, I let Sybil sit by while I fetched my lute and played to them. Later, I told the twins to put away their needles and Sybil took charge. She began by finding out how well the girls could draw, using slates to begin with, and gave them some basic instruction about taking measurements and how to make sure patterns were positioned aright.

'If you are making cushion covers, you usually want the main design in the centre of the front panel, not nearer one edge than the other. And if you are going to embroider a pair of sleeves, the pattern needs to be carefully placed and the same on both sleeves.'

After another hour, I noticed that the girls were looking tired and called a halt. 'That's enough for one day. More than enough, perhaps. We'll do some more tomorrow. Let's amuse ourselves till dinner time.'

It was a dull day for going out. Brockley had gone out to exercise our horses, but he returned just as we finished our lessons and came to tell us that he would be in the tack-room, cleaning our saddlery. We ladies repaired to the ballroom, where we took turns in playing the clavichord while the others danced. I took the opportunity of looking sharply about in case there were any doors leading anywhere I hadn't yet seen. But apart from the door into the entrance hall, the only door I could see was the one at the back that led straight into the grounds.

The grounds! The words suddenly burst into my mind. We hadn't even thought of exploring the grounds, and they might offer some excellent hiding places. But a wind had risen and was now blowing rain against the windows. We could hardly search the grounds in this.

For the purpose of practising stitchery and amusing ourselves by dancing we had all dressed in simple clothes, but the twins told us that their father liked people to wear formal clothes at dinner and said that they were going to put on their peach ensembles. Sybil and I decided to change our gowns. I didn't think it was an occasion for brocades, but I chose my favourite tawny velvet, the sleeves slashed with cream silk and the skirt open-fronted to show off a kirtle of the same material embroidered with small yellow flowers. Cream and tawny were a favourite colour combination of mine; I often wore them, in various forms, knowing that I looked well in them. Sybil selected apple green, slashed with yellow. It suited her and made her look younger than her years. Dale, observing us, also changed, into a dress which, although it was a restrained dark blue without slashings, was well set off by a pristine ruff and green-agate beads.

Our careful toilette seemed to please Master Frost, who looked at us and his daughters with obvious approval and this time took the lead in the conversation. Dr Lambert said grace, in his annoying voice, but after that held his tongue and listened with the rest of us while Master Frost discoursed on the difficulties he had had in arranging a regular supply of firewood now that the winter was approaching, and how tiresome it was that there were so many chills and fevers about. Apparently, he had a valet who was now lying sick in the men's attic dormitory and Hamble was helping Master Frost out for the time being.

I had wondered why Frost didn't seem to have a personal attendant, and now debated whether I should volunteer Brockley's services but decided against it. I was likely to need Brockley's help myself.

From time to time we all made suitable comments, and I listened attentively in case some kind of opening should arise. How *was* I to get Master Frost to talk about warships and navies? His affable manner to me didn't change the fact that he didn't like the idea of women being involved in what he regarded as men's affairs and probably wouldn't think that matters maritime would – or should – interest a lady.

The meal began with white-bean soup and proceeded in leisurely fashion through smoked mackerel to a very good dish of veal in a white wine and mushroom sauce, with a side dish of cabbage. After that came a bread pudding with raisins and ginger in it. We were halfway through that and I was wondering whether I could ask for the recipe and give it to my John Hawthorn, when I heard Master Frost remark that he would shortly be away for a few days because he needed to visit his brother in London again.

'I don't venture our little merchant ship on long voyages between October and March,' he said. 'But I still have much to discuss with my brother. I shall probably leave for London next Monday, though I should be home again by the end of the week. I believe that when we met in Guildford, Mistress Stannard, on the sad occasion of the inquest, I spoke to you of the beautiful silks I had found in Venice. I also saw some striking samples of Persian embroideries – fabrics suitable for wall-hangings. The vendor said he could obtain more if I was interested, so I placed an order with him and brought a few back. Well, I have passed both the silks and the embroideries to my brother and he has now had time to find out how popular they are with his customers, and I am anxious to know that, too. I don't really doubt that the silks will do well, but I took a chance in placing the order for more embroideries, as some of the patterns are unusual and they're certainly costly. But sometimes you have to back your own judgement, otherwise you could easily miss a fine opportunity.'

'It sounds almost like a form of gambling,' Sybil remarked, smiling.

'Perhaps it is,' Frost agreed. 'But as I said, you have to trust to your judgement and experience or you would never do any business at all. My brother and I will be travelling to various autumn fairs in big towns, so we need to make detailed plans for that, too, since we are going to cross to the Continent and attend fairs in France and other countries.'

I made a harmless remark that would point the conversation in the right direction. 'Travel by sea in the winter must have its unpleasant side,' I observed.

'Ah, well, trade can't stop on account of the seasons. The seas aren't quite empty of ships even in winter,' Frost said, and twinkled at me in a jovial fashion. I silently cursed. He knew of my reputation – which might have helped make him believe in any information I let fall – but I now suspected he wanted to ignore that side of me and regard me instead as a dear little feather-headed female. And he might well resist or resent any evidence to the contrary. I had encountered such attitudes before. If he didn't take me seriously, then he might not take seriously the information on shipyards that Walsingham wished me to pass to him.

It was going to be difficult to present myself as the Mistress Stannard who justified her reputation and at the same time avoid provoking disapproval. I had better not display an unwomanly knowledge of shipyards. How on earth, I wondered, was I to get Walsingham's misinformation across under such a handicap?

'One can usually get across to Calais without much trouble,' Frost was saying. I looked attentive and, in an innocent voice and with slightly widened eyes, asked if he and his brother used their own ship for these winter journeys.

'No, no. I lay our *Dainty Lady* up for the winter, get any repairs done and have the barnacles scraped off her. John and I just get passages across to Calais with our wares on whatever vessel is going that can carry our wagon and horses.'

Risking a little boldness, I said: 'If ever you want to replace your *Dainty Lady*, I have a cousin who works in a shipyard on the Kent coast. His company is, I believe, of good repute.

He once told me that they mostly build warships, but I know they take on private work as well for folk who want to sail for pleasure or transport goods. He made me laugh with a tale of a man who wanted a pleasure craft and kept changing his mind about details.'

Sybil and the Brockleys blinked a little as I embarked on this fanciful story, but had the good sense not to comment.

Master Frost seemed interested. 'Indeed? You must let me know his name. I will make a note of it.'

'Edwin Blanchard,' I said, snatching a Christian name out of the air and tacking my first married surname on to it. And realized that I would have to let Walsingham know about my imaginary cousin in case Frost checked up on his existence.

'I shall remember,' said Frost.

I didn't pursue the matter. One step at a time. Meanwhile, I suddenly noticed that the light in the dining hall was brightening. At the same moment, Joyce exclaimed: 'It must be clearing up. Look, the sun is out!'

Sybil said brightly: 'Perhaps when it has dried up a little, you might show us the grounds? A walk in the fresh air would be so pleasant.'

'That would indeed be delightful,' I said. 'Your daughters have worked very well this morning, Master Frost. They have more than earned a walk in the sunshine. I hope it will last.'

'I didn't expect you to slave-drive them,' said Frost, twinkling again. 'By all means go into the grounds. I take it that you all brought outdoor footwear with you? Put that on and you need not wait for the grass to dry.'

The door I had noticed at the rear of the great hall did indeed lead outside, on to a gravelled terrace. This provided a walk along the rear of the house, looking down on a square of care-fully scythed grass with a path across it. We could see that to either side the garden had wooden boundary fences stretching away into the distance. To the right of the grass lawn was a parterre garden, with neat square beds surrounded by low box hedges and all enclosed within a greater square again hedged with box. The flowers were not in their best season, but the garden was nevertheless still brave with colour: with

Michaelmas daisies, red and blue, and the purple and yellow
of the little heartsease and the pale-bluish tint of the autumn
crocus.

'That's charming!' said Sybil, stepping away from the
rest of us to look more closely. And Joyce, following her,
said: 'Couldn't we use that as a pattern for an embroidery
design?'

'Indeed we could,' said Sybil, and as they came back towards
us I heard them discussing the possible uses for such a design.
It sounded as though Sybil's first lesson had kindled real
enthusiasm.

On the other side of the lawn was another such garden,
except that the shapes of the beds were more varied and the
hedging was lavender instead of box. This was a herb garden.
I saw mint and rosemary, basil and parsley; there was a bay
tree in one corner and marjoram occupying a crescent-shaped
bed in the corner opposite. A round centre bed was planted
with roses. 'You regard roses as a herb?' I asked and was
reminded of Hugh. I found myself wistfully recalling his
beloved rose garden, which was purely ornamental.

'The people who lived here before did, I suppose,' said
Jane. 'We never used to – we didn't have a rose garden in the
Midlands – but perhaps we will now. Mrs Hamble knows how
to make rosewater perfume and rosehip syrup for coughs, and
she says she'll teach us.'

Beyond the herb garden was the side fence, with a narrow
path just inside it vanishing into a belt of shrubs. There was
also a side gate. 'It opens on to a meadow,' said Joyce when
I asked. However, we stayed on the central path across the
lawn. This also passed through the shrubbery, and after that
we came to a substantial kitchen garden. Beyond this again
was an orchard, but it only occupied half the width of the
garden. The rest consisted of trees and shrubs, with winding
paths among them, and in the midst of this, coyly screened
by a timber fence, was a garden shed.

Straight ahead was a little building in the shape of a miniature house, with a peaked roof, a door in an archway, with
narrow windows to either side, and a miniature terrace in front.

'We hope to sit here in summer,' Jane said. 'We'd have

asked to have our embroidery lessons here if only the winter wasn't coming on.'

I could see the boundary fence beyond it, closing off the end of the garden. There was, however, a gate in it. 'Where does that lead to?' I asked.

'Oh, that's one way to the home farm. Father took over the crops and bought most of the stock – it was easier than walking our cows and sheep all the way from the Midlands. We auctioned them instead, except for our stud bull. He's being walked down by easy stages. He was too valuable to waste.'

A farm, I thought. Yes, the farm had been mentioned before. Of course. A farm. Barns, cowsheds, haylofts, labourers' cottages . . . How could I possibly search a place this size?

However, when we were back indoors and had retired to our rooms to change our footwear and shed our cloaks, I called the Brockleys in to join me and Sybil for a council meeting, as it were, and Brockley dealt with my worry about the farm.

'Frost isn't likely to hide a valuable chest full of silver out there! He would scarcely put it in a labourer's hovel, nor in a barn or a feed store where there are people coming and going all the time. It would be found, for sure, and questioned.' Brockley shook his head at the idea. 'I would bet heavily on the hiding place being here in this house. But searching it *is* difficult. We can't do much by night, with all the bedrooms occupied and a dormitory in the attic. And searching by day will be just as bad – with people everywhere, and a sick man in the attic all day as well as at night.'

'If he recovers soon, we might be able to look in the attics,' said Sybil.

'Maybe. I've done some reconnoitring upstairs,' Brockley said. 'When I first came in from the stables this morning, I took a chance and slipped up to look in on the sick man and ask if I could help in any way. I could, as it happened. He wanted some more drinking water, so I fetched some for him – and took a look round while I was at it. The room where the menservants sleep is on one side, but there are three more rooms on the other side separated from the dormitory by a passage. It's a dark sort of passage, even in full day, like so

much of this house. The staircase up from this floor is very
narrow and twisting, and the stairs are wooden and rickety
and they creak! But I glanced into those attic rooms. They're
full of junk. They're as likely a hiding place as any. As soon
as that fellow is back at his duties, we'll look there. But not
until he *is* better and out of the way.'

'But there are other places,' said Sybil. 'Should we not be
systematic? I've been thinking. At night, couldn't we search
the two halls and the ballroom? What about that dais? There's
probably a cavity underneath it.'

'And Master Frost is going to be absent for a few days,
quite shortly,' I said. 'We can examine his room and his study
then. Also by night.' I gave a sigh because I had been in this
sort of situation before and did not like creeping round other
people's premises in the dark. I had had to do it in the past
and hated it, and now here we were again. 'I doubt if he is
likely to have hidden anything in any of the servants' rooms,'
I said. 'Or in his daughter's room, or Susie's. Has anyone seen
Susie yet, by the way?'

'Yes,' said Brockley. 'I have. When I was in the kitchen
yesterday evening, getting mulled wine for Fran and being
as unobtrusively nosy as I could, a very pretty young lass
came in, fetching hot possets for her young ladies. Mrs Hamble
addressed her as Susie. And that's a point. We had better be
very careful as long as Master Frost is still here. If there was
anything in the hint that young Jane dropped yesterday when
we were being shown round the house, either he or Susie
may be wandering about after dark.'

'They won't wander far,' I said cynically. 'Only across
the passageway between them. I think we can evade them
if we take care. We had better make our forays well into
the night. Once they've got together they'll probably be,
well, preoccupied for quite some time.'

Brockley chuckled softly, Sybil smiled, and Dale shook a
disapproving head. I looked at them with affection. I felt safer
for having them near.

ELEVEN
Eighty Ships by Christmas

We were cautious. I said we must wait awhile, tread softly and accustom ourselves to the household before attempting any serious searching. However, Brockley said that although he had had a brief look at the kitchens, maybe he should ask Mrs Hamble if he could be of use there. I let him do so.

'I pretended I hadn't enough work,' he explained, telling me about it afterwards. 'I groom and exercise our horses but when that's done, I told her, I am sometimes at a loose end. Master Frost's grooms don't need extra help; they're happy to feed and water my horses along with their own, and they hardly seem to welcome me when I join in the mucking out. Mrs Hamble said that I might be useful – there are things to be scoured and sometimes kegs of ale or wine or joints of meat have to be fetched up from the stores in the cellars. So I can look round the cellars while I'm about it.'

He did so, but without result. 'The kitchens aren't a likely hiding place for a treasure chest,' he said, two days later. 'And nor are the cellars. There are four rooms down there and one has to prowl about with a lantern, but I have been down several times and saw nothing resembling a chest. The stores are tidy – I must say, the Hambles have orderly minds – and they control their staff as though they were captains on a warship. Any man found in the maids' rooms – or vice versa – is dismissed instantly, and only the Hambles themselves ever drink wine. It's small ale for the rest. The spitboy sleeps in the kitchen, by the way, in front of the banked fire except in hot weather. If we do any searching by night, we must remember that he's there.'

Meanwhile, I had made a wary move of my own, by seizing another chance to talk to Master Frost about shipping. Giles

Frost himself brought up the subject at dinner on our second full day there.

It was unexpected. He began the mealtime conversation by talking to Sybil. He admired the apple-green gown she had once more chosen and asked her how the embroidery lessons were going. Both Sybil and I were able to smile at the twins and say with truth that they were working hard and clearly wanted to learn, and Sybil said she was showing them how to create a design. They were planning one based on the colours and shapes of the parterre garden, which might make an attractive wall-hanging.

But when we reached the dessert course and had started on the almond fritters, Frost turned to me and said casually: 'I was interested in what you told me about your cousin who works in a shipyard. The yard builds mainly warships, I believe you said?'

'As far as I know.' I had to keep in character. I needed to walk the tightrope between being a woman who occasionally talked indiscreetly and being such a complete wantwit that nothing I said could be taken seriously. I also had to get word quickly to Walsingham in case Frost suddenly took it into his head to find the non-existent Edwin Blanchard and tried to get him to replace the *Dainty Lady* at a discount by virtue of being a friend of his cousin Ursula Stannard.

'I can't claim to know very much about the shipyard,' I said with a deprecating smile. 'I have only met my cousin a few times, and the last time was some years ago. Much of what I know comes from things I have heard family members talk about. I was brought up largely by an uncle and aunt,' I explained, warming to my work. 'I had no father . . .' (better slip gently over that) '. . . but Uncle Herbert and Aunt Tabitha looked after my mother and me. They used to talk about Edwin sometimes.'

'And what did they say when they used to talk about him?' Frost enquired jovially. Almost teasingly, and it occurred to me that while I was trying to feed inaccurate information to him, he might well be trying to extract accurate news from me.

'They were proud of him, I think,' I said. 'And still are. They hear from him quite often and Aunt Tabitha sometimes passes his news on to me. In her last letter to me, my aunt said he had written to her that his wages had been increased in return for working longer hours. Apparently there is urgent work on hand – new ships to be built and finished before Christmas.'

I busied myself with the fritters and awaited whatever might come next. My friends were silent, letting me having the platform, so to speak.

'Really?' Frost said. 'How strange. Why such urgency? Are the vessels in question warships?'

I did my best to look blank and slightly confused, and was aware of Sybil sitting very still, and Dale wiping her mouth with a napkin to conceal a smile and Brockley stealthily but firmly letting an elbow dig into her side as a warning to keep silent.

'I suppose they might be,' I said, and then decided to get one of my tasks completed and be done with it. 'Aunt Tabitha is very particular in all matters and she said something about Edwin's letter being most untidily written – though it was probably because he was writing in haste as he was very busy on account of the rush of work, and was also preparing to travel north. He was being transferred to another shipyard somewhere up there, a new one, just opened.' (I thought that might dissuade Frost from making inconvenient enquiries about an Edwin Blanchard in Kent.)

'A new shipyard? In the north?' said Frost, frowning.

'Yes. I haven't kept the letter,' I said and I too frowned. 'Is all this gossip about my cousin of interest to you?'

'Yes, it is. I am thinking of replacing *Dainty Lady*. I am surprised to hear of this sudden demand for new shipping and of a new yard being opened in the north. It may be the wrong moment for a private order. Can you remember more about what the letter said? I wish you had kept it.'

'I will try to remember.' I made an effort to look harried. 'I think my aunt did mention – but I didn't feel it was important and I am very bad at remembering numbers.' This was a blatant lie, and I knew the Brockleys and Sybil were restraining their amusement with difficulty. 'Only I'm sure she wrote something about the number of ships that had been ordered. By the queen herself . . . Yes, I think she said it was by order of the queen – but, oh, what exactly *did* Aunt Tabitha say . . .?'

At this point, I paused artistically and sat there trying to look worried, as if I was anxiously searching for an elusive memory. 'Does it really matter?' I enquired after a moment.

'It is of interest,' said Frost. 'But of course, if you can't remember, you can't.'

'But I *ought* to remember,' I said pettishly. 'It's so absurd . . . I am trying to picture her letter, how it looked when I was reading it – and, oh, yes, I have it! *Yes!* She said that according to Edwin the queen wanted eighty new vessels in commission by Christmas! That's right! I remember thinking what a lot that sounded.' I tried to seem naively impressed. 'I recall wondering how it could be done and thinking that surely it couldn't.'

'Really? Ah, well, Her Majesty is always nervous of the Spaniards,' Frost said. 'I imagine that's what is behind this.' He sighed, with a great air of regret. 'It certainly doesn't sound like the right moment to put in an order for a small trading vessel.'

'I suppose not,' I said, a little vaguely, as though the subject were taking me out of my limited female depth. I addressed myself once more to the fritters, and gave the figure of eighty ships a chance to sink in.

'That is amazing,' said Frost. 'Quite astonishing. I wonder, though, that your cousin should put such things in a private letter. Surely it is not something to be bruited about too freely.'

I tried once more to look confused. 'I don't quite understand. After all, if the workforce in the shipyard have been told – and surely they must have been, or how would Edwin have known? – it can't be a secret. Of course I wouldn't have mentioned it if I thought it was,' I added in a shocked voice. 'Since I attend on Her Majesty at times, I understand discretion.'

'I daresay. No, I suppose the queen's command in this case isn't such a secret. But it might be best not to speak of it too freely.' Frost spoke in tones both indulgent and mildly reproving, as to a well-meaning but somewhat dim-witted child. Beneath the table, Sybil patted my knee – a signal of congratulation – while Dale concealed her mirth by taking a hurried drink of wine. Brockley was frowning at her in reproof. Joyce and Jane looked puzzled, and Dr Lambert seemed bored.

Sybil said calmly: 'I see that it's begun to rain again. Autumn

is very much on the way, is it not?' She looked at the twins.
'Shall we go on with the parterre design this afternoon? I
would like to show you how to adjust the pattern to the size
of picture that you want.'

'We'd like that,' said Joyce, and Jane nodded.

I had, I thought, done what Walsingham wanted. I had
said enough. And if only I didn't have to search for that
confounded dowry chest as well, I could have had a free mind.
I could even have invented a crisis at Hawkswood, cut the
embroidery lessons short (Dear heaven, the man could find
another teacher for that!) and gone home.

As it was, I had to stay at Knoll House. And while there,
I reckoned I had better continue playing the part assigned to
me by Walsingham. Seize any chance of reinforcing the lie
about the growth of Elizabeth's navy, while being careful not
to arouse suspicion. Go on walking the narrow edge between
being the not very intelligent being that Frost thought womanly
and a person who might have useful contacts and a degree of
worldly knowledge – a person whose gossip might be useful.

That evening I volunteered to provide some music after
supper, brought my lute downstairs and played for them all. A
neat touch, I thought, noticing Frost's evident approval. In his
mind it was quite in order for ladies to play the lute (indeed,
his own daughters had been taught to do so). It was also true
that anyone wishing to play well, needed to practise, concentrate,
apply oneself, and possess a certain amount of intelligence.

But I didn't enjoy being obliged to stay put because I had
to attempt a task I didn't want to do, in a house that was full
of shadows and an indefinable air of discomfort. And timbers
that creaked. A high wind rose that night and Knoll House
murmured and groaned as though it were a ship at sea. It kept
both Sybil and me awake until nearly dawn.

The week ended and Sunday came. Dr Lambert held a service in
the chapel but in case he wished to make a Catholic service of it,
I went with Sybil and the Brockleys to Brentvale village to attend
the nearest Anglican church. It was too far for an easy walk, so
for once Dale and Sybil had to ride pillion with Brockley and me,
but we made it more comfortable for them by taking our time.

The twins came too, though not their father. At the church, we had the pleasure of meeting Christopher and Kate, with their children. Brentvale was the nearest village to their home at West Leys, but it was still at some distance so for the children's sake they had come in a small pony cart. Little Christina had evidently recovered from her illness and was a rosy contented bundle in Kate's arms, while Susanna was as lively a toddler as I had ever seen.

'How goes it?' Christopher asked me when after the service we all paused together in the churchyard to chat. His brown eyes were anxious.

'I have done what Walsingham asked,' I said. 'As for that wretched chest, we are looking for it in an unobtrusive way. No more than that. I have to stay for a while, you know, as Sybil and I are there to instruct the twins.'

'Just be careful,' Christopher said. 'I can't quite explain it, but I really do have an uneasy feeling about all this.'

'So have I,' said Brockley, and repeated what he had said to me about too many mysteries crowding in at once.

'Brockley is right,' Christopher said to me. 'Well, call on me if you need help at any time.'

'There's one thing you could do,' I told him, and explained about my fictitious cousin Edwin Blanchard. 'Could you let Walsingham know, in case Frost really does make enquiries?'

'Of course,' said Christopher. Both he and Kate looked at me anxiously and sighed. Then the twins came to claim us and escort us home and we had to say goodbye.

On our return to Knoll House, Brockley went to the stables with our horses. And also with the twins, who collected some carrots from the kitchen and wanted to give treats to all the horses. Sybil, Dale and I went in by the front door – and stopped short, feeling awkward because in the middle of the entrance hall Dr Lambert and Giles Frost were standing face to face and Dr Lambert was rebuking the master of the house as though Master Frost were an absconding schoolboy.

'. . . I repeat, Master Frost, this is the third Sunday in succession that I have said Mass in the chapel and you have not been present.' (It sounded more like *'Aye rebeat that this is the third S'nday in s'kcession that aye hev said Bass in the chabel and you hev not beed bresent.*') 'What kind of example are you setting your household? Even your valet, though he is still not well and went back to bed immediately after, took the trouble to attend, as did all your servants. But you were absent! Not just this once, but for the third time! Explain this, please!'

'I am busy. I am leaving for London tomorrow. I have some samples with me that my brother has not yet seen, and . . .'

'That is tomorrow. This is the Sabbath. You should be receiving the sacrament of the true faith. I begin to think,' intoned Dr Lambert nasally, 'that you are not as loyal to your faith as you should be. You should remember the martyrs (*'rebember the bartyrs'*) who have died rather than surrender to the persecution of the heretics . . .'

Gingerly, we tiptoed round to the foot of the front stairs and retreated up them. Neither Frost nor Lambert took the slightest notice of us. When the stairs turned, Lambert's voice, as affected and nasal as ever, faded out of hearing – slightly to my regret as I was finding his remarks intriguing.

'Poor Master Frost!' said Sybil when we were safely out of earshot. 'I half expected Dr Lambert to box his ears.'

When we reached our rooms, Sybil and I found Susie, the twins' maid, with her head inside the cupboard where Sybil had put her underclothes and nightwear. We had got to know Susie by now. She was indeed a pretty little thing, no more than eighteen, with fair curls peeping out from under her white cap, and a pert nose and lithe figure. Her eyes were the sleepy muted blue of sloe berries. She withdrew from the cupboard, gave us a smile and a curtsey and said: 'I wasn't that busy so I axed the young ladies, could I be useful an' they said well, tidy guests' rooms. I hopes 'ee'll find all in order.'

'Very kind of you,' said Sybil rather stiffly, and when the door had closed behind Susie, she peered into the cupboard and muttered: 'All seems all right, but we've got Dale to do that sort of thing for us.'

'You don't like Susie,' I said, amused.

'I don't like her eyes. Too full of questionable promises,' said Sybil, unexpectedly.

'I expect Master Frost takes full advantage of them,' I said.

*   *   *

That evening, as we were finishing supper, Frost sent for the Hambles and made a speech to all of us.

'As you know, I shall be leaving tomorrow for a few days in London. Normally I would take my daughters with me, but they are in the midst of their needlework instruction and Mistress Stannard and Mistress Jester are here and can look after them in my absence. However, as usual, Mr and Mrs Hamble will be in charge of all other household affairs. In that respect, nothing has changed.'

The Hambles both murmured agreement. I caught Mrs Hamble's eye and gave her a little smile, as much as to say that I wouldn't interfere with her authority, and she gave me a little smile back. I was used to her by this time and Brockley was right: beneath the stiff posture and pale impassive face, she was human enough. In fact, she often looked as if she was tired and probably she was. The over-august, over-dignified Mr Hamble was far less human than his wife and I suspected that, in private, he was something of a tyrant.

In the morning, the party for London set off on horseback, with a pack pony. It included a groom and a thin, dark young man called Barney Vaughan, who had evidently decided that he was fit enough to resume his duties as Frost's valet, though he still looked pale. When they were out of sight, I sent the twins to the parlour to make ready for their lesson, and then took Sybil and the Brockleys upstairs to my room.

'He's out of the way,' I said, when we were private together. 'Tonight?'

'Ground floor and Master Frost's bedchamber and study,' said Brockley, nodding.

'We'll need lanterns,' I said.

'I've brought three,' Brockley said. 'I just hope that when that obliging little girl Susie tidied our rooms, she didn't find them and wonder.'

'I'll be thankful when it's over,' I said. 'It is just the sort of task I most dislike.'

'You have your picklocks, madam?' Brockley asked.

'Yes. I sincerely hope I won't need to use them. And I hope Susie didn't find those, either! I don't always carry them.'

'I doubt if she did much tidying,' said Sybil. '*Un*tidying

would be more accurate. When I really looked, I found that she'd jumbled up some of my things and there are two buttons off one of my pair of apple-green sleeves, which I'm sure were there when I last took those sleeves off. I found the buttons lying on the bottom of the cupboard. I suppose she might have caught the sleeve on something, and one edge of the cupboard door is splintery. I imagine she didn't want to say so. But . . .'

'Surely there's no reason why she should do such a thing on purpose?' said Brockley, picking up the hint at once, while Dale clicked her tongue and shook her head disapprovingly. 'I don't care for the girl, I must say, but surely . . .?'

'Show me,' I said, and Sybil produced the buttons.

'I'll stitch those back on for you in no time, Mistress Jester,' said Dale.

I said nothing. But I looked closely, and Sybil did the same and we exchanged glances. The buttons had not been wrenched off, but cut.

Brockley put our feelings into words. 'I said it before. There's something wrong here. Something's going on. Something unpleasant. I don't know what it is, but . . .'

'But whatever it is,' said Sybil, bemused, 'why should Susie damage my things?'

'If it really *was* Susie,' said Brockley. 'She may have tidied in here, but it isn't certain that she was the one who pulled your belongings about and cut those buttons off. It looks like her, but it isn't certain.'

'It makes no sense.' Sybil's eyes were wide and anxious. 'It's frightening. It's as though there's hatred in the air.'

I shook my head. I said nothing, because I couldn't think of anything useful to say. I couldn't understand this either, but I agreed with Sybil. There was hatred in the air. Of what or whom, and who was doing the hating, I couldn't guess. But it was there.

TWELVE
Noises in the Night

We had laid plans to take advantage of Giles Frost's absence by making an after dark search of the ground floor and Frost's bedchamber and study. But when we realized that the valet, Barney Vaughan, had got over his illness and had ridden away to London with his master, I thankfully decided we could avoid any midnight prowling. The attics would now be empty during the day and could be searched then. They were the likeliest place to look, and if we found what we were seeking up there, that would be the end of it.

But luck was against us. After supper on the day when Frost rode away, Brockley returned from seeing to our horses with depressing news, which he imparted to us after quietly asking if we would all gather in the Brockleys' room.

'I've been talking to the grooms,' he said. 'Two of them, that is. The third wasn't there. He has fallen ill with the same rheum that afflicted the valet and so, apparently, has one of the menservants in the house. The groom is in bed in the loft over the stables, but the other man is abed in the attic and likely to stay there for some time. If you are determined to make the search at all, we shall have to start elsewhere. Do you want to begin tonight after all?'

'I'd rather not begin at all, but the chest and the salt are very valuable and I have promised to look for them. I feel obliged to do so,' I said. 'Damn!' I added crossly.

Brockley's face at once became disapproving. 'And please don't look at me like that,' I said, even more crossly. 'I have to watch my tongue when I talk to Master Frost and know I must be careful with him. But I expect to feel at ease with my own people.'

'I beg your pardon, madam.'

'I grant it.' And now I just sounded weary. 'We will make a start tonight. We'll start with the ballroom. I don't believe it can possibly be there, but if we're going to search at all, let's be thorough.'

'And quiet,' Sybil put in. 'The way all the stairs here creak!'

Late in the night, equipped with two lanterns, with great caution we descended the back and only stairs to the floor where the family and the Hambles slept. Because of the creaks, it was necessary to let our weight bear down slowly with every step. Once there, we crept along the passage to the front stairs and tiptoed down them. We reached the entrance hall without mishap, and without going anywhere near the kitchen where the spitboy slept. We paused for a moment, taking our bearings. The darkness pressed on us, huge and unnerving.

The skies had been overcast earlier, but as we entered the ballroom a nearly full moon shone out through a break in the clouds and threw the mullioned pattern of the windows across the wide wooden floor. The shadow of a small tree just outside, tossed by the wind, rippled across it, looking like the shadows of little hands fluttering at the window. I shivered. The floor had been thoroughly swept – Mrs Hamble kept the maids up to their work. There were very few places where a stolen chest might be hidden, but we examined a cupboard in the wall opposite the door from the hall and peered about on the dais, more in the spirit of being thorough than in hopes of finding anything.

Then Sybil whispered: 'But didn't I say what about *under* the dais?' So we turned back and crouched on the floor in order to examine the timber panels that were the supports. Brockley crawled right round the dais on hands and knees but finally got up, shaking his head. 'It's all solid. There are no little doors leading under. It would make a good hiding place if there was any way in, but I don't think there is.'

We left the ballroom. In the hall, there was just the cupboard where the silver candlesticks stood. Brockley opened it and revealed two sets of bowls and dishes, one set silver and the other pewter (for a change).

'Great hall next,' I whispered.

Here there were the sideboards to examine, but we had already caught glimpses of their contents and we were not surprised to find no sign of the dowry chest. There were no other possibilities. I signalled to the others to follow me and led the way to the door into the chapel.

'Surely not here!' whispered Sybil. 'I don't think we ought to search here!'

'Nor do I!' Dale muttered.

'A lot of people would feel like that,' I said. 'And that would make it a good hiding place. Come along. We are doing no harm.'

At heart, I didn't like the idea either. Churches and chapels can have a strange feeling after dark, as though the prayers that have been said and the ceremonies that have taken place there have left a residue – a kind of echo that sends a frisson through one's mind and body. But I stepped forward firmly and search we did, peering into a tiny lobby that seemed to do duty as a vestry, while Brockley once more crouched down, this time by the little altar, to see if there was a cavity. There was, but it was empty. We found nothing.

'Upstairs,' I said softly as we crept back into the great hall. 'Front stairs. We'll do the master's bedchamber and his study tonight. We'll have to manage the other bedchambers somehow by day.'

We negotiated the stairs, once more, on tiptoe. They creaked all the same but not too loudly. When we arrived on the first floor, we halted. Because here there was another, quite unexpected, sound. Somewhere close at hand, somebody was sobbing.

'Is that one of the twins?' Dale whispered. 'But why isn't the other one comforting her? Or doing something, anyway? They share a room.'

'It's not coming from that direction,' Brockley said. 'It's . . .' He swivelled where he stood, like a dog trying to pick up a scent. 'It's . . . coming from Master Frost's chamber!'

We stood still, looking towards the door of the room in question. A shaft of moonlight was shining on it. It was ajar.

'We may need an excuse for being here,' I whispered. 'If necessary, I'll say I was sleeping badly. I got up and took a lantern and thought I would fetch a book of verse I'd left in the parlour. Then I heard a sound and was alarmed and fetched the rest of you. All right?'

'It's a good story,' said Brockley. 'Let's find someone to tell it to.'

This time, he took the lead, pushing the door of Master Frost's bedchamber open wide and stepped boldly through, holding his lantern up to show as much of the room as possible.

It was a big room, furnished with a four-poster bed, two massively carved clothes presses, a chest – a big one, on which my glance fell greedily at once – and a prie-dieu. The four-poster was not empty, though its occupant was not its rightful owner.

As the lantern light swept the room, someone who had been lying face down on the coverlet, embracing the pillow as though it were a lover, turned over with a little shriek and sat up, staring at us with wide, wet eyes.

It was Susie. Who, judging by this, was most certainly Frost's mistress.

'Susie,' I said, 'what in the world are you doing here?'

She was trembling. Even in the feeble lantern-light, we could see that. But she spoke up bravely enough. 'What are *you* doing here? This is Master Frost's private room!'

'I know,' I said, and recited the tale I had planned just a few moments before. 'And now,' I said, 'you had better explain yourself, young lady. You say this is Master Frost's private room. Indeed it is. And you are the maid who attends his daughters. Mistress Jester and I, being guests of some station, have a degree of responsibility in his absence. And Mrs Hamble has a good deal of responsibility. What would she say if she knew about this? I suggest that you explain yourself to us and perhaps we won't need to tell her. Why have you invaded Master Frost's room? Why do we find you crying on his bed?'

She was pretty, pert and far from virtuous, but she was also too simple to pretend. 'He's gone away and I miss him, and before he went he told me he was thinking to marry again! But he wasn't going to marry *me* – he said he couldn't do that, our stations in life don't match! He said he would give me a present and find a husband for me if I wished. He thanked me for my services . . . My *services*! I love him, I can't live without him! I came to this room to remember, to imagine, to be with him in a way . . . *I love him!*' wailed Susie and burst into tears all over again.

Brockley was inclined to berate her, but I shushed him. I went firmly over to Susie and half pulled, half lifted her off the bed. 'Someone will have to tidy that up,' I remarked in practical tones. 'But not you. Come along, Susie, go back to your own room. Remember you will have to look after your young ladies in the morning. You will feel better when it's daylight. One day you will marvel at yourself for this. You're young, and Master Frost is far too old for you. Come now. Sybil, Dale, help me with her. Hush, Susie! Or you'll wake the young ladies or the Hambles, or even Lambert! You don't want that, now, do you?'

Limply, she let us take her from the room. Sybil and Dale led her back to her own bedchamber. Brockley and I, on the pretext of tidying the bed, stayed behind. We examined the presses and the outsize chest, of which I had great hopes. Here in his own room would be a very likely place for Frost to conceal his stolen goods.

But there was no sign of the dowry chest, either there or in the adjoining study. Sybil and Dale rejoined us when they had finally got Susie settled in her own bed, and we all went quietly up the stairs and back to our own rooms. On the way, Brockley said: 'I never thought anything would come of this. The attics are the likeliest place. But how we're ever to search those with another ailing manservant up there all the time, I can't think. I suppose we'll have to wait until he's better, and hope this isn't the start of an epidemic!'

THIRTEEN
Unromantic Interlude

I t looked as though Brockley's hope was not to be fulfilled. The very next day, Dale fell victim to the complaint that had already felled three of Frost's employees. It seemed to be a kind of chesty cold. Sybil and I looked after her, in the intervals of continuing with the embroidery lessons. Sybil and the twins had developed a beautiful design based on the parterre garden and I introduced the girls to the technique of couching, in which a group of long stitches are fixed to the fabric by other stitches laid over them, crosswise and close, to make a smooth raised surface.

We were not surprised by Dale's illness since she was prone to this type of thing, and fortunately none of us succumbed. The maidservant Bessie did, but mildly and she was soon about again. Dale's attack was also quite mild. She was out of bed and attending to her duties, albeit wanly, on the Wednesday of the next week.

The manservant in the attic, however, was not so lucky, and throughout all the time of Dale's illness he remained in his bed and we had no chance at all of investigating the attics. But on the Sunday, we did not go to church and Brockley searched Lambert's room and the Hambles' quarters while Lambert was holding a service in the chapel. The twins and Susie all attended too and I made a hurried search of their rooms as well.

We found nothing suspicious, but by then we were all certain that if the chest was hidden anywhere, the attics were the place to look.

For the time being, however, we couldn't. So on the Monday, when I was sure that Dale was recovering properly, I took a day off, left her with Sybil and rode with Brockley to Hawkswood, where we collected Dr Joynings, and went on to Guildford to look in at Julius Stagg's premises and inspect the progress of the new window. I was pleased with what I saw and so was Joynings. The design was finished and the making of the glass panes under way. I had already had a chance to look at the examples of Stagg's work in the Knoll House chapel and knew it to be good. Brockley and I accompanied Dr Joynings back to his home beside his church. We then rode on to Hawkswood House to make sure all was well there and talked to Adam Wilder and Gladys, who both asked what the new window would look like. Gladys was grumpy about it.

'I shan't ever get to see that window close to. I'll only see it from inside the church, where it'll be up over my head – too far off for my old eyes to see rightly.'

Stagg had explained that when the panes were ready, the window would be assembled in his workshop and brought to Hawkswood by cart – 'A very slow cart, with a placid pony in the shafts and the window safely wrapped in lambswool.' I promised Gladys that when the cart arrived, she could be there to see it unpacked. Before leaving, I gave both Dr Joynings and Adam Wilder instructions to that effect, as I did not know if I would still be at Knoll House. If I was, then I could not be certain of getting home at any given time.

On the following evening, Master Frost returned. It was a wet, windy day and both he and Vaughan came in looking damp, mud-splashed and tired. And in Frost's case, irritable. In a loud, cross voice, he demanded hot water and clean towels, then withdrew, escorted by Vaughan, so that they could both become presentable. They presently reappeared, washed and barbered, Frost first and then Vaughan, who I suppose had had to remain damp and travel-stained until he had refurbished his master.

Vaughan was neatly beruffed and in a suit of black with shoes of gleaming leather and discreet silver buckles. His master was in a chestnut velvet gown trimmed with squirrel fur, an open-necked shirt and soft slippers. Yet it seemed to me that, though a recent invalid, the formally clad Vaughan looked the most refreshed. While Frost, despite his comfortable and informal clothes, still seemed irritable and weary.

Vaughan retired to the servants' hall and Frost joined the rest of us in the great hall, where we were awaiting supper, and sat down by the hearth. Mrs Hamble brought him some mulled wine and his daughters hovered, anxious to soothe his obvious ill humour but not sure how. It was Sybil who, in her gentle, gracious way, commiserated with him on having to travel through such unpleasant weather and asked if his business in London had gone well.

'Not too well,' he told her. 'The market for some of the goods I took to my brother is not as promising as we had hoped, and also I received news that there may be difficulty in obtaining more of the silks, which do seem to be popular. I shall face difficulties on my next voyage.'

'But that won't be until next spring, will it?' I asked politely. 'Did you not say that you lay your ship up in the winter? Perhaps things will have changed by then.'

'And you will think of new ideas,' Joyce comforted him. 'You always do, Father.'

'I daresay.' He sighed and then smiled, stretching his feet towards the warmth. 'I am a grumpy man tonight. I shall feel better when I have eaten. Shall we have some music after supper? I have hardly heard you girls play your lutes of late. I will hear you two this evening. Have you made good progress with your needles? Have you begun on the gold and silver work yet?'

'Not yet,' I said. 'I thought it best to practise all the basic stitches first, to lay a foundation of skill before tackling the art of gold and silver stitchery. It has its difficulties.'

'But we are learning much about the art of design,' Joyce said. 'Father, I hope you will like the one we are working on – the one based on the pattern of the parterre garden. I have told you about it, I think. It's full of colour. It would make a wall-hanging, either as an embroidery or even a tapestry.'

'We've never tried tapestry work,' said Jane. 'It would be interesting!'

'But to get back to this evening's entertainment,' said Frost, 'what songs shall we have? Have you practised anything new of late?'

Jane looked worried. 'I don't know where my lute is. Joyce

has hers, but yesterday I couldn't find mine when I looked for it. I thought I might have left it still in the big hamper where Susie put my summer gowns. We hadn't emptied the hamper yet. So I helped Susie to see to it yesterday, but the lute wasn't there.'

'There are still many things not yet unpacked, Mistress Jane,' said Mrs Hamble, who had just brought in some more mulled wine, this time for all of us. 'Moving an entire household is such a business! There are still some hampers and boxes in the attic, put there to be out of the way while the big items of furniture were being carried in. I fancy you will find your lute there, Mistress Jane. Perhaps it was remiss of me not to mention it before, and to leave things unopened for so long. I do apologize.'

Jane got up. 'I shall ask Susie to go up and look for it.'

Across the room I caught Brockley's eye and we exchanged silent messages. 'No need to worry about the things in the attic tonight,' I said easily. 'You can use my lute. It's dark now and it will be difficult for Susie to find things up in the attic, and not very pleasant, either. You and I can look for it together in the morning. I'll help you, Jane.' I stood up. 'I'll fetch my own lute now.'

We had a very pleasant musical evening, even though it was disturbed at times by the sound of the wind hurling rain against the windows, apparently by the pailful, and the angry splutter when the downpour found its way down the chimney into the fire. I discovered that both of the twins were skilled with the lute and that Jane had an attractive singing voice, not loud but tuneful and clear.

We had finished our entertainment, and were thinking of saying goodnight, when Master Frost suddenly said: 'I am intrigued, Mistress Jester, by this idea you are working on with my daughters, concerning an embroidery or tapestry design based on the parterre garden here. I would like to see it. Joyce has mentioned that it would make a wall-hanging. Are you planning it as a decoration in what, after all, is now my house?'

Sybil hastily began to explain that of course there would

be no thought of hanging the finished pattern anywhere without his approval; it was just that it was likely, when finished, to be suitable for such a purpose.

Frost waved all this aside. 'There is no need for apologies, Mistress Jester. I am sure you would never put up new decorations without my consent! In fact, I am most intrigued by what you have told me. May I see the design – is it far enough developed? Could you bring it to my study? Now?'

'I have drawn it freehand and in colour,' Sybil said. 'We have only just begun to draw it in a form that is ready for the stitchwork. That is a more careful business. But my original drawing does give a clear impression of it, I think. I can certainly bring it to your study. But will the light be sufficient?'

'Certainly it will.' Frost strode to the door and shouted for Mrs Hamble. When she appeared, he said: 'I want a good light in my study, at once. Bring two of those branched candelabra from the ballroom.' She hurried away and he turned to Sybil, waving her to precede him through the door. 'You fetch your drawing and I will meet you in the study. You know where it is by now, I suppose?'

'Yes, Master Frost,' said Sybil, for all the world as though she hadn't helped to search it in the small hours of a recent morning.

The rest of us collected our bedtime candles, which had as usual been set out on top of the cupboard in the entrance hall. We lit them from the big candles in the wall sconces and made our way upstairs.

Jugs of hot water had been placed in our rooms. Dale drew off my shoes and helped me out of my gown, ruff and farthingale. I washed and then she dropped my nightgown over my head and brushed my hair. 'What about Mistress Jester?' she said. 'She is still downstairs.'

'I'll help her. You go and wash before your water gets cold,' I told her. 'Leave all the candles as they are.'

I got into bed, glad to be there, for the night was getting very chilly. The wind had not dropped and it was still hurling rain at the windows, violently, as if in anger. When the door was suddenly flung open I thought for a moment that the wind had done it, until I saw Sybil standing there in the candlelight

– a wild-eyed Sybil, with a lock of hair pulled out of its coil at the back of her head and flying loose while the little velvet cap which she wore over the coil had migrated forward to hang over one eye. Even by candlelight, I could see that she was deathly pale.

'Sybil!' I was out of bed on the instant. I ran to her. 'What is it, Sybil? You've been talking with Master Frost – he surely didn't . . . try to . . .?'

'He didn't want to look at drawings,' said Sybil, blundering forward into the room and sinking on to the side of the bed. 'I put them before him, but he said he had only asked me to bring them so that we could be alone because he had something special to say to me. Then he said he wanted to marry me. I was amazed! I hardly knew what to say to him. I didn't wish to annoy him, but . . . the only answer I could make was no. I tried to say the right things – that I didn't wish to remarry, but of course I recognized the compliment . . . all the correct phrases – but he got hold of me and tried to kiss me, and I struggled away. Then he pushed me down on a stool and started telling me how he would look after me and I was just the kind of woman who would be a good stepmother for his daughters, and he promised me expensive gifts . . .'

'Sybil!'

'You know I don't want to marry again! Once was enough for me. More than enough. And besides, *this* man, Frost – when I think what he is, what he does, spying for the Spanish – the idea is appalling! I gasped out that I was fifty-eight years old and that this was ridiculous, but he laughed and said he was fifty-four; what did it matter? We were near enough in age. I managed to get off the stool in the end and kept edging away from him all the time. Finally I got to the door, and escaped from the room and ran . . .'

'Sybil! This is dreadful!'

'Well, we now know why Susie cut the buttons off that sleeve!' said Sybil. 'A fit of spite! She said he told her that he meant to marry again – and I fancy he told her that he'd chosen me, though she didn't mention that to us! As far as I'm concerned, she's welcome to him! But there was something else, too. Something I couldn't understand.'

She was shivering badly. I sat down beside her. 'Something else?' I said.

'Just as I got to the door, he . . . he stopped, backed away and raised a hand as if to say "All right, I give in, I'm letting you go." And then he said: "Well, I tried. I asked you for your hand. I gave you a chance. Now, whatever befalls you, it's your own fault. I offered you a way out and you wouldn't take it. You see, I really like you, Mistress Jester, and so do my daughters, and we could all do so much for each other. But as it is . . . you have made your choice. Goodnight."'

'Whatever did he mean?'

'I don't know! I don't understand! The way he was looking at me,' said Sybil, 'his eyes were like blue dagger points! I felt impaled by them!'

Her tone was odd, almost pensive. She seemed aware of it and shook herself as though trying to shake a bad memory away. I wondered if he had attempted more, physically, than she was telling me. 'I couldn't believe what I was seeing or what I was hearing,' she said. 'His words made no sense! He . . .'

'What's happening?' The Brockleys (I sometimes thought they had a sense of hearing to match the hearing of cats and owls) were in the doorway, looking at us anxiously.

'We heard!' said Dale, her protuberant eyes bulging, full of alarm. She was still pale from her illness and had lost weight but was nevertheless full of concern for us. 'We heard what Mistress Jester said just now . . . We heard . . .'

'Mistress Jester,' I said, 'has refused a proposal of marriage from Master Frost.'

'And,' said Brockley, 'he said something like "I gave you a chance. Now, whatever befalls you, it's your own fault. I offered you a way out and you wouldn't take it. You have made your choice . . ." What choice? A way out of what or where? What is likely to befall Mistress Jester? What's *wrong* with this house? There's a bad feeling in it, and it's not just because Susie is unhappy and feeling spiteful. It's more than that.'

To which, none of us had any answer.

FOURTEEN
A Puzzled Spaniel

Sybil and I did not sleep much that night. We talked instead. One thing seemed very clear to me – that she must not remain at Knoll House. 'If you do, you may be liable to further harassment,' I said. 'It sounds as though there is some unknown threat hanging over you. I can't imagine what it is, but . . .'

'There isn't any threat,' said Sybil. 'That's nonsense. How could there be? It was just talk, an attempt to bully me. I refuse to be bullied. I would like to go back to Hawkswood, of course I would, but we haven't finished searching for that wretched chest yet, and I have become rather interested in teaching those two girls how to create designs. Joyce seems to have quite a talent. I am prepared to stay. I shall just make sure I'm never alone with Master Frost again.'

'That may be difficult. If he is determined to approach you again, he will.'

'It's a compliment in a way,' said Sybil. 'I did acknowledge that, to him.'

I was silent. Again, something in her voice seemed strange, just as it had during her outburst when she rushed into our room. *His eyes were like blue dagger points! I felt impaled by them!* Those words had carried an undertone. Of what? Had he attacked her in a more serious way than she would admit? Or was it excitement . . .? Had Sybil not felt quite as indifferent or shocked as she wished to appear? Had something in Master Frost stirred her? Touched the heart that had been frozen for so long because her husband had ill-used her? How piquant it would be, I thought dryly, that a frozen heart should be melted – even just a little – by a man called Frost?

Even by a man who was spying for Spain!

'We had better go to sleep,' I said at last. 'Most of the night is gone already. We'll talk more in the morning.'

In the morning, as usual, breakfast was announced by the scent of newly baked bread permeating through the house. All four of us felt awkward about going down to the meal and encountering Frost, but we had to break our fasts and the appetizing aroma was a compelling summons. Dale in particular said that she really wanted her breakfast. She had eaten poorly during her illness, and her appetite had now apparently come back with a vengeance.

So, responding to an instinctive wish to keep together, we didn't go down to the great hall in pairs as we usually did, but went down as a quartet. We found Master Frost and his daughters there before us, seated at the table, but although bread and ale were set out none of them were yet eating or drinking. The twins looked serious and somewhat embarrassed and were evidently not surprised when their father rose to his feet as we entered, clearing his throat so meaningfully that we realized we were about to be addressed, like an audience. We stopped and, as we stood there in a group, drew a little closer together.

'I have something to say,' Frost declared. 'Especially to Mistress Jester, but because she has no doubt told you what happened yesterday evening, and I have myself admitted it to my daughters here, I will say it to all of you. I have to apologize. I had perhaps had too much wine at the evening meal. Yesterday evening I proposed marriage to Mistress Jester. I have acquired the greatest regard for her.' He bowed towards her. 'It was truly meant as an honourable proposal, but I'm afraid I was more pressing than I should have been. I am sorry, Mistress Jester. I will not inflict such bad manners on you again. But I will say this. The offer remains open and I do indeed implore you to consider it. I have for some time felt that I ought to marry again, for my daughters' sake as well as my own.'

He glanced aside, towards the twins, who both nodded though they did not speak.

'Joyce and Jane both like you, Mistress Jester, and I more than just like you. You are skilled in womanly crafts and have already taught them much. Before I came to breakfast this morning, I looked at the parterre pattern, which I didn't do yesterday evening. Oh yes, I know that Mistress Stannard has taught them much as well, and I would not for a moment fail to give due credit for that. But it happens to be you, Mistress Jester, who has touched my heart, just when I feared that no woman would ever do so again. I don't want a marriage of convenience. I want to wed where my heart is. So, please forgive me my bad behaviour yesterday evening, and please think about what I can offer. A steady love, a home of your own, security for life, two ready-made daughters. Please think about this, Mistress Jester. That is all I ask.'

He stepped back and resumed his seat, gesturing for us to sit down as well. Bemused, we did so. Sybil said graciously: 'Thank you for your apology, sir. I said at the time that I knew you were paying me a compliment. I am sorry, in my turn, that I cannot say yes, but I am well content with my life as it is. I will continue to instruct your daughters for the time agreed.'

As gracious in movement as in speech, she reached for the ale jug and filled his tankard for him.

For all the world, I thought, *as though they have been married for years. Was she tempted? If so, well, that's a turn of events that we never foresaw.*

For a little while, no one spoke. We helped ourselves to bread and butter and honey, and poured ale for ourselves. Then the maid Bessie, a little wan from her recent illness, came in with more bread and Hamble followed with a serving dish of cold meat slices. Breakfast proceeded in silence at first, until Jane – visibly trying to behave normally – said: 'Mistress Stannard, shall we go up to the attic presently and see if we can find my lute?'

'Certainly,' I said.

Sybil said she and Joyce wanted to go on working with the parterre design. 'You and Jane go lute-hunting,' she said.

'If Master Frost comes to the parlour . . .?' I said in a low voice, but Sybil shook her head.

'I have Joyce as a chaperone. What could be better?'

'You shall have Dale as well,' I said. 'It's still chilly, Dale, you had better keep within doors and not do too much. Stay in the parlour and don't trouble about mending or pressing anything. Jane and I will go to the attic. And Brockley too, in case we need to move anything heavy. Ask the other grooms to see to our horses. I will give you some money to persuade them with.'

Before we joined Jane to go up to the attic, Brockley said to me: 'Do you have your picklocks? I never thought to ask before.'

'Yes. I've had them with me every time we've gone searching,' I told him, and patted the skirt of the open-fronted gown I was wearing. It was one of those that have a pouch sewn inside to hold useful items for someone engaged on secret matters. Such as picklocks and a small dagger.

'We can't use them in Mistress Jane's presence,' Brockley said. 'If she finds her lute, we must somehow get her to leave us alone up there. We can say we want to help unpack Frost's belongings. If only Mistress Jane will let us do so without her!'

'We must find an excuse to send her downstairs with her lute,' I said. 'Use what's there.' I was quoting a precept we had heard more than once from one of Brockley's friends, dead now for many years, who had been a most gifted exponent of the art of seizing opportunities. I remember hearing him explain how the objects in a most ordinary room could in an emergency be turned into weapons.

Brockley chuckled and, into my ear, murmured: 'We did indeed learn from him.'

The day was not only chilly, it was also still windy. Climbing the narrow, twisty attic stairs, which not only creaked but seemed to stir a little underfoot, could not be done silently. However, there was no need for secrecy; we were on legitimate business. Jane had even brought a flask of wine and a raisin pastry with her to give to the sick man in the menservants' room. We all went in with her, commiserated with the victim, who was on his pallet, surrounded by used handkerchiefs and looking sorry for himself, though capable, I was glad to see, of eating his pastry with enthusiasm and enjoying his wine.

We left him still busy with them and went across the little passageway landing, where the stairs began, into the attics on the other side.

The first one was small and dusty, with sloping ceilings supported on heavy beams. It was lavishly supplied with cobwebs, and streaks of damp on one wall suggested that rain was getting in somewhere. There were numerous pieces of discarded furniture and other superseded household goods presumably left by the previous tenant – stools and a small table, all with broken legs, a saucepan with a hole in the base (someone had probably put it on a trivet to heat soup or water and let it boil dry), an old basket with bits of broken cane sticking out and several torn sheets stuffed carelessly into it, a pallet with straw stuffing oozing through a tear . . . Through doors to our left and right, we could glimpse other dusty, cobwebbed rooms.

Jane lifted the corner of a sheet and pulled it out. 'This isn't ours. It was here already. How wasteful! We would have mended this, and I should think that that table could have been mended, too. And surely . . . Ooh!'

Something had found a use for the pallet. A mouse came skittering out of it and dashed across the floor, veering round Brockley's booted feet and then running across my slippered toes – frightened by the boots, no doubt, but not bothered by a minor velvet obstacle. Jane squealed and the mouse vanished down a hole by the wall.

'You have three kitchen cats, I've seen them,' said Brockley, unperturbed. 'You ought to bring them up here sometime and let them have some sport.'

'Where are your own things?' I asked Jane.

'Not in here.' Jane was looking about her in some puzzlement. 'I think . . . yes.' She pointed to the door on the left. 'I think our things were carried in there. Joyce and I weren't allowed to help carry luggage about, of course. The menservants did that. But we did ask where our boxes and so forth had gone, and Barney Vaughan said go into the room to the left at the top of the stairs and then left again into another, because the first room you come to is damp. It is, too.' She pointed to the streaks on the wall. 'Father said he would get the cause of the damp traced and have it put right, but he's been too busy so far.'

'Well, let's see,' said Brockley and led the way.

This second attic room was smaller and it was dry, though there was plenty of dust. From one corner, a large spider in the middle of a web eyed us malevolently. 'Ugh!' said Jane, shuddering away from it.

I looked round. Here there were more household rejects. A couple of dented frying pans, a wooden armchair riddled with woodworm, a roll of something which, when I inquisitively picked it up and began to unroll it, proved to be a faded tapestry with moth holes in it . . .

'Those things are ours!' said Jane, pointing, and I turned to see that she meant a group of objects in the opposite corner. There were two big clothes hampers and a massive oak chest. It had a lock but the key was in it and Jane, hurrying across the room, tried to turn it. Brockley went to help her. It was stiff but yielded to his strength. He threw the lid back and Jane exclaimed with joy because there, on top of other things, was a lute case. She lifted it out and opened it. 'Oh, here it is! Lovely!'

'Jane,' I said, 'why don't you take it downstairs and tune it? It probably needs it after being up here for so long. I'm sure the air is damp in here, even though the walls are dry. And you don't like mice and spiders.'

'We don't mind so much,' said Brockley, smoothly continuing my line of thought. 'We can be useful, Mistress Jane. Since we're here, we could look through these attic rooms and perhaps find other stray pieces of baggage that ought to be rescued. I agree about the damp air. All this seems very careless, I must say.'

'Yes, of course,' said Jane. Reunited with her lute, she had little attention for anything else. 'Do please bring down anything you think may belong to us. I'd much rather go downstairs. No, I *don't* like spiders and mice – nor dust and cobwebs, either!'

As she departed, Brockley and I looked at each other and exchanged pleased smiles. 'Quick!' I said. 'What else is in this big chest? It's large enough to swallow the one we're looking for.'

'It must have been brought up here empty,' said Brockley. 'It would be far too heavy if it was full. Then things were just stuffed into it to keep them together until they could be attended to. Well, let's see what's here.'

He plunged his hands into the big chest and came up with a heavy roll of fabric. 'More tapestry . . .' He let it unroll. 'One of those hunting scenes. But the moths haven't got at this one yet. We'd better take it down. There are plenty of bare walls in this house, and Master Frost may well be pleased to see it.'

'I expect he will. Now, what's this?' I delved into the chest and hauled out a thick woven blanket.

'That looks useful. We'll take that down as well. What a casual way to treat a perfectly good tapestry and a fine thick blanket.' Brockley placed the tapestry on to the turned-back lid of the chest, which was clean, took the blanket from me, and put it on top of the tapestry. He exuded disapproval, as though we really were in the attic for the purpose of rescuing ill-used Frost property.

I remarked: 'I expect in the bustle of moving in, these things were just dumped here and forgotten, and will stay here until someone looks at a stretch of bare wall and says "Where is that tapestry with the hunting scenes?"'

'But of course we're not really here to unpack for the Frost family,' said Brockley, resuming his grip on our true purpose and turning back to the chest. 'We're here to . . . Madam!'

He was staring down into the chest. I came beside him and looked into it. Then we straightened up and looked at each other.

'It's it!' said Brockley, almost in a whisper.

And there it was, Eleanor Liversedge's dowry chest. Buried under a thick blanket and a roll of tapestry, it had presumably lain there since its disappearance from Stagg's premises.

Brockley reached down and heaved, grunting. I quickly lent a hand. The dowry chest was extremely heavy. We lifted it out and set it down so that we could see it clearly.

We both recognized it, recognized the warm red colour of the wood and its lovely grain, the spray of leaves inlaid with silver that decorated each of its sides, the pattern like a twisted rope of silver round the edges of its domed lid. It was padlocked, and there was no sign of the key.

I got out my picklocks.

The lock proved easy to open. I put back the lid of the chest and got out the salt, wrapped in cloth, inside. I freed it from the cloth and we stood contemplating it in admiration. Its amethyst decorations gleamed softly blue and lavender in the gloom of the attic.

'So now what do we do?' Brockley muttered.

'We inform Master Stagg,' I said. I began to wrap the salt up again. 'I had better . . .'

A shadow fell across my hands. Black-gowned and black-browed, Dr Lambert was standing in the doorway, staring at us.

'Just what is going on here? Do you have permission to hunt through Master Frost's attics? What is that that you are holding?'

It sounded like: *'Just what is goink on here? Do you have berbission to hunt through Baster Frost's attics? What is that that you are holdinck?'* But it would be tedious to repeat all of Dr Lambert's conversation in Dr Lambert's weird accent.

He stepped forward, took the salt out of my hands and stared at it. 'What is this? It's the bridal gift for the niece of Master Stagg, who makes stained-glass windows, is it not?'

'You have seen it before?' I said. Or rather, blurted out.

Lambert stared at me. 'When Master Frost came to inspect this property before moving in, I was with him,' he intoned. 'We found two badly cracked windows in the chapel, and I took a message about it to Master Stagg's Guildford workshop. The chapel is my charge, after all. Master Stagg had the chest there, at his works.'

'And he showed it to you?' asked Brockley, quite sharply. Sharply enough, anyway, to jerk a reply from Lambert, who said 'Certainly!' quite defensively and then went on to explain.

'I had to wait for Master Stagg in his room upstairs. One of his apprentices came in to say that his master would not be long and asked me if I wanted any refreshment while I was waiting. This chest was there under a table. The boy saw me looking at it and told me what it was. I didn't see the contents then, but the lad had apparently seen that salt when Master Stagg first acquired it and he described it to me. He was greatly impressed. "Amethysts!" he said, in such an awed voice. He told me he had asked Master Stagg what they were because he'd never seen an amethyst before. When Master Stagg came, I mentioned what the lad had said to me and he showed me the salt. I recognize both it and that rosewood chest.'

He stopped and seemed to recollect himself. 'Why am I troubling to explain all this? It is none of your business. What right have you to question me? I have caught you interfering where you should not. You are the ones to explain.'

I had pulled myself together by now. I said: 'Mistress Jane could not find her lute yesterday and thought it might be in some luggage that had been put up here during the move and not yet unpacked. We came up here this morning to help her look. She found her lute in this big chest and took it downstairs. We – that is, Brockley and myself – thought that probably there were other things up here that ought to be unpacked and Mistress Jane agreed. She wanted to go down and retune her lute somewhere more comfortable and gave us permission to look around to see if anything else ought to be taken downstairs. That is what we were doing when you came in. I assure you that we are here with Mistress Jane's permission. I must say, I am surprised to find Mistress Liversedge's dowry chest here. We too recognized it, having seen it at Master Stagg's place.'

The mention of Jane obviously mollified Lambert. The suspicion faded out of his face; instead, he now seemed bewildered. I realized that I was looking at him properly for the first time. Hitherto, he had been a thin man with a dark gown and cap and an irritating voice. Now, it occurred to me that here was a man who was worried. His brown eyes were the anxious eyes of a spaniel trying to understand the speech of its human owners. Eventually, he said: 'Well, I suppose Master Frost knows his own business best. Perhaps he is looking after the salt for the time being. He and Master Stagg are old friends, after all.'

We stared at him in such surprise that he noticed it and asked: 'Why are you astonished? Did you not know? I know little about it myself, as I have only been Master Frost's chaplain for a few months. But when he told me that we were to move down to Surrey, he said that it would be pleasant to be near his friend Julius Stagg, a master glazier living in Guildford. Only two days after we arrived here, Master Stagg came to dine. And a fine muddle it all was!' There was a retrospective amusement in his voice, and I realized that Lambert's speech was suddenly less weird. Interested in what he was saying, he was forgetting his affectations.

'It was all arranged so quickly,' he said, 'that the preparations needed to entertain a guest had to be done in a rush. Half of the kitchen utensils still hadn't been unpacked, and the Hambles had to be sent out to Guildford early in the morning to buy extra victuals. They had trouble finding sugar and cinnamon and couldn't find any fresh fish at all. By the time they'd bought what they could and brought it back, the cook was going out of his mind because he had a leg of mutton on the spit and was waiting for capons, needed the ingredients for some special sauce or other, and couldn't start on the desserts without sugar . . . The whole house was upside down in panic! No one who was here is likely to forget the day that Master Julius Stagg came to dinner.'

'But . . .' I said, and then stopped. This was utterly at variance with what Stagg had told us. He had said that he had only come to Knoll House to work and had lacked sufficient social status for anything more. I sensed that Brockley's mind was following the same bewildered track.

'We will leave things as they are,' I said at last. 'You are right, of course. Master Frost must know what he is about, and the same applies to Master Stagg.' With Lambert standing there, I could not use my picklocks to secure the padlock so I turned away, leaving it open.

'I will mention the matter to my employer,' said Lambert. This time he remembered to intone, and he seemed to be soothed.

Which is more than either Brockley or I were.

There was no question of going straight back to the parlour and sitting down for a quiet morning of instruction in needlework.

I told Brockley to bring Dale to my room and then called Sybil to join us. 'Please forgive the interruption,' I said to the twins. 'A private matter has arisen. Go on with what you are doing until we return.'

Once I had all three of them in my bedchamber with the door closed, I told Sybil and Dale what we had found in the attic and what had been said when Dr Lambert caught us. Bewildered, Sybil observed: 'Master Stagg said he came here just as a workman. But now the chaplain is saying that they're old friends!'

'I know.' I felt just as confused. 'We're supposed to be here because Stagg says he can't just come here himself and make any kind of attempt to do his own searching.'

Brockley said: 'I think we should simply tell Stagg what we've found and what Lambert said about it, and leave it at that. With your permission, madam, I'll ride over to Guildford straight away and do so. Yes?'

'No,' I said. 'At least, not on your own. I shall come with you.'

FIFTEEN
The Call of the Wild Geese

I excused my absence that afternoon by saying I wished to ride out for exercise and ought to make another visit to Hawkswood, to see that all was well there and also to find out when the new window was to be installed. Sybil could continue instructing the twins, who in any case were eager to concentrate on the parterre pattern. It sounded natural enough.

Once more, I encouraged Dale to sit in the parlour with them. She always seemed to have some mending to do, and could do it there. She looked depressed because I was going off alone with Brockley, even though she knew quite well that such expeditions were in no way a threat to her. Dale couldn't help her jealous nature. I always did my best not to arouse it; and so, I think, did Brockley though we never discussed the matter.

'We'll be back before supper,' I said as we got ready to set out. 'Thank goodness, the weather has changed for the better.'

It had indeed, and we had a pleasant ride through cool autumn sunlight. There were few flies to annoy us, but the sky was like blue enamel and the trees were still in leaf although the first signs of bronzing had begun. The going was damp but firm and we made good time. In an hour and a half, we had reached Hawkswood.

We called at the house first, to be greeted delightedly by Harry who at once informed me that a buyer had been found for Philip's mare. Then I enquired into the progress of the new window, and Adam Wilder told us it was actually being installed at that moment.

'Dr Joynings came up from the village on his pony to tell us that Master Stagg and his workmen had arrived. He has only just gone. And, madam, would you believe it,' he said with amusement, 'old Gladys has got it into her head that someone from the house ought to be there to watch. I don't know why, but she got the vicar to take her to the church on his crupper. Does she think Master Stagg is going to install a window that ought to go into another church altogether, or put in a cheap imitation then charge you for good work and sell your beautiful window for a fine profit elsewhere?'

'I promised she should see the window unpacked when it arrived,' I said mildly, 'as she wanted to view it close to. Have you seen it yourself? Will I be pleased with it?'

'Yes, madam. Master Stagg sent a few days ago to ask if Dr Joynings would like to go to Guildford to make sure all was in order before the window was delivered. Dr Joynings invited me to go with him and I did. You are sure to be pleased with it. What that Gladys has got into her head I can't imagine! Whatever you promised her, madam, I still think she made too much of a to-do about it.'

'Gladys loves making a to-do,' said Brockley. I nodded but, although I didn't say so, I once again experienced the uneasy feeling that had troubled me at the very beginning of this business – the odd combination of the broken window, Walsingham's secret commission and Stagg's extraordinary one. These things seemed to have no connection with each other, but Brockley himself seemed to *feel* that they were connected. By the sound of it, Gladys was experiencing something similar, and I didn't dismiss that as merely the vapourings of an aged and cantankerous Welshwoman. I had learned from experience not to discount Gladys's ideas.

'We'll go to the church,' I said. 'I wish to see Master Stagg anyway, and I suppose he is likely to be there if the work is still going on.'

'I think it is, madam,' said Wilder. 'It will be quite a task, getting the boarding and the remains of the old window out then securing the new one in place, and it will require careful work.'

He was right. When Brockley and I reached the village, we found a cart drawn up in front of the church. The horse was dozing with a hind hoof languidly propped on its toe, and the church door was open. Standing around and staring with immense interest were a number of villagers of both sexes, some of whom should certainly have been in their workshops, parlours or kitchens or behind their counters. There were several children, too, all agog and full of shrill comment.

We dismounted, tethered our horses and went inside, where, alarmingly, the first sound to greet us was that of breaking glass. But then we saw that Dr Joynings was there, standing back to watch, looking quite unperturbed. The boarding over the window had gone and two of Stagg's men, clad in leather aprons stained with paint and putty, were up on ladders outside, knocking out what was left of the old glass and leading. The pieces were raining down on to a big sheet of canvas placed ready to receive them, on which the splintered boarding already lay. Through a hole already made in the glass, I could see that one of the men looked very young and was probably an apprentice. He was also exuberant and Stagg, standing below and clearly much more anxious than Dr Joynings, seemed to be worrying about him.

'Steady with that hammer, Jude! Slow down! We don't want any accidents! And we don't want shards of glass all over the floor. They've got to fall on the canvas. What do you think the canvas is there for? Shards of glass are like daggers. Watch what you're doing!'

'Sorry, sir!' The youth began to use his hammer with exaggerated caution. Stagg shook his head and clicked his tongue, and then noticed that we had arrived. He gave us a nod of acknowledgement, before turning back to give his attention once more to the work in progress. Joynings had also seen us and was inclining his head in greeting, though a moment later his gaze was back on the window – clearly the only thing he was really interested in just now.

The light had changed. Since the boarding was gone, bright daylight could now pour through. The new window, swaddled in thick, soft fleece, had been brought inside and placed on a long trestle table. Some of the new benches had been pushed aside to make room for it. Seen closely, the size of the window was impressive. Carrying it inside must have been a very cautious business. They would have had to tilt it to get it through the doorway.

The knocking out finished, and the men came into the church

to begin folding the canvas over the bits of broken glass and board. Master Stagg gave a satisfied nod and turned again to us. At the same moment, I caught sight of Gladys, who had appeared from the other side of the church and had lifted some of the protective covering to peer at the window. Dr Joynings had moved to her side and was pointing something out to her. Stagg glanced at them and laughed. 'The old woman is from your house, I think, Mistress Stannard? She wants to inspect things on your behalf!'

'She's a nosy old soul, but harmless,' I said, though softly so that Gladys wouldn't hear. 'Master Stagg, I am very pleased that I happened to come home on the right day to see the window arrive, but it's pure chance. I really came on another errand entirely. I wanted to tell you that we have found the missing bridal chest. It's as you feared. It's in an attic at Knoll House. I just wanted to inform you. What you do about it is up to you.'

'You've found it!'

'Yes, that is what I said.'

'She's *found* it!'

I started. I hadn't realized that Eleanor was there too. She had been inside the small chapel on the south side. In these Protestant days it wasn't used as a chapel, but housed the tomb of Hugh's grandfather – by his own wish, Hugh had told me. The tomb had a flat top where flowers were often placed in a couple of big vases, and as I looked through the pointed arch that led to it I saw fresh flowers in the vases. Eleanor had presumably been arranging them.

'You don't mind?' she asked me anxiously. 'I came with my uncle to see the window go in and saw that the vases were empty. As we came into the village, I noticed some late-flowering roses in one of the gardens and asked if I could take some for the church. The woman there said yes, and told me that her neighbour who usually sees to the vases had been ill. I've put in some red roses with ferns for greenery, though they're beginning to turn bronze. You don't object?'

'No, of course not.' From where I stood, I could see that the flowers and ferns were well arranged. Eleanor clearly had a good hand with them. 'It was a very kind thought.'

'Pretty notion,' remarked Gladys, who was still peering down at the window, which Dr Joynings had now unwrapped completely. In it, the righteous were being welcomed to the presence of God and the unrighteous were being led away to damnation. I went to stand beside Joynings for the closest possible look. The colours were rich and beautiful and the theme was dramatic enough to strike awe but not crudely frightening, as the former window had been.

Pleased, I turned away and went back to Eleanor, who made a charming little reverence to me. She raised her large grey eyes to my face. They were full of pleading.

'You have found the chest,' she said. 'I am so relieved! Dear Mistress Stannard, can you get it out, privately, and bring it to us? Please say you can. My betrothed will be visiting me soon and I do so long to have the chest there for him to see.'

'And above all, we don't want him thinking that we have been involved in anything . . . unsavoury,' said her uncle, coming to her side and drawing her arm through his. 'This match is very pleasing to Eleanor, and also to her stepfather and me.'

I had been afraid of something like this. I took a deep breath and said firmly: 'Master Stagg, your private affairs are your own. And Mistress Liversedge, the same goes for your personal business, too. I cannot agree to undertake the removal of the chest. For one thing, apart from the sheer impropriety of taking something from my host's house without his consent, we could only do so by night, as the house is too populated by day. Also, the chest is both heavy and bulky, and it is up in an attic next to the dormitory where the menservants sleep, and if we got it past them we would still have to carry it past the room on the floor below where the women servants sleep. Impropriety apart, it would be impossible to get it out in secret.'

'Quite right.' Brockley came over to us, followed by Gladys, hobbling arthritically, who made an uninvited comment. 'Quite wrong,' she said, causing us all to stare at her in astonishment. She stared back, sharp dark eyes gleaming from either side of her beaky nose. 'I can deal with sleepy maidservants and a crowd of men, easy as winking, indeed I can. Just give me the word.'

'Please,' said Eleanor. And once again, the big grey eyes brimmed with beseeching tears – the tears that seemed to come to her so easily. 'It means so much to me. Please. Please. *Please!*'

And that was the moment when I forgot to be a respectable middle-aged lady, and became again the adventurous young woman I had once been.

It was a mistake.

We had provided ourselves with a good supply of clothing when we set off to stay at Knoll House but, as is so often the case, found we had left behind things that we would have liked to have had with us, including gowns that we missed, clothes ideal for autumn weather, and extra underlinen and the like. Brockley had been regretting a favourite doublet and its matching hat. After we left the church, we went back to Hawkswood House not only to have a little refreshment before starting for Knoll but also to collect and pack these items. We didn't stay to see the window actually installed, though Gladys did, saying that Dr Joynings would bring her home when it was done. 'Only, don't you leave afore I come. You'll need me.'

We took our time, fortifying ourselves with ale and warm chicken patties, before collecting the fresh clothes, along with a few other items that I had instructed Brockley to fetch. I was aware all the time that although Brockley did what I asked him to do without comment, he was silent and tight-lipped. Presently he came to my room to announce that he had finished packing, and because his room overlooked the courtyard had seen Gladys come back, riding behind the vicar.

'Joynings went straight off again. I heard him calling goodbye to someone, and Gladys has gone to the kitchen. I looked out and saw where she went. To prepare her wretched potion, I suppose. I'll start carrying things down if you have anything ready . . .'

And with that, his bottled-up feelings burst into words.

'Gladys almost rules this house. It's time we were on our way but – oh, no! – we have to wait until her potion is made and we can't set off until it is. Madam, do you really intend to go through with this? Yes, I've fetched those wine kegs up from the cellar as you asked, and told Eddie to harness Rusty to the cart. Madam, I realize that it isn't my place to criticize anything you do or plan to do, but I have to say it. Are you really set on this course of madness?'

'It was sensible to choose Rusty,' I said calmly, pretending that I hadn't heard the fury in his voice. 'He is our quietest horse and the kegs mustn't be jolted. Eddie can drive and bring the cart back home.'

'That wench Eleanor,' said Brockley angrily, 'turns the fountain on to order. Dear God, those great big grey eyes full of tears! They're as mournful as the North Sea in a rainstorm. By the sound of her betrothed, he isn't a man who will be patient with such a weak link.'

'Meaning that it might be as well if he did break it off?'

'Yes,' said Brockley tersely. 'So must we go through this . . . this performance?'

'I've given my word,' I said.

And so I had. Stagg had drawn me, Eleanor and Gladys away from the others and guided us into the chapel. Brockley tried to come too, but Stagg waved him back. 'This is a private matter, my man!' Brockley looked angry but we could hardly create a noisy scene in a church and in the presence of the vicar and the workmen, so he couldn't interrupt the ardent pleas for me to spirit the chest out of Knoll House.

The onslaught was like a verbal trident. What with Gladys – I think under some perverse impression that I would welcome her assistance – kindly offering to assist the business with a poppy potion, Stagg anxiously coaxing me, and Eleanor weeping as she pleaded with me, I finally gave in. Eleanor's tears in particular distressed me. She made me feel I had no choice. I now wished I had been more resolute. Indeed, I had been wishing that ever since we left the side chapel with Eleanor earnestly thanking me and still weeping – in gratitude this time – and came face to face with Brockley. He understood at once that I had given in and his expression told me what a fool I was. I should have told Gladys to mind her own business and treated both Eleanor and Stagg with a healthy mixture of reason and callousness. I had done none of these things.

Brockley was now saying: 'That chest is heavy even on its own, and with that salt in it *very* heavy. When it was taken to Knoll House, I doubt if it was carried up those awkward attic stairs with the salt inside. I fancy the salt was carried up separately. The chest is valuable too and part of the gift, or so I understand, so we'll have to move them separately – up and down that narrow creaking, twisting stair in the dark, one at a time. I don't like the idea!'

'Nor do I,' I said. 'But I've given my word now, and with Gladys's potion . . . How long does that damned potion take to prepare? I wish she'd got back from the church sooner! We'd better get our own things down to the cart, anyway.'

'I'll see to that, madam. And hurry Gladys up as well.'

I looked with fondness into the face of the manservant who was also my friend and my comrade. 'I know you don't approve of this, Brockley. Why are you so willing to help?'

'I have to help you,' said Brockley. 'I can't leave you to undertake such a wild scheme on your own!'

'It isn't all that wild,' I said, somewhat defiantly. 'If Gladys's poppy potion does what she claims for it – and it will because she's given it to me when I've had a migraine and couldn't sleep, so I know it works – then we should be able to get that wretched chest and the salt down from the attic and out of the house during the night without disturbing anyone. Stagg says he will wait for us, with a cart, just outside the side gate that leads from the herb garden. He'll take the chest to Eleanor, and it will be there when her prim and proper suitor comes to see her. I wonder if her stepfather knows about all this? Stagg hasn't mentioned him.'

'As I've said before, there have been too many odd things about this business, far too many,' said Brockley. 'And this is just one more. Why are those two so anxious to get you to move the chest? If you had any sense at all, you'd leave it alone. If Stagg and his niece want that chest back, let them collect it. According to Lambert, Stagg *does* know Frost socially – they're supposed to be friends. Stagg was lying when he said he had only been to the house as a workman and therefore had no chance of being able to search the house himself. Why did he lie? I'd like to know the answer to that.'

'That may be it,' I said. 'I mean, if they are friends, Stagg may not want to issue a challenge, or an accusation. He just wants the chest to . . . to vanish from the attic of Knoll House and reappear in Eleanor's home. In a way I can understand that. I'm sorry, Brockley. I'm committed now. I have to go through with it, even though you think I'm out of my wits.'

'Not out of your wits, madam,' said Brockley. 'It's just that you've heard the wild geese call.'

SIXTEEN
Drinking After Dark

The Knoll House mastiffs knew us by now and, although they always bounded up to greet us when we went into the grounds, they would only bark when we returned from the outside world. All the same, the fewer chances we took, the better. I had made arrangements to deal with them. 'I've been as thorough as I can,' I said reassuringly to Brockley as we unloaded the cart. 'I think – I hope – it will all go smoothly.'

Eddie helped us carry our various boxes and hampers and the two wine kegs up to my room before leaving to drive the cart back to Hawkswood. Mrs Hamble and two of the maid-servants saw us and glanced at our burdens with mild interest, but no one asked any questions. Dale helped us with the unpacking but there was no sign of Sybil. 'Where is she?' I asked Dale. 'With the twins? Are they really still creating parterre patterns?'

'They're getting quite excited about their parterre embroidery,' said Dale. 'I believe Mistress Jester has pointed out that in making it they can practise all their stitches and the couching you have been teaching them, ma'am. They have started the actual embroidery and are working on it now. But Mistress Jester isn't with them. Mrs Hamble fetched her. Master Frost wanted to see her about something.'

Suddenly worried, I went out of the room and made for the back stairs, which had a window overlooking the gardens. There they were, Sybil and Master Frost, walking on the lawn, apparently deep in talk. As I watched, I saw that Sybil was shaking her head and pointing to the house as if saying she wanted to come indoors. Then she glanced up and saw my face at the window. I waved, and Sybil at once and decisively said goodbye to Frost and walked purposefully towards the

house. I withdrew from the window and went back to our
room. A moment later, Sybil joined us.

'What was all that about?' I asked her.

'Master Frost was offering his hand and heart. Again,' said
Sybil shortly.

'No!' said Dale. 'I mean . . . was he really? But surely you
didn't . . .?'

'No, I didn't. Of course I didn't.' Sybil, visibly upset, burst
out: 'I wish we didn't have to stay here!' and then, obscurely,
added: 'I wish so many things were different!' She stared
round at the various objects we had brought from Hawkswood.
'Whatever is all this?'

'I'm wondering that, as well,' said Dale.

Brockley and I explained our plan, and the reasons for
bringing some of the things that were now scattered about the
room. The two kegs respectively contained a warm red
Mediterranean vintage, and a thinner white wine from Germany.
We had also brought a large set of earthenware goblets; a flask
of pale green-tinged liquid mixed for us by Gladys, created
mainly from the juice of a certain species of poppy; and two
small lamb joints. John Hawthorn, the Hawkswood cook, had
mourned aloud when I demanded these from his stores, and
positively howled when I said I was going to feed them to the
Knoll House mastiffs. 'They're beautiful joints,' he protested.
'Much too good for dogs!'

'All these goblets!' said Dale wonderingly, as I set them
out on the small table at my side of the bed. 'Aren't they from
Hawkswood?'

'I can't very well rifle the Knoll House cupboards,' I said.
'And in any case, here in Knoll House I've seen no nice brown
earthenware cups. They're mostly silver. Master Frost really
does love silver! And pewter's no better for our purposes. So
I've brought some brown earthenware goblets from home.'

'But why do you want brown goblets?' Dale wanted to
know.

'Because they'll conceal what we put in them,' I said.

Back at Hawkswood, when the potion was ready, I had
conferred with Brockley and Gladys about my plans. Brockley
had immediately thought of a snag. 'It's highly likely,' he said,

'that the servants we are trying to drug will invite whoever brings the wine to take a drink with them. I think I would. That could make things very tricky. We can't just put the drug into the pitcher.'

'We could fill the goblets beforehand and bring them in on a tray,' I said. 'It would mean preparing special goblets for us, without any potion in them – and we must make sure we know which ones they are.' I paused and thought for a moment. 'I'd better take the wine to the women, while you, Brockley, serve the men in the attic. We had better keep the rule of the house, about the men and women never entering each other's sleeping quarters – except for Susie and the master, of course.' Gladys emitted a wicked cackle and Brockley gave his rare, expressive, grin. 'I imagine,' I said, 'that Sybil won't want to deliver the women's wine, and Dale probably won't, either.'

'Madam, I wouldn't allow Fran to take part,' Brockley told me. He was frowning. Then he said: 'Filling the goblets in advance won't be a problem with the women servants, they're on the same floor as us. But I would have to carry a tray of filled cups up to the attic, up those twisty, awkward stairs, and some of the wine would spill. I don't see how it can be done.'

'There's stupid, you are,' said Gladys rudely. 'It'll be dark, and you'll be serving by candlelight. Got eyes like cats, have they, these Knoll House folk? What you want is dark goblets, and we've got brown earthenware ones here. Take them along empty except for a spoonful of my poppy juice in the bottom of each. That's all you need. It's got no colour to speak of – you'd hardly see it in broad daylight, let alone by candlelight! All the goblets'll *look* as if they're empty. But yours would *really* be empty and you'd best take care you drink from the right one. It takes about half of the hour to take effect. There'll be time to drink with the servants and get away before they even start yawning.'

Now, in my room at Knoll House, I explained all this.

'How many people do we need to give the potion to?' I asked.

Brockley looked at Dale, who said: 'There are three maids, not counting Susie. The youngest one, Mary, always works in the kitchen. The other two, Bessie and Cath, help there but also clean and make beds, and such. Cath, the oldest one, is called the linen maid and she supervises the wash and does repairs. They all share the dormitory. Susie sleeps on the floor below, of course.'

'And the men?'

'There are six who sleep in the attic,' said Brockley. 'The cook and his second and a junior cook, that's three – the spitboy sleeps in the kitchen. Then there's Barney Vaughan, who attends Master Frost, and two others. They do heavy jobs, like carrying buckets of water, fetching kegs up from the cellar and bringing in fuel. They also help serve at meals (you've seen them). That's the six. There are three grooms but they don't come into this, as they sleep over the stables. And the porter and his lad don't come into it either, as they have a room in the gatehouse. But we'll need a goblet for the spitboy. He's bound to know about the wine being given to the other kitchen servants, and will very likely complain if he's left out. So he'd better have a good night's sleep like all the rest, even though we're going to avoid going near the kitchen.'

I counted on my fingers. 'Three maids and seven men who need wine. Ten, and then you and me. We need a dozen goblets.'

'You're taking such a chance!' said Sybil. 'I do think . . .'

'That I have lost my wits,' I said. 'I know.'

'I agree,' said Brockley with emphasis. 'The coincidence will be noticed. That the night we give treats of wine to the servants is the night when they all sleep amazingly well and the chest disappears. Someone will smell a rat. Someone will smell a whole colony of rats!'

'Firstly,' I said, 'it may be quite a long time before Master Frost realizes that the chest has gone. Secondly, if and when he does realize, he may not connect it with any particular night. And I doubt if he will want to raise a hue and cry. After all, if he stole the chest in the first place . . .'

'But why did he steal it?' Dale burst out. 'It doesn't make sense! Not since him and that Master Stagg are supposed to be friends. And if they are friends, then why are they pretending they're not? There's something wrong – something very, very wrong! Someone's been lying to you, ma'am. I keep on thinking that, over and over.'

'Yes, Dale, I think so too!' Sybil declared.

'By taking this decisive step,' I suggested, 'maybe we'll find out what it is that's wrong. We've all felt from the beginning that something's amiss. This may be our opportunity to get it out into the open – to unlock the mystery at last.'

Brockley, Dale and Sybil all looked at each other.

'Wild geese!' said Brockley, once again, and the others nodded. Their expressions suggested that they regarded me as suffering from some incurable disease.

'All right,' I said. 'You think I'm out of my wits. Perhaps I am. But will you do your part?'

'I feel,' said Brockley, 'that as your loyal servants, madam, we should all refuse to undertake this, and in your best interests should lock you in your room until you come to your senses!'

'Do that,' I said calmly, 'and when I have released myself with the help of my picklocks, I will dismiss all of you. Unpaid.'

'I doubt it,' said Brockley candidly, and then sighed. 'I suppose we shall do as you wish. As always.'

It was a pattern that I knew so well. At heart, Brockley was as enamoured of wild geese as I still was in spite of the years, even though I was no longer the passionate young girl who had eloped with my cousin's betrothed by climbing out of a window and sliding down the slope of a lower roof into his arms. My lovely daughter Meg had come of that first union with Gerald Blanchard and I had never regretted it. And my wild streak had served me well both then and on other occasions too – it had led me into acquiring two fine houses and also led me into marriage with my dear Hugh.

Besides, there really was a mystery here that needed explaining, and my scheme might achieve that. Perhaps I had been right to give in to Eleanor's tears, after all.

'I can't take part,' said Sybil. 'I hope you don't mean to ask me, Ursula. I can't bring myself to do it, and *you* shouldn't! You really shouldn't! Nor should you, Brockley.'

'If we don't help her,' said Brockley, 'madam is quite capable of undertaking the whole thing herself! Though how she would carry that heavy chest down those attic stairs on her own . . .'

'I wouldn't find it easy,' I said, 'but I would manage it somehow. If need be, alone.'

'I would do it wrong, anyway, I know I would!' Dale looked as frightened as though I had already handed her one end of a heavy chest or a trayload of soporific goblets.

'I have already told Mistress Stannard that I wouldn't let you try,' said Brockley. 'You're my wife and I won't have you caught up in this.'

Sybil said: 'I can't understand *anything* about this! Why should Master Frost steal from a friend? Why should they pretend they hardly know each other? I know I'm repeating what's already been said, but . . .'

'We're going in circles.' I cut her short. 'And haven't I said that perhaps by taking firm action we may find out what's at the back of it? Anyway, it's all arranged. Stagg will be there tonight, waiting outside the side gate. He'll be there from two o'clock onwards. It's settled.'

'If only it could be done during the day,' said Dale. 'Then there'd be no need for potions and tiptoeing about in the dark.'

'There are always people about,' Brockley said. 'Even when the attic is empty, people come and go. Look how Lambert suddenly appeared when we were looking for the chest! And early this morning I saw Mrs Hamble coming down the attic stairs, carrying a hamper. I daresay she'd been up to see what else still needs to be unpacked. No, we had better wait until nightfall.'

The timing had to be right. We had to choose a moment when the servants would have retired to their dormitory but were not likely to be already asleep.

After supper, Brockley remarked that it might be as well to prime the pump and slipped off to the kitchen to whisper to its staff that by order of Mistress Stannard, who realized that she and her companions must be causing extra work, a goblet of wine would be served to each of them before they went to sleep, and would they let the rest of the indoor servants know.

'I told them that my mistress thought that you would like wine as a gift, as you are not allowed to have it as a rule, but a single goblet each wouldn't do anyone any harm. I said I would take one to the kitchen for the spitboy and that you, madam, would yourself take a tray to the women servants, while I served the men.'

In my room, later, we set out the trays; red wine for the men, white wine for the women. 'Most of the women would prefer the lighter wine, I should think,' said Brockley. We took great care over positioning the goblets on the trays. 'I think,' Brockley continued, 'that it would look best, madam, if we say straightaway that we wish to drink with our . . . guests. And we should then pour for them, as gracious hosts – we should just do it without discussing who is going to pour. But we must be very, very careful to pour our own wine into completely empty goblets and be sure we know which ones they are.'

'You need a tiny mark,' said Dale. 'Something no one would notice but you.' She looked at the trays. 'Look, some of them are old and have little chips in the rim. And here's one on Roger's tray with a little chip off its foot as well. Put that one nearest to you, Roger. Like this.' She moved the goblet with care. 'And ma'am, here's one with two chips on the rim, close to each other. That can be your marked one.'

'Thank you, Dale,' I said.

Brockley had moved to the window and was looking out at the sky. 'It's starting to rain,' he said. 'It may be a very dark night. Madam, you have only to walk across a passageway with your tray for the women servants, but I shall have to carry mine up those attic stairs in order to serve the men and can't manage without light. I need a lantern but I shall have my hands full with the tray, so will need someone to light my way. Not you, Fran. I have said so from the start. Not even on madam's orders.'

He turned and gave me a challenging look but I shook my head. 'You are within your rights, Brockley, and I certainly shan't try to insist.' In fact, I never had any intention of letting Dale take an active part in the night's adventure. She was too nervous, and I had visions of her stumbling on the attic stairs, letting her lantern slip from fingers sweaty with fright and setting fire to the house, or else bumping into Brockley and sending

the tray down a flight of stairs with an almighty clatter and an
overpowering smell of wine . . . No, it wouldn't do.

'Mistress Jester . . .' Brockley essayed.

'No,' said Sybil. 'I am not taking part in this, in any way
at all. I think the whole idea is madness. And in any case, I
can hardly believe that Master Frost would do anything so . . .
so cheap as to steal a bride's dowry chest, least of all when
her uncle, who is giving it to her, is his friend. I have talked
with him – or he with me, rather – and I can't believe that he
is that sort of man. There is something very, very wrong here.
I am sorry, Brockley, but I will not light your way; and, Ursula,
please don't ask me to change my mind, because I shan't. I
can't.'

'I'll light your way, Brockley,' I said. 'We'll take your tray
up first. I'll leave you there and come down to see to the
women servants.'

When the moment came, I nearly lost my nerve and almost
called the whole venture off, but Brockley now seemed calmly
assured about it. He had let Dale help by pouring the potion
into the goblets and positioning our undrugged cups in exactly
the right way. A goblet had been set aside for the spitboy, and
we had drugged the lamb joints for the dogs.

'I'll deal with those and the spitboy first,' said Brockley.

The expedition went smoothly. Brockley disappeared down
the back stairs, with the spitboy's drink in one hand and the
lamb joints slung over his shoulder in a bag. In a very short
time he was back, looking pleased with himself. 'The spitboy,'
he said, 'will have to enjoy his treat all on his own, poor lad.
But he doesn't seem to mind. And the dogs gobbled their meat
as though they'd never had a square meal before. It was easy.
Now, which tray is for the attic?'

'This one,' Dale said, pointing. 'The one with red wine in
the jug. And that's *your* goblet.' She touched the chipped one
where it stood, just a little apart from the others. 'Don't make
any mistake!' she implored him.

'Trust me,' said Brockley.

Again, it was easy. We went up the awkward twisty attic
stairs very slowly, with Brockley in front carrying the tray,
while I walked just behind him holding the lantern up so that

it would light his way. He had a second lantern on the tray, unlit, to use on his way down. I saw him safely into the menservants' quarters, and then withdrew and went back to my room alone.

Now it was my turn. Dale handed me my tray. 'Four goblets arranged two by two,' she said. 'Yours is this chipped one just a tiny bit out of line. I've put the potion in the others.'

'Thank you, Dale,' I said, and picked up the tray and made off with it, without giving myself a chance to think about it any more.

I had no stairs to worry about. It was only a few steps across the passageway to the door of the women's dormitory. Balancing my tray with caution, I tapped on the door and it was opened at once by a middle-aged woman I recalled seeing about the house with armfuls of sheets and towels. This was obviously Cath. She smiled and stepped back to let me through.

I found myself in a long chamber with a row of three pallets along the far wall. Against the opposite wall there were clothes presses, and at the far end of the room a long table with ewers and basins on it. A number of candles stood about, flickering because the room was somewhat draughty. All to the good, I thought. Mary and Bessie were sitting on their pallets, looking expectant. Wine really was a treat for them.

I set the tray down on the table with my own goblet nearest to me and said: 'Good evening to you all. I know that having guests in the house means extra work and thought a drink of good wine would be a graceful thank-you. As well as, and not of course replacing, your gratuities when we leave! This is a light white wine that I hope you'll all like. May I share it and drink with you? I've brought a spare goblet.'

There were murmurs of 'Yes, of course, ma'am, madam . . .' Cath did seem doubtful about the propriety of all this, but young Mary smiled at me sweetly and Bessie, who had bold brown eyes and a knowing grin, said: 'Shame we couldn't have a proper party with the lads from upstairs!' Which caused Cath to bark: 'And shame on you, Bess, for saying such a thing! The master'd never allow that sort of behaviour, and well Mistress Stannard knows it.'

'He's not so prim himself,' Bessie said unrepentantly. 'Ask

our Susie! Well, she's missing this, though I daresay she gets her share elsewhere.'

'Stop it!' said Cath sharply. 'I'm sorry, madam. Bess here is too sprightly for her own good. May I pour?'

'One is only young once,' I said, smiling. 'But allow me to serve you. I am your hostess this evening, after all.'

Yet again, it was easy. I poured their wine and handed the goblets round. I filled my own innocent goblet, took a seat on the end of Cath's pallet, and drank and giggled with my guests-cum-victims. Then I said 'Goodnight and God bless!', gathered up the goblets and piled them on the tray, and took my leave. As I went out, I noticed that Mary was already settling back into her pallet and Bessie's eyes seemed drowsy.

As I crossed the passage, Brockley appeared from the far end of it, having just come down the stairs from the attic.

'All well?' I asked him softly. 'No one seemed suspicious?'

'No one. I handed the drinks round to our unwary friends and all went as smoothly as cream. Too easy by far. Let us hope things go on that way.'

SEVENTEEN
Mystery Unlocked

Since Sybil and Dale were not to take part in the business of removing the chest, only Brockley and I set out when the time came, just before two o'clock in the morning. We left them sharing my bed, with their heads under the covers. Dale whispered: 'Good luck!' as we started for the door. Sybil did not.

The house was silent as we crept into the passage and turned along it to reach the attic stairs. I had charge of the lantern and I made sure that it did not cast any beam under the door of the women's dormitory. We moved noiselessly, not even whispering to each other, round the corner to the foot of the attic stairs and then up them. There were two sharp turns that had to be stealthily negotiated. We trod with the utmost care. Not that creaks mattered much, for tonight was once again windy and the whole house was creaking. At the top, we halted and listened. The sound of several people snoring in different tempos and various keys came reassuringly from behind the door on our right. We turned left.

Once inside the relevant attic, I swept the beam round and found the chest, which had been left out on the floor. I found something else as well.

'Rat droppings!' said Brockley with distaste. 'I'm glad I'm not a manservant here. The brutes probably get into the sleeping quarters as well.'

'They have cats downstairs,' I said, 'but maybe they aren't good hunters. I must offer the family one of Whiskers' kittens. Or Diana's.' Whiskers was a notable huntress, and her progeny took after her. We had kept one of her daughters and named her Diana after the Roman goddess with legendary prowess at hunting (though there was nothing of the virgin about our

Diana), and between them mother and daughter kept
Hawkswood House very free from vermin.

We went over to the chest. There it was, looking innocent,
its padlock back in place and fastened. I stooped to use my
picklocks. 'We're moving the salt first, I take it?' I said.

'Yes. I'll carry it. You light the way. I can handle the salt
on my own all right,' said Brockley.

He lifted it carefully out and then set it down and looked
inside the wrappings. 'Just to make sure this really is the salt,
and that nothing's been substituted for it.'

'Do you think that's likely?' I whispered, in surprise.

'No, but we're dealing with some curious characters,' said
Brockley. 'I don't want anyone making worse fools of us than
we already are.'

But the salt was there, as expected. Brockley swathed it
again and carried it out to the stairs. I followed. As silently
as possible and slowly, for the sake of caution, he carried it
down the stairs, while I shone the lantern from behind to show
him where to put his feet. Once we were down on the second
floor, we took it to the Brockleys' chamber, empty now because
Dale was spending the night with Sybil in my room. We put
it in the clothes press then once more set out for the attic, and
a few minutes later we were standing beside the empty chest.

'Right,' said Brockley. 'Now, this is a bulky, awkward thing,
but if you light my way and we go slowly we should be able
to manage.' He stooped, pulled the chest towards him
and pushed his fingers beneath it to lift it. And then he
desisted and muttered something like a curse.

'What's the matter?'

'Although it's empty, it's still heavy!' Brockley straightened
up and turned to look at me. 'I should have realized. It's good
solid timber and it's awkward to grip hold of, too. If Frost's
groom moved this on his own with the salt inside, well, he
must be a good many years younger than I am and exceptionally strong at that. This needs two pairs of hands.'

I stared at him in dismay. 'I can't hold one end of the chest
and manage the lantern as well. I haven't got enough pairs of
hands.'

'If only we had some light apart from the lantern!'

'Wait.' I was trying to think, taking my imagination step by step. 'If I go down first, on my own, to the first turn and put the lantern there, it will cast some light upwards. Perhaps just enough. Then we can work our way down holding the chest between us. I'll take the lower end of the chest and go down backwards, first. Then when we get to the lantern, we'll have to put the chest down somehow, while I go down to the second turn and put the light there . . . Do you see?'

'It won't be much of a light.'

'Let's test that first.'

In fact, when we carried out a cautious reconnaissance on the attic stairs, we had a little luck – or perhaps it wasn't luck but the result of a past householder's common sense. There were hooks in the timber wall at both the turns, which looked as if they were intended to hold lanterns and had been placed where they would cast light both up and down, above and below the turn.

'We can do it,' said Brockley. 'We'll get the chest to the top of the stairs. Then you go down and hang the lantern above the first turn and come back, and we'll move the chest down that far. We can rest it on the stairs at the first turn, while you move the lantern down to the next. I think it will work.'

So far our night's adventure had been easy, but this was not. We did have light, but there were still misleading shadows. Furthermore, not only was the width of the stairs narrow but they had narrow treads as well, and in these restricted circumstances the chest seemed to grow in size and bulkiness, tilting wilfully and slipping a little because my fingers were sweating. I had thought that Dale would have had sweaty fingers, but I seemed no better. We descended gingerly one step at a time, with a certain amount of whispered acrimony.

'It's leaning to the left, straighten it up . . . My left, madam, please!'

'I can't! My thumb's caught against the wall . . . Ow!'

'Don't make such a noise! Hoist it up a bit . . .'

'It won't . . . Yes, got it! Now it's steady . . . Oh, God, where's the next step down . . .?'

'Don't lurch! I'm being thrown off balance.'

'I'm not lurching on purpose! Brockley . . .?'

'What is it? Why have you gone rigid?'

'I'm sure I heard something!' I whispered. 'Up the stairs, behind us.'

For a few breathless moments we stood absolutely still, but there was no sound beyond a creak as a gust of wind swept round the house. And then, distant now because we were almost at the first turn, there came a faint snore and after that a scuttle of rodents' feet.

'That's what you heard, rats and snores. Here's the turn. Put your end down, madam, and move the lantern.'

'There's no point in addressing me as madam while you're giving the orders!'

'Just do it, madam!' said Brockley through his teeth.

Eternity passed, punctuated by more irritable phrases, and muffled complaints of caught fingers and bumped elbows while feet wavered nervously in search of shadowy treads.

But then, at last, we were down, carrying our burden out on to the passage. The next part was much less difficult because we were able to use the front stairs to get to the ground floor, and they were wide and fairly shallow. As we passed our rooms, Brockley had slipped into his to fetch a second lantern. It was easy enough to place lanterns in strategic places, and now we had two.

We reached the entrance hall without incident, set the chest down and then went softly back to fetch the salt. Candlelight showed under the door of my room, and as we carried the salt out into the passage Dale and Sybil peered round the door. 'All's well,' I said softly before they withdrew.

'If only nothing dreadful happens now!' I whispered to Brockley.

'We should be all right. I can manage this on my own. And you can light the way . . . madam,' said Brockley and grinned, and once again, it was there, the secret rapport that we had so carefully, though not always successfully, hidden from Dale. For one long moment, in the lantern-light, our eyes met and things that might have been quivered in the air between us. But only for a moment. The past was the past, and the present had set the pattern for the future. We set off on the final stage of our exhausting expedition.

We carefully avoided going near the kitchen door. The spitboy was asleep in the kitchen, but Gladys had warned me that people could sometimes wake up after one of her potions. 'If they want to ease themselves, like, or there's a big enough noise.'

Instead, we carried first the salt and then the chest through the great hall and let ourselves out through the door at the garden end. The rain had ceased and the sky had cleared, but there was no moon tonight to help us. However, out of doors there was still some natural light and we could manage without lanterns. As we came through the great hall, I had held mine up for a moment and seen that the silver clock on the wall showed the time as twenty past two. We put the lanterns out and left them by the door. Then we carried the chest across the terrace and down to the lawn, and through the wet herb garden to the side gate. I stayed beside it while Brockley went back for the salt. We returned it to the chest and then carefully, quietly, I eased back the bolts on the gate. It swung open and Brockley stepped outside. In a low voice, he called: 'Master Stagg!'

Nothing stirred. The side gate opened on to a path which led away across a meadow to join a lane at the far side, making the shape of a T. From where we stood, we could just make out the hedgerow that was the boundary on the far side of the meadow. There was no sign of anyone at all.

'He's not here yet,' said Brockley, stepping back. 'Or he's given us up.'

'We're a little late,' I said. 'But I warned Eleanor that we couldn't be precise about time. He said he would be here from two o'clock and that he would wait. He must have been delayed.'

'I don't like this,' said Brockley. And then, with a horrid jerk in the pit of my stomach, I realized that I could see his face much too clearly. I turned to see why and discovered that a lantern was shining on us both.

'Good evening, Mistress Stannard, Master Brockley. Or should I say good morning?' said the voice of Giles Frost. He stepped forward. 'Perhaps,' he said politely, 'you would care to explain the meaning of this?' He pointed to the chest and then leaned down to flip the lid back. I had not padlocked it, thinking that Master Stagg would want to verify the contents. Frost lifted the wrapped bundle out, opened a fold of wrapping and peered at the salt. 'Yes, indeed,' he said softly, as he replaced it in the chest. 'What can be the meaning of this?'

The question was rhetorical. I knew it, and knew that something dreadful was about to transpire. Brockley said steadily: 'Master Stagg knows the meaning of this perfectly well. He is coming to receive these things, which belong to his niece Eleanor and which he says have been stolen from her. They are a bridal gift from Master Stagg himself.'

'What a remarkable story!' said a second voice, and Stagg himself appeared, emerging from the shrubbery and holding up another lantern. Other shadowy figures followed, resolving themselves into Barney Vaughan, Susie and the Hambles.

'It is, isn't it?' said Frost affably. 'You were quite right, Julius. It is amazing, but you were perfectly right.'

'What are you talking about?' I said sharply.

Frost, incredibly, said: 'Julius warned me that you might attempt to steal this. He overheard you planning it, after he – somewhat carelessly, I fear – let you see it when you called at his workshop, where it was then being kept. I found it hard to believe but after all, Mistress Stannard, you have embarked on a most expensive project, to replace a big stained-glass window at the Hawkswood parish church. I can believe that you have need of extra funds.'

'I'm not in the habit of ordering work I can't pay for!' I snapped. I wanted to say more, to end what was surely some frightful confusion but I couldn't find the right words. My tongue was hindered because my ears were telling me things I couldn't believe. And therefore couldn't refute. I had never in my life been so bewildered. It was as if the very ground beneath my feet was dissolving into water and I was sinking, drowning, in its depths.

Brockley, however, still seemed to be in possession of his wits. 'Master Stagg there,' he said, 'told us that the chest and its contents had been stolen and were likely to be found here. He asked us to search for it and his niece Mistress Eleanor desired it to be retrieved for her. She wanted no scandal because her betrothed would object very much to such a thing.'

Stagg, unbelievably, said: 'Pooh! What a taradiddle!'

'Because of Master Stagg's suspicions,' said Frost, 'a watch has been kept on you. We know you have prowled about at night. Many a night, Mr Hamble and Barney here have been on guard to see what you were about. Then when Dr Lambert told me that he had found you in the attic, examining the chest, our suspicions hardened. And tonight, you were glimpsed taking wine to the servants. *Very* suspicious. I alerted Vaughan and the Hambles here, and Susie too. She has been on guard at her window – from which this side gate can be seen. Thank you, my dear; you performed your part excellently well. I had also instructed Dr Lambert to be on watch at his window, and he saw you creep out from the great hall. I was in the garden, and Barney was upstairs, hidden in the attic. He followed you down.'

'I *said* I heard a noise!' I managed to speak at last. 'But we thought it was snoring and rats.'

'One rat anyway.' Brockley said, with meaning.

'You watch your tongue!' said Mr Hamble, and Mrs Hamble clicked hers in audible disapproval.

I was very angry by now, and also afraid. 'I don't understand any of this,' I expostulated. 'Master Stagg knows very well that he and his niece Eleanor asked us to find the chest and bring it out of Knoll House for them! Why he is now pretending otherwise, is beyond me. What is the point of all this nonsense, this denying of things that Master Stagg *knows* are true?' I stared straight into his face. 'How can you pretend that you and your niece didn't ask us to do this for you, and why did you say you were not friendly enough with Master Frost to be able to visit his house? You know you said that. My maid Fran Brockley and my gentlewoman Sybil Jester know, too.'

'Servants, dependants, all such people will naturally take their mistress's part and accept what their lady tells them,' said Frost dismissively. 'I am happy to let Mistress Brockley be, though no doubt she will be questioned when this matter comes to court. As for Mistress Jester, for her I feel great pity, for I believe her to be a truly honest woman and tomorrow she must wake to realize what a wasps' nest of dishonesty she has been living in. I intend to rescue her and protect her as far as I can from any unpleasant consequences. She has been taken advantage of in a most cynical and improper manner. I mean to look after her and give her the protection of my name. I . . .'

'*No!*'

Susie's outraged shriek cut across the darkness like the screech of an owl or a streak of lightning. She darted forward and seized Frost by the arms. 'You promised me you hadn't meant it when you said you meant to marry. You promised me! Only yesterday you said that all right, you'd thought of it, but the Jester woman had said no and you'd changed your mind! You swore that to me! You promised! And I've sat up at night, never mind how tired I was, keeping watch on these people for you. You . . .!'

'Susie, *Susie!* What are you about, child? Is this the way a young maidservant behaves? Come here at once . . .!'

Mrs Hamble hurried forward and tried to drag Susie away from Frost. Susie held on, shaking his arms, crying aloud. The next words she screamed shook everyone. 'You can't throw me away! You can't, you can't, I'm carrying your child!'

Mr Hamble had joined his wife and between them they hauled Susie away from Frost. Then we heard exclamations from the garden and there were more lanterns waving and figures like ghosts in pale flowing garments running towards us, and the twins, their white dressing robes billowing over their nightgowns, were there.

'What's happening?' Joyce panted. 'We heard such strange sounds from our room. People hurrying about, voices calling . . . And then we looked from our window and saw lanterns. What's going on?'

'Susie, what's wrong?' Jane, gentle and compassionate, had gone to the frantic maid, who merely wailed all the more.

Into the uproar, I said again, and very loudly: 'What is the point of all this nonsense, this denying of things that Master Stagg *knows* are true! What's it all about? Why are you lying, Master Stagg? I want to know why!'

It was Susie who replied, in a voice in which hysteria was mingled with a wild laughter. 'Stagg? His name's not Stagg! I'll tell you who he is . . .!'

She stopped, perforce, because Frost had reached out and grabbed her, slamming a hand over her mouth. 'Be quiet, you silly wench!'

'Silly wench is right! That's just what she is!' shouted Stagg. 'She'll make up any daft tale now out of spite, say anything with no sense to it. That's what silly wenches do.' He stepped forward, looked down into the open chest and then, in his turn, lifted the salt out and put back its wrappings. 'Well, I'm glad to see this safe. It's a pretty thing and I wouldn't have liked Eleanor to miss it. Lovely workmanship. These little drawers work as smoothly as cream.' He flicked at the drawers, which did indeed slide in and out with ease, and silently.

Inside my head a horrid realization exploded. I remembered how Walsingham had spoken to me of Simeon Wilmot, the leader of the gang who had kidnapped my son and tried to turn me into an assassin and been hanged for it. Simeon Wilmot, with the agile fingers – those unnaturally long fingers – that could flick through a deck of cards as if they were made of water.

Simeon Wilmot who had a half brother called Anthony Hunt. In my brain, Walsingham's voice spoke. *I have heard that this man Hunt has made threats against you. He apparently wants to avenge his brother.*

The very first time I saw Julius Stagg, I had noticed how elegant his hands were. Those same elegant hands were testing the smoothness of the spice drawers now, before my eyes. Those tapering artistic fingers too were unnaturally long and very, very agile.

Brockley was also looking at them. Then he turned his head, put his mouth close to my ear and whispered: 'Madam! Julius Stagg. Why did he choose that name? Think! If he's really Anthony Hunt . . . Julius Caesar and Mark Antony. Stag. Hunt. Staghunt!'

I gasped. I now saw the yawning pit to which I had been led step by step and into which I had now fallen. And now the tricks that had brought me here paraded through my mind like a cavalcade of demon horsemen.

Someone had broken that window in St Mary's. Why? To give Master Stagg a way into my life, and then bring the chest and the salt to my notice? He had probably broken the window himself.

And then . . . I had not summoned Master Stagg to replace the window. He had presented himself. He'd said he had got the news of the broken window when he met an acquaintance from Hawkswood. That might well be genuine, but if he hadn't met the acquaintance no doubt he would have invented some other excuse. Of course! said the second demon rider, leering at me.

How did he make sure I would see the chest in his workshop? Or come to visit it? He had invited me. All along, he had been guiding me towards disaster, *this* disaster.

And then he had pretended that the chest had been stolen, and Eleanor had wept. She was in it too, and I had been fool enough to pity her! Oh dear God, I had . . .

I wanted to retch. I could have evaded the trap if I had had more sense. If I had held to my first decision and simply told Stagg that we had found the chest and left the rest in his hands, then we would have been safe. But I had not. I had let Eleanor's tears move me. And I had let that something in me, that unregenerate part of my nature, which had run me into trouble so often before, rule me again. I had heard the call of the wild geese, and like a fool I had followed.

But Brockley's mind was running on a different track. He was glaring at Stagg and Frost. 'My son Philip was part of the plot that Simeon Wilmot laid. Is his death part of this? Did one of you kill my son?'

Silence can be an expressive thing. No one answered the question or even attempted an answer. No one said 'What's all this about?' or 'Who's this Philip and what's he got to do with anything?' No one spoke at all.

It was enough.

'I see,' said Brockley grimly. 'So you did. Why? Did you want him to help trap us, and he said no and then tried to warn us? And did you realize he was about to do so? And watch him and find that he was setting out to visit us, and take steps to see he didn't get there? Am I right?'

At that point, Frost did say the words which an innocent man should have spoken sooner. He said: 'What on earth is this man talking about? Who is this Philip?' But he had delayed too long. And Brockley, as Susie had done a few moments earlier, sprang.

Vaughan and Hamble dragged him off. Mrs Hamble, clicking a shocked tongue, started to hurry Susie and the twins away. All three were in tears and Susie was angrily resisting. As they departed through the herb garden, Frost said to Stagg: 'We must remember that Mistress Stannard is half-sister to the queen and her children are the queen's niece and nephew. We shall therefore have to act strictly within the law. This isn't a case for a local constable; in the morning we will send word to Sir Edward Heron.'

'Quite. He will be shocked,' said Stagg sanctimoniously. 'What a terrible thing, that a connection of Her Majesty should behave in such a tawdry fashion. Stealing a bridal chest, indeed! Shameful!'

'What hypocrisy!' Brockley muttered, in the grip of Vaughan and Hamble.

After that, there was no more talking. Brockley and I were hustled away and marched back to our rooms. We protested all the way and Sybil and Dale met us at the door of my chamber, candles in hand and wide-eyed with alarm. Sybil said: 'Giles, what is all this about?' and was told not to worry, he would see that she came to no harm, and if she wanted to know the whole story, no doubt I would tell it to her.

I was thrust into the room, and Dale was roughly shoved into the one she shared with Brockley. Then the doors were locked on us.

I sat down wretchedly on the side of the bed. Sybil set her candle down nearby.

'What happened?'

'I have been blind,' I said. 'I have been the greatest wantwit in the world. Julius Stagg is Anthony Hunt, and from first to last this whole business of the stolen chest has been a scheme to ruin and discredit me. Or possibly to get me hanged.'

EIGHTEEN
Unknown Quantity

Throughout all this, my picklocks had remained safely in my concealed pouch and no one, it seemed, had ever thought to wonder how, when Dr Lambert found us examining the silver, we had managed to open the padlock.

When I had finished explaining things to Sybil and she had drawn me to sit beside her on the bed with her arms round me and rocked me for a few moments, as if I was a grieving child, she said: 'Can we join the others? Do you have your picklocks?'

I pulled them out. In a few minutes I had opened our door and let us into the Brockleys' room. They greeted us wanly.

'A fine tangle we are in now!' Brockley said grimly.

'Surely it's not so bad?' Sybil was calm and soothing. 'We can prove that we were asked to retrieve the silver and that Eleanor and Master Stagg wanted it. Gladys heard them ask us! Heard Eleanor plead with us, and cry. She was there!'

'And she's about the least useful witness we could have,' I said bitterly. 'Old, devoted to us because we've saved her life once or twice, and with a bad reputation. She's twice been charged with witchcraft, and every respectable physician and vicar for miles detests her. Even Dr Joynings doesn't like her, though he doesn't make a parade of it. And Heron doesn't like *me*! It will be: "Ah, well, the testimony of grateful old servants with criminal pasts can't really count for much." And perhaps it'll also be what Stagg said just now and he'll say it again, oh so sadly, more in sorrow than anger: "What a shocking thing, such a tawdry crime for a woman of standing to commit . . ." And he may add: "Ah, but women in middle age do sometimes do strange things. We must plead with the law to be merciful."'

'But the law won't be merciful,' said Dale, trembling. 'Ma'am . . . Roger . . .'

'Those two,' said Brockley, 'will do all they can to see that the law moves fast, before anyone can intervene. And probably nobody can intervene anyway. Even Walsingham can't just override the law.'

'We need to get word to him,' I said. 'To tell him who Stagg really is.'

'But will it make any difference?' Dale asked, trembling. 'Ma'am, if you and Roger are found guilty of stealing a valuable chest and an even more valuable salt . . . will you ever have a chance to explain what's behind it? And if there's only Gladys as a witness . . . what then?'

We were all silent. We all knew. It could be a hanging matter. If it was not, then it could be prison, a squalid cell for a very long time. It could be the horror of public chastisement at the cart's tail. Even if we could prove that Julius Stagg was really Anthony Hunt, who had made threats against me, that wouldn't amount to proof that Brockley and I were innocent of theft. Nor could we prove that Philip had been murdered by Frost and Stagg. And Dale, my maid and Brockley's wife, might well be dragged in too, no matter how we swore to her innocence. She knew it. She was crying now with fear, for herself as well as for me.

I thought of her, terrified, imprisoned, beaten, even . . . Oh God, what had I and the wild geese done? Even if she did escape accusation, she might still be left without Brockley. I thought of Harry, left without me; of Meg, grieving for me. Thank God, she at least had her good husband, George Hillman, to look after her.

My mind skidded wildly into the future that must follow my death or accompany long incarceration. Perhaps Meg and George would care for Harry until he came of age and could take control of his inheritance. If he had one; if my property wasn't confiscated. If it wasn't, then looking after my two houses, Hawkswood and Withysham, and the stud would be a heavy task for George Hillman . . . A good overseeing steward would be needed. Adam Wilder was getting on in years. Someone would have to be appointed . . .

I thought of my good, faithful, dear Brockley, dying or suffering because of his loyalty to me.

Because of his love for me.

Brockley was no doubt thinking the same things. And he was also thinking of Philip, his son, who had once betrayed us but had very likely lost his life because this time he had tried to warn us of our danger.

Dale had turned a tear-streaked face towards the window. She said: 'It's so dark. It's as if the whole world's died.'

'It's the dark before the first signs of dawn,' said Brockley. 'Daybreak will come before long.'

I wondered what it was like to see the dawning of one's last day on earth.

After a while, I said: 'That little Susie could be a witness for us. She was about to blurt out Stagg's real name. She never actually said it because Frost stopped her mouth, but she must have meant that it was Anthony Hunt. What else could it be? What else would make Frost so determined to keep her quiet?'

'Would it make any difference?' Brockley asked. 'Perhaps Stagg is Anthony Hunt and perhaps he has uttered threats against Mistress Stannard and myself, but we were still found creeping out of Knoll House with valuables that aren't ours.'

'I will plead for you,' said Sybil. 'With all my heart!'

'Will he listen to you?' I asked, and then said: 'Well, I have heard you call him Giles. Are you on such close terms with him?'

'I don't know. I will try. He has told me to call him Giles,' said Sybil. 'He has repeatedly pressed me to marry him. More than you know. I didn't want to talk about it. I didn't want to tell you how nearly I agreed.'

I stared at her. 'Have you actually considered it?'

Even in the candlelight, I saw her flush indignantly. 'I would never have gone through with it. Not really. A man who has been selling secrets to Spain! Never! Not even if I wanted to marry again, and I don't. One bad experience was enough. And now, when it seems that he has plotted to destroy you and Brockley and may have been concerned in Philip's murder . . . But I was attracted. He is attractive. I am still a woman.

I don't like or trust him, but when I am in the same room with him my eyes keep being drawn to him. I am ashamed of that. Ursula, if need be, I will marry him – but only as part of a bargain to save you.'

'*Sybil!*' I had never been so taken aback. Brockley said: 'Madam, you and Mistress Jester should go back to your own room. You must not be caught here. Your picklocks might be found and taken away, and you never know when we may have a use for them. We should all try to sleep.'

Sleep was impossible, of course. Sybil made use of the prie-dieu and said a prayer for me and Brockley, but I didn't join her. If anything saved us it would be human intervention, by someone who wanted to get at the truth, but we would be lucky to find anyone who could see past the undeniable fact that Brockley and I had been caught creeping around the premises with a valuable chest and a silver salt.

When Sybil had finished, we pulled off our outer garments and lay down, then drew our rugs over us and tried to doze. But we couldn't. Outside, the dawn began at last to break, and the sky became cloudy again. The wind, which had dropped for a while, once more buffeted the windows, and I saw a cloud of leaves blow past, torn from the trees in the grounds.

Where would I, where would Brockley, be spending Christmas?

Presently, the door was unlocked and the Hambles came in with trays, bearing small ale and some bread with a small pot of honey. Not much of a breakfast, though it could have been worse. Mrs Hamble said as much.

'I said, let them have honey,' she remarked. 'It's likely to be the last honey you ever taste, Mistress Stannard. And the master says Mistress Jester's not part of what you tried to do, though how he can be so sure, I can't guess.'

'You're soft,' said her husband. 'I've no sympathy for them, but I suppose there's no harm done. They'll be gone from here soon enough. Master Stagg slept in this house awhile last night, but he'll be off within the hour to call at his niece's home and tell her the chest is safe, and then he'll ride on to see the county sheriff, Sir Edward Heron.'

The Hambles, I reckoned, were not privy to their master's schemes. He had no doubt told them that Brockley and I were thieves, but he was protecting Sybil. Would he spare Dale? If only he would do that . . . If only that much could be saved from the wreck! Sybil would look after her. So would Meg. My mind went round and round, confused and frantic.

The Hambles went out, locking the door behind them and we heard them going into the Brockleys' room next door. Listlessly, we drank our ale and did our best to eat the food. The bread was fresh and the honey was sweet. I tried to appreciate them. Mrs Hamble was right: I might well never taste such things again.

About two hours went by. No one brought us any water for washing. Sybil and I combed each other's hair and we dressed.

Then we were startled by a sudden disturbance. There were raised voices coming from a distance – from the ground floor by the sound of it, but loud enough to be audible in our room. And then feet were coming up the stairs and Master Frost was saying something loudly and crossly, and our door was being unlocked.

It was flung open and there stood Frost, with a face of thunder. 'You are wanted in the great hall. Come!'

We stepped into the passage. Brockley and Dale were there already, pale and alarmed. Without another word, Frost led us down the front stairs into the entrance hall and then into the great hall.

The morning was cold and a good fire was already burning in the hearth. Several people were already in the room. One of them, who was standing in front of the fire, caught my eye at once because he did not belong to Knoll House. He was young but richly dressed, resplendent in cherry velvet with silver slashings, and looked like someone of position and responsibility. After a moment, I recognized him. He was Master Taverner, the glassmaker I had met in Greenwich, from whom I had bought a blue glass jug and six matching goblets. Another man, his valet, to judge by the quiet smartness of his dark-brown doublet and hose, stood attentively close.

Close to Taverner, side by side on the right of the hearth, were Julius Stagg and Eleanor. Eleanor seemed to be shrinking from our eyes – even though the room was warm enough, she was still huddled in her outdoor cloak and keeping the hood drawn over her head. The Hambles were absent and so was Dr Lambert, though a deferential Barney Vaughan was there. He and Frost were to the left of the hearth. Together, they amounted to a formidable row of accusers . . . I felt as if I and my companions had been thrust into a cage of lions.

And then I noticed that one pair of eyes was not accusing but seemed to be puzzled. Perhaps one of the lions might be friendly. Taverner, surely, had not helped to set the deadly trap into which weepy Eleanor and her devious uncle had coaxed me. The gentleman in cherry velvet was an unknown quantity and just might be an ally. Giles Frost stepped forward and opened his mouth to speak, but I spoke first.

'You are Master Taverner,' I said, ignoring Frost and looking straight at my acquaintance from Greenwich. 'We have met.'

'Indeed we have, Mistress Stannard. My full name is Martin Taverner and I am betrothed to Mistress Eleanor Liversedge. I am here because extraordinary things seem to be going on – things I wish to hear about in greater detail.'

So this was Eleanor's too fastidious future husband! I said: 'It seems strange, but although Master Stagg and Eleanor mentioned you to me, neither ever told me your surname. Eleanor spoke of you as Martin, that's all. Does she know that we have met?'

Frost glanced back and forth between me and Taverner. He was frowning. Taverner's thin eyebrows had risen. 'Yes, she does,' he said.

Eleanor gave a little gasp, but he did not turn towards her. 'Are you suggesting,' Taverner asked, 'that although Eleanor knew we had met at court, she did not wish you to realize that I was her betrothed?'

'I think we are,' said Brockley grimly.

'No!' Eleanor, for once, was not crying, but by the shake in her voice I suspected that she was close to it. 'No, it's not true. I just called him Martin, as I always do. Martin, I don't understand. Why do I feel that I'm being accused of something?'

'You aren't,' said Stagg, putting an arm round her. 'It is

these people who are being accused, who have tried to steal the chest and salt intended as part of your dowry. Master Frost had taken charge of it for me, as I had nowhere secure enough in my home.'

Brockley addressed Taverner. 'Can we know just what has happened? How do you come to be here, sir?'

Taverner answered his question, but because of attempted interruptions from Frost, Stagg and Eleanor, it was a confused explanation. I will simplify it as best I can, as it would be pointless to repeat all the contradictory words of four argumentative people.

Martin Taverner had intended to make a surprise visit to his prospective bride. He had set off from London with his valet and groom, expecting to reach Eleanor's home, Brookfield House, before supper. But they had been delayed when the groom's horse went lame, and finding a stable where the horse could be cared for and another animal hired had taken so long that in the end, as it was getting late, they had found rooms in Woking, about four miles short of Brookfield. They had ridden on early next morning.

On arrival, everything seemed normal at first. The groom took their horses to the stable while Taverner and his valet presented themselves at the front door. However, it was an unusually long time before it was opened, and the butler who opened it looked worried. And somewhere in the house, there were raised voices.

The butler sent the valet at once to the kitchen and asked Taverner to wait in a small parlour, as the master and Mistress Eleanor were engaged just then. But at that point both of them suddenly appeared, Daniel Johns in his wheeled chair, pushed by a manservant with a face as blank as a sheet of unused paper, and Eleanor expostulating and in tears.

'As usual,' whispered Brockley.

Taverner said that Stagg had been walking behind them, red in the face, clearly very angry, and that the trio seemed to be quarrelling about something to do with a chest and a salt. Master Stagg was saying it had been stolen. Daniel Johns was saying that he had never heard of any such chest or its theft, and what was all this going on in the midst of his family that had been kept from him? A good thing he had just happened to ask his man to wheel him into the breakfast parlour in time to hear what his stepdaughter and brother-in-law were talking about!

Taverner had stood where he was, listening with astonishment and also with all ears. At this point, the trio realized that Taverner was present, and Daniel Johns promptly repeated to him what he had overheard Stagg and Eleanor saying to each other.

'He told me,' Taverner said to us, 'because I was betrothed to Eleanor and was therefore an interested party.'

Stagg, it appeared, had been telling Eleanor that her dowry chest had been safely recovered and that he would now ride on to see Sir Edward Heron. If Sir Edward should question Eleanor later, she *must* remember that, as far as he was concerned, her uncle Julius had put the chest and its contents in the care of Master Giles Frost of Knoll House, who had caught his guests making off with it. 'And *that* is the tale you must tell and hold to.' That was the moment, said Taverner, when Daniel Johns had been pushed through the door to confront his stepdaughter and his brother-in-law.

At this point in Taverner's account, Stagg intervened with fury.

'What are you talking about? You've got it all wrong! I was simply telling Eleanor about the gift and explaining that Master Frost had been looking after it and had caught Mistress Stannard and Brockley trying to steal it. Eleanor hadn't known about my gift before. I'd meant it to be a surprise for her, but when it was stolen from Master Frost I knew there would be such a to-do that it couldn't very well be a secret any longer. I was explaining all this to her when Master Johns burst in.'

'Rubbish!' Taverner didn't shout. He merely used a voice that would carry and silence opposition. 'Master Johns repeated to me, without doubt or hesitation, every word that he had overheard only a very short time before. And they were the words of deception. Eleanor *must* remember that as far as Heron was concerned the chest was in the care of Master Frost, at Master Stagg's wish, and Master Frost had caught his guests making off with it. *That* is the tale she was to tell.'

The tale!' said Taverner with emphasis. 'One does not think of recounting the truth as telling a tale. What Master Johns heard – what he well knew he had heard – was Eleanor being instructed to tell lies to Edward Heron. I want to know just what is going on. I am here on Johns' behalf to find out.'

'But will anyone believe the truth when they hear it?' Dale whimpered, pressing herself against Brockley's side. Sybil was standing aloof, holding herself stiffly, head high, her mouth set, her hands clasped in front of her. But I saw that they were trembling.

'These people were caught creeping out of my house with that chest,' said Frost. 'As far as I am concerned, they are thieves.'

'Once again,' said Taverner, with an air of patience, 'was it necessary to remind Eleanor that she had to remember that "as far as Heron was concerned"? If it's true, what else would she say, to Sir Edward Heron or anyone else?'

It was high time to declare the real situation. I drew a deep breath, stepped forward and used my most commanding voice. 'I believe that all this has been a deception aimed at me!' Everyone turned towards me and I seized my audience, especially Taverner. 'Last night the maid Susie tried to shout out that Master Stagg's real name is Hunt and Master Frost prevented her. But I think . . .'

'What is this nonsense?' Frost cut in sharply. 'Master Taverner, this woman is appealing to you as if you were a judge on the bench. Well, are you?'

'I have to admit,' said Taverner, looking more bemused then ever, 'that I am not. But I would like to hear more.'

'Hunt is the brother of Simeon Wilmot, who was hanged for kidnapping and treason, and I was mainly responsible for getting him hanged,' I said succinctly and quickly, before anyone could interrupt me. 'I believed Eleanor when she told me her chest had been stolen. Oh yes, she knew about the chest all along. She came with Master Stagg and told me that it had been stolen from her uncle's house by Giles Frost and, since I was to stay at Knoll House, implored me to try to get it back quietly, because she was afraid that you, Master Taverner, might not go through with the marriage if any breath of scandal were to touch it.'

'*What!*' shouted Taverner. 'Eleanor, what in hell's name is Mistress Stannard talking about? What sort of man do you think I am?'

Frost said: 'I regret to observe that, as well as being a clever thief, Mistress Stannard is also a clever and extremely inventive liar.'

'*Eleanor!*' thundered Taverner. 'Did you ask Mistress Stannard to retrieve the silver for you? And did you say the fear of scandal might drive me away? As though I would hold you responsible because something of yours had been stolen?'

Eleanor went to him, pawing at him. 'Of course I didn't ask anyone to steal the chest for me! It's all lies! But I did know about the chest and knew it had disappeared. And yes, Martin, I was afraid you would think the whole business scandalous and be upset. Perhaps I was wrong. I'm sorry.' Predictably, she broke down all over again, shedding anguished tears, like a child.

'Stop that wailing, for the love of heaven! Could you really believe . . .!'

'We didn't wish you to know anything about this,' said Stagg. 'That much is true. You couldn't be expected to like it. I had good reason to fear that Mistress Stannard and her associate Brockley might have designs upon it. I overheard them talking about it when they saw it at my premises. They said: "Oh, we could pay our bill easily if we could lay hands on *that* . . ."' I gasped indignantly but Stagg ignored me. 'The lady has ordered some costly work from me and I fear she may not have the wherewithal to pay me. That is why I placed the chest and the salt in what I thought would be the safe care of my friend Giles Frost. I was alarmed when I learned that Mistress Stannard was actually going to stay in his house. I warned him, and a watch has been kept upon these people.'

I gasped again. It was a wild, loose fabrication. A tapestry with more holes than fabric in it that would be remarkably hard to substantiate, but it might just hold. I was sure now that all this was an offshoot from the mad plan to force me into becoming an assassin. It had the same hallmark of being ramshackle and muddled – and yet also a trick that might just possibly succeed if Stagg, Frost and Eleanor were all prepared to stand together and tell lies. Frost was still talking.

'Mistress Stannard and Master Brockley here were caught stealing that chest. There is no more to be said, and they will be tried for it. I will add,' Frost continued, in a forbearing sort of voice, 'that I do not hold Mistress Sybil Jester responsible for any of this, nor the tirewoman Frances Brockley. Mistress Stannard and Roger Brockley are the guilty ones. Guilty in every way, and Sir Edward Heron must be informed . . . What are you doing here?'

He was responding to a new interruption. The door to the entrance hall had opened while he was speaking, and the twins had stepped inside. They looked as if they had dressed in haste. Joyce's cap was not on straight; and Jane had put on yesterday's gown, which had a mark on the skirt, and she was still fiddling with a cuff button. Their father looked at them in consternation. 'I ordered you to stay in your room! You should not have come down. Return to your room at once, or sit in the parlour if you wish, but leave this hall instantly.'

'But what is happening?' asked Jane in her gentle voice. 'Why is our dear Mistress Stannard here, looking as though . . .? We heard you call her guilty! What do you think she is guilty of?'

'Yes, what do you say she has done? We want to know. We are fond of her!' Joyce backed her sister up.

'She has been so kind to us, and so has Mistress Jester,' said Jane, smiling towards us. Then she seemed suddenly to notice Martin Taverner and at once became touchingly formal – a young thing suddenly shouldering an adult duty. 'We are sorry, sir. You have not been properly received. We have no mother and so must fill her place as best we can. Have you been offered any refreshment?'

'Yes, indeed!' Again, Joyce supported her sister. 'You are a stranger to us, sir, but clearly a guest here. May we know your name? And indeed we must ask if you need any refreshment?'

'It is very early,' said Jane. 'Have you breakfasted, sir?'

'*Jane!*' shouted her father. 'Cease this play-acting! Go back to your room, I say, both of you . . .'

'The young ladies are more courteous than their father,' Taverner remarked. He inclined his head towards the twins and smiled at them. And then his gaze lingered. On Jane.

I saw it happen and, although at the time I didn't realize what I was seeing, I nevertheless remembered it, and later on I understood. Looking back, yes, I saw it happen. I saw the moment when Martin Taverner, master glassmaker in the City of London, and Jane Frost, daughter of courtier, minor landowner and possibly traitor Giles Frost, looked at each other, light-brown eyes meeting greenish hazel ones, and fell in love.

It can be like that. I have heard it variously described. Some say that it is like being struck by lightning or knocked over by a runaway wagon. Some say it is like falling down a well but falling towards light and not into darkness. For others, it is like coming indoors out of a snowstorm to find a bright fire on the hearth and a friend there waiting.

It was something like that between me and my last husband, Hugh, though that was gradual, not instantaneous. But I have known the lightning too – known what it is to be knocked off your feet. That is how it was the first time I set eyes on my first husband, Gerald Blanchard, when he was introduced to me as my cousin Mary's betrothed. It was mutual. And so was this.

It was also interesting, or so I have since thought, that the personable and authoritative Taverner gave his heart not to the stronger-minded Joyce, with her dashing near-auburn looks, but to the gentler, less colourful Jane. But give his heart he did, and immediately. In that moment, the lachrymose Eleanor lost her chance with Martin Taverner for ever.

Brockley was muttering something in my ear. I turned and looked at him, blinking. Because of the confusion that had reigned since the moment we entered the great hall, and because my own fear and anger had muddled my mind, I had let myself be distracted from something obvious. But Brockley had not and was reminding me.

'Joyce and Jane,' I said, 'Where is your maid Susie?'

'We left her in our room,' said Jane, 'brushing things.'

'A pity you didn't let her dress you properly,' said Frost acidly. 'You look as if you scrambled into your clothes more or less by yourselves.'

'We did,' said Joyce. 'We heard footsteps going by, a lot of people going downstairs, and then raised voices from down here, and Mistress Stannard's voice . . . We had to know!'

I raised my voice again. 'Will you summon Susie and bring her here? I have something to ask her.'

NINETEEN
Bringing Up the Artillery

The twins turned at once and went out together. As they closed the door behind them, I said to Master Taverner: 'When you have heard what the maid Susie has to say, it may make a considerable difference. But if . . .'

'What is all this? What can Susie possibly have to say that is to the point?' demanded Frost. 'She is a silly little thing who imagines herself in love with me, and a great embarrassment it is. She will tell any foolish lie to hurt me because I have rejected her. She . . .'

'If you will forgive the interruption,' said Taverner, in a tone which strongly implied that he didn't care in the least whether he was forgiven or not, 'I would like to hear the rest. I have to say that I am in something of a daze. There appears to be no doubt that Mistress Stannard and her manservant were found trying to get a chest of silverware out of this house, but her own explanation was interrupted, partly by me – for which, my apologies, Mistress Stannard. It ought to be heard, and in view of Mistress Stannard's standing, her relationship to Her Majesty the queen and her past reputation, of which I know a good deal, I feel that we should consider the matter more fully.'

'Indeed, yes!' said Brockley. 'It is time our side was given a hearing!'

In a patient voice, I repeated: 'Susie may make a difference.' I turned to Taverner. 'Sir, if this matter can't be cleared up quickly, I would wish someone to take the news of what is happening to me to my people at Hawkswood, where I live. It is only nine miles away. Will you do it? My steward Adam Wilder needs to know and so does my stud groom, Laurence Miller. I would also be glad if you could give Adam Wilder

a message from me. I wish him to tell Christopher Spelton
what has happened to me. He is an old friend, I want him to
know.'

Taverner looked relieved by such a reasonable request.
'Naturally your people should know,' he said. 'I will take your
message to your steward with pleasure.'

'Who's Christopher Spelton?' demanded Stagg in a loud,
suspicious voice.

'He is a friend of Mistress Stannard,' said Frost. 'As she
has just said. Naturally she will wish to inform such people.
Whether they remain her friends for long, we shall see.'

I ignored this and said: 'Thank you,' to Taverner.

It was the best I could do. My friend, a Queen's Messenger
and occasional secret agent, Christopher Spelton might be able
to help. He would certainly try. He would surely send a report
on the matter to both Cecil and Walsingham. So would Miller.
They might come to the rescue. Unless Susie did.

Susie appeared only a few moments later, brought by the
twins, who urged her into the hall ahead of them, then followed
her in and stood resolutely behind her, obviously intending to
block her way out. Their father looked at them with annoyance. Fearing that he was about to order Susie out, I spoke
first.

'Susie,' I said, 'last night, you were about to tell us what
Master Stagg's real name is. Will you do so now? It is
important.'

Frost drew a hissing breath and Stagg went crimson. He
glared at me and opened his mouth. And then shut it again
and glared at Susie instead. The twins looked bewildered.
Susie's eyes were resentful, and when she glanced at Sybil I
read hatred in them. Then she said stonily: 'Dunno what you
mean. He's Master Julius Stagg, that's who. That's all.'

'That's not what you said, or began to say, last night,' said
Brockley sternly.

'And Master Frost stopped you,' I said.

'I just wanted to stop the whole silly rigmarole!' Frost
barked. 'You had been caught stealing a valuable chest, and
what Julius's surname is or was could hardly have had less
importance.'

'I think it could be of great importance,' I said, in my silkiest tone. 'Susie . . .'

'Susie behaved very foolishly last night and talked wildly,' said Frost. 'Susie, you know very well that though I am no angel I would wish to recognize and support a child of my own getting. At least, provided that the baby's mother was discreet and made no trouble.'

He turned to Sybil. 'I am sorry. As I said, I am no angel. I have had my affairs and Susie is one of them. But my feelings for you are of a different nature and I still hope I can persuade you to look upon me favourably.'

Sybil said nothing. And I felt bitter. I knew what I had just heard: Giles Frost had bribed Susie. Her mouth was now firmly closed. He had promised to support her child, and presumably Susie herself, as long as she made no trouble. She would not now betray Julius Stagg's real name. I was as sure as I could be that he was Anthony Hunt, but I had no proof.

'Lock them up while I go to see Heron,' said Stagg to Frost. 'That's my advice.'

'And I will be on my way to Hawkswood,' said Taverner. As he made towards the door, Eleanor stepped towards him, reaching out a hand, but he did not look at her and her hand dropped. Seeing her gazing forlornly after him as he went out, I felt a trace of pity for her. She had been extremely foolish; even if she was, as I suspected, a niece of Simeon Wilmot as well as a niece of Julius Stagg, and even if she was really fond of both her uncles, she should have had more sense than to let herself be entangled in this. However, she was very young and perhaps she really was in love with Taverner.

But I couldn't spare much time or energy over feeling sorry for Eleanor. It looked as if Frost did not intend to accuse Sybil or Dale. But Brockley and I were in great danger. We were standing close to each other, side by side. Softly, so that no one else could hear, I said to him: 'Brockley, I'm so sorry. This is my fault.'

'I knew I was right when I said your loyal servants should lock you up until you came to your senses,' Brockley muttered back. 'The trouble is,' he added, 'I was quite enjoying the challenge. Until now.'

No censure. Only a declaration of partnership. Dear
Brockley!

This time, we were all incarcerated together, in my room, the
larger of the two. 'You can wait here,' said Frost, before he
closed the door on us, 'until Master Stagg gets back from
seeing Sir Edward Heron. He may bring Sir Edward with him.
That one of you is unfortunately half-sister to the queen does
make things awkward. What a way for a queen's sister to
behave!'

'We have to rely on Laurence Miller and Christopher Spelton
now,' I said to the others as the key turned in the lock. 'They
will inform Cecil and Walsingham. They may help us. Perhaps!'

'But they didn't instruct you to smuggle any chests full of
silverware out of Knoll House, did they?' said Sybil. 'Walsingham
sent you here to tell lies about shipyards.'

'They know perfectly well that I wouldn't steal,' I said.

'But they can't override the law at will,' Sybil said. 'Maybe
even the queen can't . . . or wouldn't. It would set a bad
precedent. Oh, *why* have things had to go so horribly wrong?'

We had all been standing about in the room, too unsettled
to sit down or make ourselves comfortable in any way. But
now Sybil did sit down, on the side of the bed, and burst into
a flood of tears which almost outdid Eleanor's. Dale went to
her and put a kind arm round her shoulders. 'Oh, don't cry
so. It will be all right. You'll see. Mistress Stannard will
manage, I know she will. Oh, please . . .' She produced a
handkerchief. 'Mistress Jester, dry your eyes on this. It will
be all right, I tell you!'

But the swift glance that Dale gave me, from blue eyes
more protuberant than usual because of anxiety, expressed
only hope. There was no certainty.

'I'm sorry!' Sybil gasped. 'I'm sorry. I don't understand
myself! But except to help you, Ursula, I'd never marry a man
who's been selling secrets to Spain. I'd never marry a
man who is threatening you! I'd never, never do that. *Never!*'

'But Sybil, dear Sybil, whoever thought you would?' I too
went to her. 'It's not your fault that Giles Frost has pursued
you. No one blames you for that.'

'I know, but I blame myself. It's no use and I would never give way to it but . . .'

'You find him attractive,' I said. 'You have told me so. I do understand.'

'It's worse than that! I dream of him at night,' Sybil said miserably. 'I long for him. I crave for him. I . . . I love him. I have prayed; pleaded with God to take this unholy love away from me, but He hasn't answered me. *I love him.* It isn't simply lust. You must finish with me, Ursula. When we're out of this, you must send me away; I'll go to my daughter in Edinburgh. Perhaps there I will be able to forget, in time. I *will* get over it. I know too well what a bad marriage is and once you're wed, if things go wrong there's no going back, you are trapped. Even now, when I'm mad with love, I don't think I could force myself to go through a wedding ceremony, knowing the power I would be putting in a man's hands. I'm sorry, I'm sorry, I'm not making sense but . . .'

I said firmly: 'When I was married for the second time, to Matthew de la Roche, I was passionately in love with him but we were never happy because he was Elizabeth's enemy. Just as Frost is. I know exactly what you are going through, because I've been through it too. There's no need to be sorry and of course I wouldn't send you away. Dale is right. You must dry your eyes and we will all sit together and try to think of ways to get ourselves out of this. Come along, Sybil. No more of this *mea culpa*! You're a woman like other women and suddenly you've been reminded of it. That's all.'

'I've been thinking that I am going mad . . .'

'No, my dear, you are not.' I handed her a second handkerchief. 'Come, try to calm yourself . . .'

'Mistress Jester isn't the only one who has been doubting her own sanity,' said Brockley, startling us all. 'I have been thinking of something that is tying my mind into knots.'

'What do you mean?' I asked.

'Frost and his associates murdered my son Philip. I am sure of it. But how can I bring them to justice? I can't see a way, but – he was my *son!*' said Brockley, his voice harsh in a way I had never heard from him before. It sounded as though it were made from pieces of iron that were being dragged over a bed of flint, grating and grinding and striking sparks.

'We will do it,' I said. 'I hadn't forgotten. We will do it somehow.'

'I can't see how,' said Brockley, still in that curious, harsh voice. 'I've been thinking and thinking and tying my brain in knots and can't see a way. But whatever happens to me, I pray I will see them dead, both Frost and Hunt, before I die myself!'

'I understand,' I said. But then added: 'I would be happier if the only deaths were theirs, not ours. What can we do to save ourselves?'

Unknown to us, Martin Taverner was doing it.

We were left to ourselves for the rest of the day. Food and drink, in the shape of cold meat, bread and small ale, was served to us twice. That night, we three women squeezed into the bed, while Brockley found a truckle bed underneath our own and slept on that. I used my picklocks to fetch him some bedcovers from his rightful room next door. Early next morning, I quietly returned them. None of us had slept well, anyway.

Breakfast was cold lamb chops, yesterday's bread and more small ale. A couple of hours went by. And then, in the distance, we heard hooves and voices and we were fetched to the great hall. There we found the sheriff in person, Sir Edward Heron, with a couple of his men, awaiting us.

I never learned the names of the two men. They were not the ones who had come when Philip was killed, though both pairs of men wore helmets and carried swords. Of these two, one was hefty and sandy with a pugnacious face; the other was short and wiry, with fair curly hair, round blue eyes and a deceptively angelic air. I privately named them Pug and Saint. They stood a respectful two paces behind their master, and he, of course, I knew. Sir Edward Heron was a tall, thin man with cold eyes and a long nose of a faintly yellow tint. In fact, he did actually look something like his name. He didn't like me and showed it immediately.

'Ah, Mistress Stannard. Once more I find you embroiled in violent and questionable events. You would be so much happier if you would confine yourself to your still-room and your needlework, as a lady should.'

'Sir Edward,' I said, making him a curtsey. 'Good day. I assure you that I have been staying at Knoll House only to instruct Master Frost's daughters in embroidery.'

Sir Edward raised his arched eyebrows half an inch or so higher and said: 'I am glad to hear it.' On the occasion when I successfully obliged him to withdraw a charge of witchcraft, I knew he had felt defeated. He had wanted me to be guilty because he disliked the kind of woman that I was. Like Walsingham, he did not consider that it was a woman's business to undertake secret missions for the queen.

But he had his virtues. Sir Edward Heron might dislike me, might indeed be biased against me, but no one had ever accused him of dishonesty. He was a man of integrity. If the evidence cleared me, he would not try to falsify any facts.

The trouble was that Stagg and Frost, and probably Eleanor too, would falsify facts with a will. Yes, the danger was real. The ghost of Simeon Wilmot was in the room with us.

Sybil was invited to sit down and Dale was told to stand at her side. Brockley and I were left standing in the middle of the floor. The table had been pushed back to make room. Heron, Stagg, Frost and Eleanor were seated on a bench, facing us. Dr Lambert was present this time and he, along with Barney Vaughan and Susie, all standing, were ranged on one side of the bench. Heron's men stood watchfully upon the other. Eleanor had reddened eyes, as though she had been crying again, which was no surprise. Lambert didn't look happy, either.

Frost called on Dr Lambert to open the proceedings with a prayer for guidance and the discovery of the truth. Under his breath, I heard Brockley growl: 'Hypocrite!' The prayer was short and exceptionally nasal, as if Lambert was reciting the words but could put no heart into them. Did Lambert have a bad conscience? I wondered. How much did he know? Anything? Nothing? Or all?

The proceedings began. It was not a trial, of course, but a preliminary enquiry. Heron wanted to know the facts before he actually invoked the law. He tried to conduct things in a dignified and official manner, calling on first one and then another to speak, and silencing interruptions. But the enquiry never really got under way. We were still listening to Stagg explaining, outrageously, how his suspicions had been aroused by the cost of the window I had ordered and what he called my covetous expression when I saw the chest while visiting his premises, and what he claimed to have heard Brockley and me whispering to each other, when there was an interruption.

It began with the sound of hoofs and the rumble of wheels and Heron called a halt while he sent Pug to ask who had arrived and why. Pug returned looking astonished, and he was followed by Taverner, leading a small procession. First came Christopher Spelton, pushing a wheeled chair in which Eleanor's stepfather Daniel Johns was seated. After him came Dr Joynings and behind him, glowering and clumping along on her stick . . .

'God's Teeth!' muttered Brockley. 'They've brought the artillery!'

Last in the procession was Gladys.

Taverner and Johns between them managed to present a most authoritative front. Politely, having removed their hats and bowed to Sir Edward and then collectively to everyone else, they presented their companions in formal fashion. Johns stated that he had decided to leave his valet, who usually pushed his chair, at home, since Master Spelton was willing to assist and the matter in hand was so delicate. He then announced that he and Master Taverner had a favour to ask. Taverner did the actual asking. In the least humble voice imaginable, he said that he humbly begged that Mistress Stannard should be allowed to put her side of the story. They had brought witnesses who might be able to bear some of it out, and it would shorten the proceedings if it were possible to go straight ahead with this.

Sir Edward pursed his lips, and then spoke quietly to Frost and Stagg, presumably asking for their agreement. They shook their heads quite violently, which had the effect of making him look at them sharply. Then he turned to Johns and Taverner.

'Your request is granted. Mistress Stannard may speak.'

I did so, as I had tried to do the day before. Then, I had been interrupted and contradicted. This time I was heard out. I put everything as plainly and briefly as I could, so as not to waste time or confuse anyone. When I reached the stage of explaining why Frost and Stagg desired my downfall, they both clearly wanted to interrupt but Heron ordered them to keep silent, and when Saint and Pug placed ominous hands on their sword hilts the attempt to interrupt ceased abruptly.

At the end, Heron said: 'So you claim that you were told that the dowry chest had been stolen, and that you were asked to find and retrieve it quietly, ostensibly because Mistress Liversedge feared that her betrothed husband would be shocked by the scandal of having the chest stolen, even though she was the victim and not the perpetrator. He denies this . . .'

'I most certainly do!' said Taverner. 'And I am so appalled at being used in this offensive manner that I have broken my betrothal off.' Eleanor at once began to whimper and he rounded on her. 'Oh, don't begin that again, Eleanor, please! You will dissolve into a puddle soon!'

Eleanor produced a handkerchief, blew her nose and wiped her eyes. She stood trembling, but refrained from any further demonstration of grief.

'And Mistress Stannard, you claim,' said Heron, 'that the entire request was a trap, aimed at getting you caught in the act of committing a theft. Aimed, in fact, at your ruin. Because you also claim that Julius Stagg is actually Anthony Hunt, brother of Simeon Wilmot, who was hanged for his involvement in a plot which you foiled, and that Master Stagg – or Hunt – therefore seeks revenge.'

'Yes, Sir Edward. And I – we, all of us – also suspect that Philip Sandley, who was recently found murdered not far from Hawkswood, was aware of the plot against me and was coming to warn us, but was prevented. We have reason to suspect that he was actually involved in Simeon Wilmot's plot, and that Hunt and Frost thought they could involve him in this one. Perhaps they had some scheme that needed his co-operation and had to change their plans when he refused. He and his father, Roger Brockley, had by this time formed a bond.'

'It hangs together very well,' Heron conceded. 'But where

is the supporting evidence? Is there any at all to uphold this matter of Philip Sandley, which you have brought up so very unexpectedly? And is there any at all to support your version of how you came to be found removing the chest and the salt from Knoll House?'

'I have something to say,' said Christopher.

'You, Master Spelton?'

'I paid a call on Mistress Stannard shortly after she was visited by Master Stagg and his niece with their extraordinary request. When I entered the parlour where she was sitting, she was in the company of Gladys Morgan, whom you see here, and in fact it was Gladys who told me about their visit. She had been present throughout. She confirms Mistress Stannard's account of that visit.'

'Gladys Morgan? I know of her,' said Heron. 'A loyal family servant who owes Mistress Stannard much and, or so I understand, is also grateful to Roger Brockley. It is common knowledge in this district that in the past they protected her from charges of witchcraft, which I myself strongly suspect were justified. A loyal, aged and possibly dubious servant is not the kind of witness I find convincing. I cast no aspersions on your honesty, Master Spelton, but you are offering no more than hearsay and not from any reliable source.'

Gladys lifted her stick and banged it three times on the floor, making us all look towards her. 'Enough of calling me dubious, whatever that means. There's rudeness, anyway. I know it. But I can tell you that that man Stagg hates Mistress Stannard, and there's proof of that. Summat I can *show* you. Hates her so much, his very hands betray him.'

'And I can speak to that,' said Dr Joynings. 'Gladys has shown me.'

I stared at them in amazement. Brockley, Sybil and Dale were fairly gaping. None of us had the least idea what this was about.

'It'll mean a journey to Hawkswood,' said Gladys, obviously enjoying herself. 'But you can see for yourselves, indeed you can.'

'She is right,' said Joynings. 'She has shown me. It is something in the church. She has shown Master Spelton, too.'

Christopher nodded vigorously and Daniel Johns said: 'Master Spelton has told me about it. I believe him.' Eleanor's wet eyes were wide with incomprehension, and Stagg and Frost clearly just as flummoxed.

'Got the Hawkswood coach outside,' said Gladys, looking smug. 'Been a fair old game, it has, people riding hither and yon all yesterday. Me getting Master Taverner to put me on his crupper so we could call on the vicar and I could be showing them what I want to show you all now, and then Master Taverner going off in the coach yesterday to fetch Master Johns so we could all travel here together this morning, and the vicar here galloping off on his fat old skewbald to fetch Master Spelton and show *him* what's to be seen. Well, who's coming along to see for theirselves?'

TWENTY
The Face of a Damned Soul

'There is no need for us all to go,' Sir Edward said, testily. 'We are not going a'maying. The party will consist of myself, the accused – Mistress Stannard and her manservant Brockley – Julius Stagg and Giles Frost, the woman Gladys Morgan, of course, Dr Joynings and Master Taverner. That is all.'

'I am coming as well,' said Johns. 'I got here in the Hawkswood coach and if there's no room for me this time, then I'm sure the Knoll House stables can provide me with transport. A plain farm cart will do. And Eleanor comes with me.'

'So do I,' declared Christopher. 'I am a witness to what Mistress Stannard told me before she came here. In fact, I advised her not to get involved. My wife was once her ward and I also have the status of a Queen's Messenger. I came here on horseback and intend to go back to Hawkswood the same way, with or without an invitation. Anyway, Master Johns will need me to push his chair.'

So, in the end, it was a sizeable party that set out for Hawkswood that morning, though there was no need for any farm carts. Johns travelled in the coach, which turned out to be driven by my groom Eddie. Gladys and Eleanor also journeyed in the coach and, on Heron's orders, so did Brockley and I. With five of us squeezed in along with Daniel's chair we were very much wedged together and far from comfortable. The chair bumped my shins all the way. Heron and his men rode around the coach, encircling it and forming a guard. 'We're virtually under arrest,' Brockley said to me as the party set off.

'I know,' I said grimly.

Dale and Sybil, who had both been left behind, knew it too.

Our last sight of them had been two forlorn women with white faces standing outside the house to watch the coach depart. I glimpsed the twins trying to join them and caught sight of Mrs Hamble and Dr Lambert trying to draw them back. The twins must be frightened, too, I thought. Their father had not been officially accused of anything, but I had myself brought him under suspicion.

The rest of the party were all mounted and rode behind. We formed quite a cavalcade as we covered the nine miles to Hawkswood. We did not go to Hawkswood House, but straight to the village and the church, where the riders dismounted and tethered their horses.

Brockley and I got out of the coach, and Eddie, descending from the driving seat, chivalrously helped Eleanor out. Brockley and I hadn't felt inclined to do so. Christopher then lent Eddie a hand in getting the wheeled chair out, guiding Daniel Johns down into it, and fetching a rug out of the coach to place across his knees. When everyone was finally assembled, Heron took the lead as we filed through the gate, then along the short path to the church and into the cool interior of St Mary's.

'Well,' said Heron, swinging round to look at his clustered audience. 'Here we are. What is it that we have been brought here to see?'

Gladys hobbled forward and used her stick to point to the last window on the south side. 'That's it. You look close at that one. That's the Last Judgement, that is, and there're the demons taking the damned to hell. You take a good hard look at those. Can't see it from down here; those windows are too high. You'll want ladders.'

'I left a ladder in readiness,' said Joynings. 'There it is, propped in the corner beyond the font. Master Heron, perhaps your men could . . .'

Pug and Saint were already doing it. They brought the ladder out of its corner and set it carefully beneath the window Gladys had pointed to. 'I've been up there,' said Joynings. 'I've seen what Gladys Morgan means and . . .'

'And how did Gladys get up there?' enquired Heron. '*She* can't climb ladders!'

'There's silly talk,' said Gladys in her rude way. 'I was here when the window was brought inside the church and I saw it then, close to. After the mistress had gone, I stopped on. Wanted to see the window go into its place, I did. Only I were in that little chapel, looking at the flowers in there and Master Stagg didn't know I were still there. But I was, and I was at that there chapel door, about to come out, when, just as the men were putting ladders ready to help them get the new window into place, Master Stagg strolls up to it, says: "Ah yes, one final touch!" – and with that, quick as lightning, he knocks out one pane, just one, puts another in its place, gets it fixed, and then tells everyone to wait, it's got to settle. "We'll break for a meal," he says. "It's all ready at the inn. Got to wait a bit now before we move the window."'

'That's true enough,' Stagg interrupted. 'It had all been a rush, getting ready to deliver the window and I forgot to see to a pane that I thought should be replaced. The colours weren't right in the one already there, didn't perfectly match colours in other panes they ought to have matched. I'd got the new one ready myself, working late for two nights. And then, would you believe it . . .'

'No,' muttered Brockley.

'. . . I was so tired that I overslept, and in all the to-do of getting the window wrapped and on to its cart I almost forgot the new pane! I remembered at the last moment, and I like a job to be perfect. So I picked up the new one and brought it with me. I didn't want to mention any of this to the customer, though! I knew Dr Joynings would want to see the window before it went into place, so I waited for him to come. Then Mistress Stannard came too. Well, good. I let them both see all they wanted to see and when they'd gone, I saw to replacing the unsatisfactory pane. What's all this fuss about?'

'I waited till they'd all gone,' said Gladys, unimpressed. 'But afore I left, I took a look. And that new pane, it worried me. Couldn't think what were amiss with it, I couldn't, but summat was. Even dreamt about it at night. And then, night afore last, it were, as I woke up, I *realized*! Plain as the sun in the sky! Them goats have people's faces, but there was one face that was different in that new pane and all of a sudden I knew why. But I didn't know what to do about it, not till

Master Taverner got here with his wild talk about Mistress Stannard there being arrested, and that's when I saw. That man Stagg, I thought, he's at the bottom of this, and I got Master Taverner to take me to Vicar Joynings here and I told him what I'd seen and he got out his ladder and took a look and, well, everyone as can ought to take a look, too!'

Heron was, as I have said, a fair man. He might not approve of me but he was not going to refuse to look at evidence on that account. Without another word, he gripped the sides of the ladder and began to climb. Pug and Saint took hold of it to keep it steady.

'It's bottom left,' Gladys called after him.

'I'm there,' Heron shouted down to her as his head topped the lower edge of the window. 'What am I supposed to look at?'

'The damned!' shouted Gladys. 'Look at their faces!'

'They're goats!' Heron shouted.

'They got humans' faces. And one of 'em's a face you ought to know! You *look!*'

There was a silence, while Heron peered. Then, slowly, he backed down the ladder. His expression was grave. He looked at me, for once with no sign of dislike, but with something more akin to sympathy. 'Mistress Stannard, can you climb that ladder?'

'I think so,' I said. In fact, I was determined to climb it. If anyone had a right to know what had so obviously shaken Heron, I had.

I did not find it easy, even though I was physically quite strong, having always ridden regularly and been often busy about the house and garden. I had climbed ladders in the past but not for a long time now, and in the intervening years I had grown older. I knew that Heron's men were holding the ladder, but still it quivered under me and made me nervous.

But I had to know. My breath was coming short when I reached the window, but I had managed it. I turned a little and looked where Gladys had said, at the bottom left-hand corner, where the demons were dragging the damned to their eternal torment.

I stared in amazement. I had seen and approved the design

in Master Stagg's workshop and I had seen the window close to when it was delivered, but I had not seen this. On the contrary, I had been pleased to see that the design was restrained. The entrance to hell was a black cavern mouth, but nothing worse, and the damned were shown as goats with sad human faces. Although they were being escorted by two black horned demons with pitchforks, only one of them was actually prodding a goat.

The change was in the goat that was being prodded. It had a new face, and it was the face of a woman bound for hell. Her mouth was distorted, a taut, gaping rectangle of pain and fear. She was surely screaming. Tears flowed from her distended eyes. The second demon was in the next pane but for his clawed hands and they now clutched her throat.

That face of terror and anguish was my face. The hair was dark, the eyes, very cleverly done, were a mingling of brown with bits of glittering green: hazel eyes, my eyes, deeper in colour than the hazel eyes of the twins. I recognized the way they were set, the shape of the dark eyebrows above them; I recognized too the cream and tawny of the goat's coat, the exact shade of my favourite cream-and-tawny colours which I had been wearing, as it happened, every time I met Stagg. And I recognized the topaz pendant round the goat's neck.

Stagg was good at portraiture, I thought. The human face of that goat was certainly mine, depicted as only someone could who hated me with every fibre of his being, body and soul.

He had been careful to make sure that if I or Joynings inspected the window before it was put in place, as indeed we did, we would only see the original pane. He had made the change at the very last moment, after we had come and gone. He knew that once the window was in place, it would be hard to see that agonized face.

The window was high and the faces of the goats were small. The details of their expressions wouldn't be obvious. Wouldn't, indeed, be obvious at all except to people who knew my face well and perhaps not very plain even to them.

A stained-glass picture of a goat with a human face, and the features of a living person were so very different. Glass and paint for the one, flesh and blood for the other; the one static in a church window, the other walking and talking. Even Gladys, who knew my face well, had not recognized it at first.

It would be Stagg's nasty little joke, though he would have to keep it to himself. His emotions had been so strong that he hadn't been able to keep them out of his work. He hadn't been able to resist the temptation to record me, for all time, as damned. I might never realize – indeed, I was not intended to realize – that it was there, but he, Stagg, would know, and rejoice in secret.

I shuddered. It was a frightening thing to find oneself the target of a hatred as intense as that.

I backed down the ladder, not minding it now for I was far too shocked by what I had seen to care. I stepped off and turned at once to Heron.

'If you please, Sir Edward, I would wish everyone to see that window who can climb up to it.'

I glanced at Stagg. His face had gone leaden, bloodless.

'Perhaps Master Stagg himself should look,' said Sir Edward. 'We will see what he thinks of it now.'

Stagg made an effort. He licked his lips and said he didn't understand.

'Go up!'

We watched him climb. I looked at the long, sensitive fingers gripping the sides of the ladder. Simeon Wilmot's fingers. Why had I been so slow to recognize them? Even the lines of Stagg's back looked familiar now. They too were the same as Wilmot's.

He reached the top of the ladder and then called down: 'But what am I to look at?'

'The damned, as well you know, look you!' screeched Gladys.

More temperately, Heron called: 'Left-hand corner.'

Stagg looked. Then he came down the ladder. His face was now as pale as a white linen sheet. He did not speak. Christopher said: 'I have seen it already.' But he went up all the same to view it for a second time, and came down with such anger in his brown eyes that I felt alarmed, even though the anger was not directed at me.

Taverner, who had also seen the window already, declined

to take a second look. 'I was horrified enough the first time. It's despicable.'

Dr Joynings too had seen the window, but Heron signed to Brockley and he in turn tackled the climb. He descended with his lips pressed together and a disquieting glitter in his blue-grey eyes. It boded ill for someone.

'I can't get up there,' said Daniel Johns. 'But the window has been described to me and you all look thoroughly appalled by it. It is evidently most objectionable. Well, Master Stagg has had time now to consider his position. Has he not, Sir Edward?'

'I don't understand,' Stagg said again. 'I didn't mean . . . I never intended . . . I suppose Mistress Stannard's face was in my mind. She has a most pleasing countenance . . .'

While Johns was speaking, Frost had climbed up to the window. He now descended, scowling, and said roundly: 'Julius, I think you must have let your brains go begging.'

'I want to see!' Eleanor suddenly interrupted. Without waiting for permission, she went swiftly up the ladder. Young and lithe, she climbed like a monkey. She looked, gasped, and came down even more rapidly than she had gone up. 'Uncle Julius, how could you?'

'Hatred,' said Brockley sternly. 'Only someone who hated Mistress Stannard could perpetrate such a thing.'

'I don't hate Mistress Stannard, that is nonsense!' Stagg now burst out in self-defence. 'It was just that her most pleasing features were in my mind, and the colours in the first pane were wrong. I suddenly thought that one face at least should express the true feelings of a damned soul. I find Mistress Stannard's features most striking and memorable, and . . .'

'You did *that* to them? To features that pleased you?' Brockley strode over to stand face to face with Stagg. 'What I saw there, my friend, was *hatred*. It may seem odd that Julius Stagg, maker of stained glass, should hate Mistress Stannard, but it wouldn't be at all odd if Anthony Hunt, the half-brother of Simeon Wilmot, did! Would it, Master Hunt?'

'My name isn't Hunt. I don't know who this Wilmot is and . . .'

'You have his fingers,' I said. 'And his back.'

'His *fingers?* His *back?* What in the name of heaven are you talking about, madam?' Stagg was blustering.

'I have said it before.' Brockley's voice was grating again – grating, I thought, with rage. 'Someone murdered my son Philip. I think that you and Frost did it. If not, who did? And why? Well? It was you, wasn't it? *Wasn't it?*'

'Don't be . . .'

Once again, as at the side gate in the pre-dawn garden, Brockley sprang. His target this time was Stagg. They rolled on the ground, shouting, Stagg bellowing 'Get off me!' and a stream of swear words, Brockley exploding into vicious epithets and using his fists. Heron and Taverner leapt forward to try to separate them. Eleanor shrieked. Heron's men ran forward as well, but hesitated as they saw that their master was himself entangled in the conflict.

The struggling heap of angry men crashed into one of the new benches, thrusting it sideways and nearly knocking Dr Joynings off his feet. Joynings had so far been watching the whole business in silence, but now he came to outraged life and began to shout. He waved his arms wildly and kicked vainly at the combatants, cutting a figure both comical and impressive at one and the same time.

'This must stop! Stop it at once! I will not have such violence in my church. This is holy ground, consecrated to a loving God. This is an indecency, I will not tolerate this . . .!'

I can still see and hear it all, inside my mind: the battling heap on the floor; the open mouths and horrified eyes of the onlookers as they sidestepped and backed out of the way; the disordered benches, several of which had now been hit and two completely overturned; Dr Joynings' scarlet face and flying cassock; Christopher standing back with arms stolidly folded; and then, absurdly, in a moment when Joynings had paused to draw breath and only snarls and grunts were coming from the struggling heap, and even Eleanor had briefly stopped screaming, the sound, beyond the open south door, of sparrows twittering.

Finally, Sir Edward Heron broke out of the mêlée and raised his voice in command. His men rushed in and the fighting trio were yanked apart, jerked to their feet, shaken into silence.

Brockley's nose was bleeding and Martin Taverner had a cut
lip. Stagg looked as though he would have a black eye by the
next day.

'I want to hear more,' thundered Sir Edward, 'about
the murder of Philip Sandley. And about Anthony Hunt.'

Stagg and Frost both began to shout at once. Johns caught
his stepdaughter's eye and beckoned her imperiously to come
to him. When she did so, he seized her arm and rattled off
some angry questions. Because Stagg and Frost were making
such a noise, I couldn't hear what he said and nor, I think,
could anyone else except Eleanor.

Who lost her head.

Breaking away from Johns, she screamed: 'What's all this
about murder? No one ever said anything to me about murder!
I know nothing about it, nothing . . . It was just to pay the
Stannard woman back for the death of my poor uncle Simeon.
She deserved it, but there was no talk of murder.' She rushed
at Stagg and grabbed him by the elbows. 'It isn't fair, it isn't
fair! You never said anything to me about murder!'

Heron said something and the cherubic Saint marched over
to Eleanor and pulled her away. She was weeping wildly.
Taverner went to her, and Saint let him take her. In a rough
and ready way, Taverner pressed her face against him to muffle
the tears, and after a moment she quietened. He then detached
her, except for continuing to hold her by one elbow. Joynings,
who had witnessed the scene with obvious distaste, looked as
if he would very much like to dig a hole in the flagstoned
floor and bury himself in it.

Stagg and Frost stopped shouting. They stared at Eleanor.
So did Heron. 'I think, Mistress Liversedge,' said Sir Edward,
'that you have things to tell us.'

'I think so too,' said Daniel. 'And by God, young lady, I
order you to tell them!'

Eleanor gulped, sobbed anew for a minute or two, was
shaken by Taverner, not violently but reprovingly, and was again
told by Daniel Johns to speak up and no more nonsense. Joynings
echoed him. And, at last, the truth was told.

Sullenly, Eleanor said: 'I was fond of my Uncle Simeon. He
was hanged and that Stannard woman was responsible – and it

was all because he was in a plot to help England and protect the queen. To protect Her Majesty! What was so wrong about that? He and some friends . . .'

'Including Master Frost?' snapped Sir Edward.

'No, no. Other friends. They made a plan to make the Stannard woman . . .'

'Mistress Stannard, if you please, young woman!' barked Brockley.

'All right, Mistress Stannard . . . She has a certain reputation for . . . for undertaking things. They wanted to make her kill that Scottish queen who's so dangerous to the realm, but she wouldn't do it. Instead, she got them arrested and my poor uncle was hanged. Uncle Anthony was angry. He loved his brother, and why shouldn't he? He moved his stained-glass business from Somerset to Guildford and changed his name. And he told me why. He said if I would help him, I could have a costly dowry from him and all he meant to do was avenge his brother by discrediting Mistress Stannard. I only had to pretend that the chest had been stolen and beg Mistress Stannard to get it back, then he would see she was caught trying to steal it and accused of theft. Serious theft . . . Even if she wasn't hanged for it, she would be ruined and serve her right!' bawled Eleanor, ending her account in a howl of protest against the unfairness of her relatives and the law.

Silence fell after that. Then Daniel, oddly authoritative despite his wheeled chair and the fur rug over his knees, said: 'It seems to me that my stepdaughter has been a very foolish wench but nothing worse. I cannot criticize her for feeling affection towards an uncle, though I certainly criticize her for lending herself to an ugly and remarkably inefficient scheme of vengeance against those who brought him to justice. I know nothing of this murder which is said to have taken place, but I believe her when she says she knew nothing about it either . . .'

'Nor did I, until it was too late!' Frost's face had once again turned leaden and he was sweating. Stagg glowered at him. 'Well, I didn't!' protested Frost. In a shaking voice, he added: 'You have lost. We have lost. It's all over.'

Stagg seemed to pull himself together. 'I must say this. I

am not prepared to see my niece tried for helping in a murder. It is true that Eleanor knew nothing of Sandley's death, and indeed it was never intended. Sandley was part of the original plot against Mary of Scotland, of which my brother Simeon was never ashamed. We believed that Sandley was true to us and asked him to play a part in our new undertaking. I believed him to be estranged from his father and the plan was for him to claim he had overheard a conversation between Brockley and Mistress Stannard, scheming to get their hands on the dowry chest. But instead, he said he was going to betray us, the silly innocent! I told my workmen I was ill and was going to stay in bed, but really I was out keeping watch on him. And when the very next day he set out and took the track for Hawkswood . . . well, I knew where he was going and went to intercept him. I wanted to argue with him, to persuade him to turn back. But he wouldn't listen, and even drew his dagger and . . .'

'You shot him from cover, with a bloody crossbow!' shouted Brockley. 'Then, I suppose, you played the part he should have played!'

'It was self-defence!' Stagg bellowed.

'You're a liar! He never carried a dagger!' Brockley thundered. 'Were the stakes, to your mind, so high you needed to kill him?'

Stagg gobbled, but didn't reply. His temples were streaming with sweat and he was looking about him like a hunted beast at bay. Then I said: 'Anthony Hunt had made threats against me. Sir Francis Walsingham told me that. He will confirm it.'

'I can confirm that, too,' said Christopher. 'I knew of it from Walsingham, as Mistress Stannard did.'

Heron turned to his men. 'Place Master Stagg – or should I say Hunt? – and Master Frost under arrest. As for this girl, Eleanor . . .'

'She has been foolish and dishonourable,' said Daniel forcefully. 'She is not of my blood but I am responsible for her, and I have affection for her and a desire for her well-being. She has not deserved the horror of a fetid prison, though she should pay somehow for what she has done. What does it amount to, after all? In exchange for a dowry chest, she implored Mistress Stannard, weeping – she's good at that – to retrieve the chest from Knoll House. She knew the plan was meant to ruin the lady's reputation, but she fancied that that was justified because she had loved her Uncle Simeon and thought him unjustly condemned. If you will leave her to me, I will see that she pays a suitable price for her behaviour, but in private. She is only a silly young maid, not a criminal.'

Eleanor, who had been listening to him with a look of hope, now let out a squeal of fright and he gave her a sharp glance. 'Don't burst into tears again, girl! Not now. Save them for when we get home – *if* you are allowed to go home. My legs may be useless but my right arm is not, and the birch will use up all the tears you can spare. Sir Edward? What do you say?'

Sir Edward ruminated. At last, he said: 'I agree that she is a silly young girl, little more than a child. Take her home and deal with her as a father should. Hand her to her stepfather, Taverner.'

For once, I thought, Sir Edward Heron's poor opinion of the female sex had worked to female advantage.

Brockley had come beside me and was speaking into my ear. 'There's something I still don't understand, madam.'

'What's that, Brockley?'

'I think Frost told the truth when he said he didn't know about Philip's death. I think he must have been at court when my son . . . died. On the day of the inquest, which was the twenty-first of August, didn't he say he'd been at court since early August and had only just returned? Philip died on the thirteenth. Which means Frost can't have murdered Philip, and it's probably true that he knew nothing about it until it was too late. Stagg must have acted on his own. I think Frost really is innocent of murder.'

'What I can't understand,' I said, 'is how did Stagg – Hunt – and Frost ever come to be fellow conspirators. Frost is a Catholic and was passing information to the Spanish, whereas Hunt was the brother of Simeon Wilmot, who wanted to protect England from the Spanish by getting rid of Mary Stuart. Whatever brought those two together?'

TWENTY-ONE
Unanswered Questions

I attended part of the trial, as a witness. But I was not present for all of it, nor did I wish to be. In December, I was surprised to be unexpectedly summoned to Greenwich to speak with Walsingham – and still more surprised to find him in an apologetic mood.

'I must express my regrets,' said Her Majesty's Secretary of State, almost humbly. 'I believed I was taking advantage of a harmless search for an embroidery teacher. It seemed to be a good opportunity to plant a source of inaccurate information at Frost's very table, and doing that was important. There have been plots, Ursula, plots to call on Spain to help Mary Stuart on to the throne of England. We have defeated them, but there will be others. I wish with all my heart that the queen would let me detach Mary Stuart's head from her body. I took Frost's desire for an embroidery teacher as a golden opportunity. He even mentioned your name as a possible choice. Perhaps that should have made me smell danger! It was only a bait to draw you into a hornets' nest. And to think I had warned you against those same hornets! I am not often so deluded!'

'It all turned out well,' I said forgivingly, rather enjoying the chance to be magnanimous towards the most ruthless man in Elizabeth's council. 'But I was surprised to hear that Giles Frost may not be in the Tower for very long. The Hambles passed me a letter from him.'

'There are reasons,' said Walsingham. 'Even the queen – who can be difficult about these things – has consented. Frost is very useful, and he was not responsible for the death of your man Brockley's son Philip. He has been heavily fined, of course, but he is more use to us free than in prison. We have also freed that fool of a chaplain of his. It seems Dr Lambert knew nothing of the plot.'

In most of the royal palaces beside the Thames, Walsingham not only had an office but also a private suite where he could entertain guests. He had invited me to dine. We were almost alone together, though Dale and Brockley were in the adjoining room having a meal with some of Walsingham's servants. Another manservant was waiting on us, dispensing dishes from the sideboard, where they were being kept warm on tripods over beds of charcoal.

I accepted some wine and said: 'But Stagg – or Hunt (I keep wanting to call him "Staghunt") – will die for killing Philip. You say he has admitted it?'

'Yes,' said Walsingham. 'The Tower has a power of its own. Guilty men lose their nerve when the walls close round them. Master Hunt has been talkative.'

I sipped the wine, glad of its warmth in my throat, because thinking of Hunt made me shudder. 'Anthony Hunt hates me,' I said. 'He hates me poisonously. It chills me inside to think of that. All I did was to try to save my son without committing a serious crime. But when I was in the courtroom at the trial, in the same room with him, I could feel his hatred coming at me in waves. He wanted me to be disgraced – hanged, if possible – and would like to see me dead at his feet. I suppose he loved his brother and would say that was his excuse. But . . . it gives me the shivers.'

'You should not be so sensitive,' said Walsingham. 'There are plenty of people who hate me that much, but I don't worry about such malice and nor should you. I know Hunt's family background. As I said, he has talked! So did Wilmot, but with Hunt it has been a positive torrent. He has filled in all the spaces. It's interesting. Believe me, they are a passionate family. That's how it begins. Many years ago, an innkeeper, a childless widower in his forties, fell wildly in love with the young daughter of a master glassmaker in London. Master craftsmen who are members of London guilds don't usually match their daughters with innkeepers, but Joan Ames was daughter number five and her father was feeling harassed about providing a dowry and finding a husband for her. He'd used up all the sons in his social circle, so to speak. And he himself had a maternal grandmother who came from a respectable clockmaker's family but had eloped with a strolling player who had a gift for card tricks. More passion, you see. Anyway, Master Ames wasn't very rigid in his ideas.'

'Card tricks!' I said. 'So that's where Simeon Wilmot got his knack with cards from. He had such long, agile fingers. And so has Anthony Hunt.'

'They had long fingers? I never noticed. Anyway, Joan was allowed to marry Samuel and they had a son, Simeon Wilmot – who eventually inherited the inn – and a daughter, Eliza. You know all about Eliza. She was the mother of Eleanor, who is now in the care of her stepfather. But Samuel died when Simeon was only ten and Eliza just eight. Their mother married again, a Thomas Hunt, glassmaker – it was arranged through her father's contacts – and Anthony Hunt is their son. Thomas Hunt was a healthy and vigorous man with a liking for spirited horses. One of them threw him and broke his neck for him when Anthony was two. After that, his mother, Joan, showed no desire to marry a third time. So there were the three fatherless children. Simeon was the oldest and seems to have felt responsible for both Eliza and his half-brother Anthony. In turn, they very nearly worshipped him. To an extreme degree. As I said, they were a passionate family. And there,' said Walsingham, 'you have it. Passionate in love, passionate in hate. You stepped into the path of an avalanche.'

'I was dragged into it!' I said with asperity. 'So was Harry. And poor Philip. Poor Eleanor, too,' I remarked. 'I mean that. She was obviously very attached to her two uncles, both Wilmot and Hunt. She has already lost one, and now she must lose the other as well.'

'But her stepfather, Daniel Johns, is conscientious,' said Walsingham. 'He has disciplined her, as is his duty. In fact, there was a kind of deal done with Sir Edward Heron.' I nodded, having witnessed it. 'Heron has a soft place in his heart for young girls and he settled with Johns, who sees himself as responsible for Eleanor's welfare, that she should not be prosecuted but would not escape unscathed. I have spoken with Heron, and he tells me that Taverner has backed out of the betrothal. But Johns will find Eleanor another suitor before long, and when she has a family of her own she will not need to pine for her uncles. You too have a soft heart, Ursula, I believe?'

'Perhaps,' I said, wondering about Walsingham's own heart. I had not met his family but he was said to be a devoted, even passionate, husband and father. It was difficult to imagine.

'And now,' he said, as the manservant came to offer us slices of meat and some beans in an aromatic sauce, 'I hear that you have accepted the task of looking after the Frost girls until their father can rejoin them. I believe that is what he wrote to you about.'

'Yes. They have already arrived at Hawkswood. Joyce told me that they have cried bitterly for their father, and then said primly that they are willing to do whatever he thinks best for them. She also said that they understand that I have not done anything wrong. I think they haven't been able to bring themselves to face the fact that he was prepared to see me and my good Roger Brockley ruined or even hanged – why, I don't know and would very much like to know! When the girls arrived, we were very awkward with each other. Sybil is looking after them now and perhaps she will manage better. After all, Frost was proposing her as their stepmother. Well, he is to be set free before long and the bad feeling may pass. I hope so, they are likeable girls. I must say, I am astonished that Frost should choose me as their guardian. He can't have very kindly feelings towards me. And I'm not very clear about what will happen after his release. I suppose he will want them back.'

'I think not,' said Walsingham. 'Because of the fine he has to pay, Knoll House will have to be sold. He will have no home for them and at times he will, of course, be away on his voyages. I imagine he will stay with his brother in London and then find himself somewhere to rent, but it wouldn't be much of a background for the girls. Hawkswood is a better one. However, he did save something from his ruin,' Walsingham continued with a saturnine smile. 'His brother visited him while he was awaiting trial, and went away with instructions. Frost owns – or owned, I should say – a parcel of land in the Midlands. It's divided into three smallholdings, rented out

separately. He apparently told his brother where to find
the deeds and asked him to see that the smallholdings were
made over, respectively, to his two daughters and a girl called
Susie Hopkins, who was their maid. I believe she is carrying
his child. Fine goings on in the household I sent you to! We
found out all about it, naturally . . .'

Naturally, I thought with wry amusement. Walsingham probably knew when Frost last had a cold in the head and how
often he filed his toenails.

'We have always kept an eye on activities at Knoll House,'
said Walsingham, unaware of my private commentary. 'And
after his arrest we questioned his lawyer in London about his
affairs. We learned what he had done with his Midland property.
Susie Hopkins has gone home to her parents, but I suppose she
will now have an income, and a dowry if she marries. And the
Frost girls will have dowries too. He moved so fast that the law
had no chance to confiscate the smallholdings, and in the
end contented itself with a fine.'

'He'll probably do well out of selling his silver collection,'
I said dryly. 'Do you think I am now likely to become the
permanent guardian of the twins?'

'You will probably end up having to arrange their marriages.
Meanwhile, I suppose you and Mistress Jester will continue
to instruct them in embroidery.'

'I shall do my best,' I said. 'But Sybil . . . has been much
upset by this whole business. She has decided to travel to
Scotland to make a long stay with her married daughter,
Ambrosia, in Edinburgh. She will be welcome there, apparently, as she can help Ambrosia with her young family, and
is looking forward to it.'

'I am sorry,' Sybil had said, only a few days before I left
Hawkswood in answer to the summons from Walsingham.
'But I have made my mind up. As soon as you heard from
Master Frost and learned that he will be home again in a few
months, I knew what I must do. I have exchanged letters with
Ambrosia and her husband. I hired the fastest courier I could
afford and he brought back a most cordial invitation. I can't
. . . I can't bear the thought of what has happened lately.

Ursula, I spoke the truth when I told you that I was – still am – in love with Giles Frost.'

She paused. I smiled at her. She gave me a small, tired nod. 'Yes, Ursula. In love. Not just attracted. *In love.* I never thought I would ever – *ever* – feel like that again, and feel it for such a man. A traitor! A Catholic! Someone who has tried to trap you, ruin you, dear, dear Ursula! But it's the truth. I . . . am hungry to be with him, not just to be in his arms, but to talk to him, share everyday life with him, become part of him. It's disgraceful. I can't believe such a thing has happened to me – that I could let it happen! I feel as though I too am a traitor and ought to be in the Tower . . .'

'Sybil, please don't! Please! Falling in love isn't something one can help. It just happens. It happened to me!'

'But when it came to the point of choosing between Matthew and Hugh, you chose Hugh. In the end, your head and your integrity chose the right path. I must let mine do the same. It would be better if I were in Scotland. I intend to spend Christmas with my daughter and her family, and I will probably stay on.'

'I see,' I said, and tried to smile again but failed. 'It seems that no one can wreck a female friendship more thoroughly than a man!'

We had been together for . . . I tried to work it out, and realized that it was seventeen years. And as friends and companions, we had been through so much. I would have cried myself to sleep that night, except that after I had gone to bed Gladys appeared, armed with a potion.

'I knows all about it,' she said. 'Mistress Jester, she told me what she'd told you and said look after Ursula, it'll likely bring on a migraine. She said she was sorry but she couldn't help it. So you drink this and you'll sleep quick and wake up calm. Nothing lasts for ever. I shan't be here for ever, either. And seeing that I can't walk right and I've that many aches and pains, I won't be sorry when it's time.'

'Please don't talk like that, Gladys.'

'You might not believe it,' said Gladys, 'but I'm mighty sorry for what I did.'

'What *you* did?' I had never seen Gladys contrite before.

'Offering that potion to put the Knoll servants to sleep. Whole thing was my fault. I might of bin your death!' Her voice dropped to a whisper. 'And Master Brockley's too!' said Gladys miserably.

'It's all over now. And it *was* what I wanted,' I said. 'In a way I was a fool, and I am sorry too. If only I had stuck to what I planned to do at first and just told Stagg – Hunt – where the chest was and refused to do anything more, his plan would have collapsed.'

I felt bitter, but mostly with myself. I was horrified now at the easy way I had been got to agree, against what I even then knew was my better judgement, to remove that chest. The disaster that had so nearly overtaken me was far more my fault than Gladys's.

She was right in saying that nothing lasts for ever. Sybil and I had been close friends for seventeen years, but they were over now.

'Before you return to Hawkswood,' Walsingham told me. 'Frost wants to see you. Will you visit him in the Tower? His accommodation is quite dignified. He isn't in a dungeon.'

'If he wishes it,' I said, puzzled.

'I wish it,' said Walsingham unexpectedly. 'There are still things that are unclear. He admitted – and so did Anthony Hunt – that they colluded in that shocking scheme to discredit you, but what Frost has never explained is why he was willing to be involved. You have said yourself that you'd like to know the answer to that.'

'Yes, I would,' I agreed.

'Frost is Catholic,' said Walsingham, 'and sells information to the Spanish – whereas Hunt's brother, Simeon Wilmot, was so against the Catholics and Spain that he tried to get Mary Stuart assassinated. When Wilmot was executed, Hunt was enraged. I have learned that Hunt has never known about Frost's faith. He thinks the services held in the Knoll House chapel are in accordance with the law. And yet Frost knew perfectly well why Hunt wanted to attack you. So why did Frost agree to help him? What was in it for him? He will not say, and I can only justify the rack as a means of making criminals confess *what* they have done. Not simply to ask *why*. But I would like to know, and so would you.'

His dark eyes suddenly gleamed with the grim sense of humour that occasionally surfaced in him. 'Well, we know all we need to know about Hunt. Your Gladys Morgan did wonders for our case when she showed us your caricature in that window. He really does hate you so much that he couldn't resist declaring it somehow. He couldn't say it aloud, so he said it through his artistic fingers. I wish we had had your Gladys in court,' he added wistfully. 'You did well to have the offending pane of glass removed and brought to be inspected by the jury, but Gladys's testimony would have been as salty as the ocean if she had had a chance to give it. I wish we could have heard it.'

'Gladys behaves better these days than in the past,' I said. 'She quietened down after she was nearly executed for witchcraft. But I still always fear that if provoked, she will curse people. She was best kept away from the hearing – her curses are exceptionally lurid! I will see Master Frost, since you wish it and he has asked. Though why he should talk to me when he won't talk to his questioners, I don't know.'

'Well, you were the intended victim. He may feel differently about you now. And since he has requested a visit from you, he must want to tell you something.' There was a pause while an apple tart was brought in. Then Walsingham said: 'Have you had a new pane of glass put into the church window at Hawkswood?'

I shook my head. 'No. I felt such a distaste for that window that I have had the whole thing removed. The place is boarded up once again. There is another maker of stained glass in Guildford – an old established business run by a man called John Hines. He has taken over some of Stagg's craftsmen, so they haven't suffered too badly because their master is in the Tower. Hines is making a complete new window for me. It isn't going to be too costly and, of course, I haven't had to pay Stagg.'

I didn't mention that, although I had paid Hines for the new design, Sybil had decreed the details, fairly standing over him to make sure he was using her ideas. She said that this was her farewell gift to me, and she had given of her best. The resultant picture did include some demons with pitchforks, and once more they were driving not people but a flock of brown goats towards the mouth of a cavern. But this time the goats were simply goats and there was pity in the faces of some of the blessed. These were dressed in white, with golden haloes, and were climbing a golden stair towards heaven, led by an angel, as before, but some of them were looking back with obvious compassion at the unhappy goats.

Sybil had said: 'Why should the blessed not pity the damned? Their own friends, even members of their families, could be among them. If it's heretical – well, I'm prepared to argue about it.'

'It's beautiful,' I said, as I explained this to Walsingham. 'It makes its point, but it isn't ugly or crude. No small children will be disturbed by it. My latest adventure has at least had one good outcome!'

Walsingham laughed out loud. 'I have never approved of a woman doing the things that you have been doing for so many years, Ursula, but I must admit you do them with style.'

'I'd much rather not do them at all,' I said. 'I would prefer a quiet life at home. But I will visit Frost today.'

'I have prepared a pass for you,' Walsingham replied.

TWENTY-TWO
The Value of a Merchant Ship

I had visited prisoners in the Tower before and it was never a pleasant business, even when they were not chained up in dungeons. Frost was in a tower room and he was better housed than some since he had a fire, though not much of one, and also a bed, a table, a wooden chair and a few books. The narrow window, set slantwise in the thick wall, gave a view, albeit a restricted one, of the river Thames. But the room was barely large enough to contain the meagre furniture and its walls closed us round: grey stone, grim and unpitying, silent witnesses to the terror and despair of those they had imprisoned before. There were names cut into them here and there. I averted my eyes from them, and tried to avert my thoughts from the sound of the turnkey locking me in. Brockley and I might well have found ourselves in a place like this, or perhaps a worse one. And here I was, alone with one of the men who had tried to put us there.

Frost was reading, seated on the chair, but he closed the book and rose as the door was shut behind me. He tossed the book on to the bed. 'So you came,' he said.

'Yes. Sir Francis said you had asked to see me.' I detested this man but I spoke pleasantly. When I thought of what had so nearly happened to Brockley and me, I shuddered with anger, but I did not want to be harsh towards a man in the Tower.

He was thinner and very pale, probably because he hadn't been out of doors for a long time. He looked more than ever as if he had been left out in a blizzard.

He said: 'I asked for you to come because my daughters are in your care and there are things I must explain to you. I hope they are behaving well. I wrote to them – the Hambles took the letter for me – and made it plain that I wished them to become your wards. I told them not to be angry with you, for you never intended harm to me – indeed it was I who intended harm to you.'

'They are safely at Hawkswood,' I said diplomatically and decided not to enlarge. They were good girls who had been taught that they must obey their parents, so were obeying their father. But the twins who arrived at Hawkswood were downcast and, although perfectly polite, looked at me askance, even though Frost had written to them telling the whole truth.

'Everything came out at the trial,' Joyce had said to me, soon after their arrival. Her voice was calm but cool and she did not look me in the eyes. 'He knows that it would reach us sooner or later. He preferred that we should be told at once, accurately and not through gossip.' Then she did look at me, and there was accusation in her eyes. 'Why did you let yourself be led, like a calf to the butcher? Why didn't you just tell Master . . . Hunt . . . and Eleanor Liversedge that you had found the chest and then left it to them to decide what to do about it? *Why* did a woman of your age and dignity play the fool, stealing the thing, creeping out of the house with it – causing all this?'

'I am sorry,' I said inadequately. I did not say: 'I heard the call of the wild geese.' Joyce would have thought I had lost my senses. Instead, I said: 'Eleanor cried.' I think Joyce decided I had lost my senses anyway.

Now, in Frost's room in the Tower, I said: 'I am happy to look after your girls.' He looked relieved and I found myself actually in sympathy with him. Naturally, he would be worried about his daughters. I smiled at him and tried to lighten the air by saying: 'I am glad I don't have to shelter Susie as well. My youngest maidservant, Margery, would like to train as a tirewoman. She will attend to the girls. I understand that Susie has gone home.'

'I have provided for her. In time she will forget about loving me, though she doesn't believe that now. She'll marry, and I have made sure she has a dowry. You and Mistress Jester need not concern yourselves with her.'

'Mistress Jester is going to Scotland,' I said. I was finding it quite easy, after all, to talk to him in an amiable fashion.

'She has family there and has decided to live with them in future.'

'Because of me?'

'Yes.'

'I don't think I ever really expected her to marry me,' said Frost. 'But I greatly wished it, and dared to hope.'

We were silent for a moment. Then I became businesslike. 'Master Frost, you say you asked for me to visit you because you wished to tell me something concerning your daughters. On my side, I agreed to come here because there are questions that I want to ask and that Walsingham would like me to ask, too. Which shall we deal with first?'

'Let me explain matters in my own way,' said Frost. 'But I would ask you to realize that there are things that I don't want shared with Walsingham. Can I trust you to be discreet?'

'Provided you aren't about to confess to a crime – another crime!' I said with emphasis.

'No, I'm not. Very well. It may sound as though I am wandering round the houses, but if you bear with me all will become clear. First, I daresay Walsingham has told you that I have agreed to become one of his agents. To continue passing information to Spain, but to do so knowing that it's inaccurate – all in the interests of defending England from the Spanish and from Mary Stuart.'

'Yes, he has. And that Master Hunt must hold those same opinions. At least, his brother Simeon Wilmot did, and Hunt wished to avenge Wilmot's death. They can hardly be your opinions, and yet you conspired with Hunt to harm me. One of the questions both Walsingham and I wish to ask is why?'

Frost had been sitting on the bed, having waved me to the chair. He rose, walked across the room and then came back.

'This is complicated. What you want to ask me and what I want to tell you are tangled together. Initially I had reasons for disliking you, or thought I had. Until you actually moved into Knoll House and began to teach my daughters – and did it so well – I knew little of you, except that you had habitually involved yourself in things that are not a woman's business. When Hunt asked me to help him to . . .'

'Entrap me?'

'All right, to entrap you. When Hunt sought my help, I agreed because I believed that you were something that I disapproved of, the kind of woman I was willing enough to see set down—'

'*Set down!* You nearly brought Brockley and me to . . . the gallows!' My buried anger spurted out of me. 'And you were willing enough to make use of my skills with a needle.'

'I know. I am truly sorry,' he said wryly. 'At the time, I remember hoping you wouldn't give my daughters any wrong ideas. After all, you weren't to be in my house for long – you were only supposed to be there for a week or two, until the plot came to a head. But once you were under my roof, Mistress Stannard, I found I couldn't dislike you.' He shook his white head with an air of surprise. 'I had expected you to be hard, mannish, dictatorial, and you are not. And your friend Mistress Jester was enchanting. I had a complete change of heart. You know,' he said thoughtfully, 'that was when things began to go awry. I realized that far from being a dubious person, you were just the kind of woman I would like as a guide for my girls. But by then it seemed too late to stop. I just hoped it would all be over quickly and told myself, well, although she knows how to create a good impression, she *has* dipped a finger into some pies that no woman should concern herself with.'

'Oh, really!' I said, exasperated.

'I think I hoped that perhaps you wouldn't let yourself be caught. Perhaps you wouldn't try to make off with the chest.'

He had no idea how much I wished I hadn't!

'Everything seemed to slow down,' Frost said wearily. 'Indeed because of the succession of invalids in the attic, I thought you would *never* begin to search there – until dear Jane came to the rescue.'

'You surely don't mean . . .?'

'What? No, no! Jane is as innocent as an angel, she simply wanted her lute. But to get back to the point, I have to tell you that I am not on the side of Mary Stuart and Spain. I am not a Catholic, or anything else, now. I was a Catholic once, but I lost my faith.'

Evening was near and the daylight was fading. But the firelight played over his pale face, tinting his skin and hair with red, as if he was becoming flushed. Perhaps he was, I couldn't tell. 'I see,' I said. 'Or rather, I don't see.' Anger was being replaced by incomprehension. Confused, I asked: 'How did it happen?'

'It began on a starry night, with a crescent moon and thousands upon thousands of stars. I began to think: "Can all this just be a setting for human beings?" And then I read some books about stars and planets, and it all seemed so huge, so vast – all that, and just us in the middle, with all our faults and flaws and muddles . . . Then I woke up one morning and knew I didn't believe in my religion, or any religion, any more. It was odd, and I struggled against it at first. For some time, in fact. It felt so strange, like losing a foothold or falling off a cliff. Then at last came the sense of freedom. And for years,' said Frost, 'I have been falsifying the information that I've been passing to Spain.'

'You've been . . .?' I was too astounded to finish the sentence.

Frost nodded. 'Yes. Even before that shattering starry night, I had been becoming horrified by what I had heard of the Inquisition and knew I couldn't go on supporting Spain. I have no wish whatsoever to see their beliefs enforced here in England. Or any belief, come to that – but certainly not theirs. That is why I have agreed to work for Walsingham. But he mustn't know my real reason – my loss of faith.'

'Why not?' I said, bewildered. 'If it has led you to work with us . . .'

'Loss of faith is a dangerous thing to admit, even to Walsingham. He opposes the Catholics but he is ardent enough in his own beliefs. And we are all supposed to obey our sovereign and accept what religion we are told is right. I needed to explain my secret to you in private because you must not be confused about the way you are to guide my daughters. The girls don't know about my changed beliefs, though I suspect that Lambert guessed something. He has upbraided me at times for being lax about Catholic observances.'

'I overheard him doing so once,' I said.

'Did you? I have dismissed him, of course. He knew nothing of the plot, by the way.'

'I know. Walsingham said as much to me. Dr Lambert,' I said reminiscently, 'always reminded me of a puzzled spaniel. I think he may have sensed that something was going on but didn't know what.'

Frost said seriously: 'Although my girls are unaware of my changed beliefs, they do know about the plot against you. They had to know, since I was consigning them to you. But I have lain awake wondering what they now think of me, and fearing that you will be unkind to them because of me. One reason why I asked to see you was so that I could beg you to promise that you will not. Please promise that! Please promise me that you will not! Please!'

'Of course I promise!' I found I was surprised that he needed to ask, so far had I been from intending anything else. Indeed, I had been worrying over how to overcome *their* hostility.

'I hardly knew what else to do with them while I was away,' said Frost. 'They are too young to be left without guidance. Also, I fear that society may look sideways at them on my account. Your social position may protect them, and they know you and have some respect for you. Those were among my reasons for choosing you. Moreover, after getting to know you myself, I found that I trusted you.'

'You can,' I assured him.

'Thank you. I am truly grateful. Now, I must tell you how I wish you to guide them. They have been reared as secret Catholics. But now, for their own safety and happiness in a dangerous world, I ask you to encourage them to adopt Protestant beliefs. I wish you to find Protestant husbands for them. Guide them well, I beg you. I had to explain this – and to request this – face to face. I am sure you understand.'

'Yes, I do understand,' I said. 'I will try. But please, Master Frost, you have still not told me *why* you agreed to help Hunt. That I *can't* understand. It wasn't just because you disapproved of my reputation, surely? And why did you go on with it when you had changed your mind about that? Were you afraid of Hunt? And how did you even get to know him?'

'We met when he was visiting his brother, Simeon Wilmot, here in the Tower. I was also visiting a friend who was a prisoner here – a foolish former tutor of mine, a Protestant minister who had preached an unwise sermon before the queen when she was supposed to be going to marry a Catholic prince. He rebuked her and got himself locked up. He's free now, and I trust won't make that mistake again. He tried to tell me that he was prepared to face martyrdom for the sake of his faith, but I told him he would change his mind when he was on the scaffold. I think it had an effect.'

'Wise advice,' I commented.

'I think so, too. That day, by accident, I met Hunt. We liked each other. We became friends. But he never realized that I had a Catholic household. Lambert was always discreet in the presence of people he didn't know well. I was sympathetic when I learned how Hunt's brother had tried to rid England of Mary Stuart. She is dangerous. She is the key that could unlock England for Philip of Spain. I understand why you didn't want to—'

'Murder her,' I said coldly. 'I have undertaken many secret tasks for the queen but never that!'

'Quite. But I still rather wish you had made an exception for Mary Stuart. I am sure you would have been most competent.'

'Thank you!' I said. And not at all in a grateful voice, but Frost didn't seem to notice.

'You say,' said Frost, 'that you doubt that I really joined in Hunt's plot against you just because I disliked your unwomanly reputation. You may be wondering what else was in it for me. Well, there was an inducement. That is what kept me to the plan even when I had ceased to disapprove of you and had even begun to hope that you would escape my toils.'

'What was it?'

'My ship – well, our ship, since I share her with my brother – is old. She needs too many repairs, too often. I really do need to replace her, and Hunt offered to do so at his own expense. My brother could be told that I had prevented some dishonest person from stealing valuables that belonged to him, and that this was a practical form of thanks.'

He spoke in a perfectly ordinary tone of voice as though such a mundane, mercenary reason for endangering two lives was quite reasonable. For a moment, I was staggered into silence.

Then I said: 'Now I know my value and Brockley's. Our combined worth is that of a merchant vessel. Well, well. No wonder you don't want Walsingham to know everything!'

There was a moment of tension in the room. It emanated from me. I was recoiling from this snowman of a man with his twisted ideas. He seemed to regard religions as if they were organizations that one could join or resign from as a matter of convenience, and he seemed quite unable to understand – or even recognize – the horror of the danger that Brockley and I had faced. He seemed indifferent to it, even though he had faced that danger himself. I was trembling with hatred.

With a giant effort, I kept myself still and quiet and let my outrage settle, and then I said: 'I have agreed to be discreet. And I don't want your daughters to be caused any more pain. For their sake, I will do nothing to blacken your name further in Walsingham's eyes. When I report on this meeting, I shall tell Walsingham that you wished to discuss your daughters' education, and that you also told me that tales of the Inquisition gradually convinced you that you were wrong to spy for the Spanish so that already, on your own account, you have begun to pass them false information.'

'Yes. Thank you.' He smiled broadly, looking amused. 'You told me a tale of eighty warships being made ready before Christmas, did you not? Was that false information?'

'Yes,' I said shortly.

'I thought so. But I was ahead of you. I didn't mention shipyards in the north, but I had already warned Spain that a hundred and five warships were likely to be ready early in the new year.'

I did not know what to make of him. I loathed him, and yet not only had I intended to speak to him politely during this conversation, at first I had even found it quite natural to do so. He had brought Brockley and me near to a dreadful fate for a shockingly inadequate reason, and yet I still couldn't regard him as wicked. My simmering hatred kept faltering, drowning in bewilderment. He was foolish and insensitive, but despite being beset by prejudices and mercenary temptations and a sorry lack of imagination, in a confused manner he had looked after Susie, cared for his daughters' safety, been shocked by the Inquisition, and faced and accepted what his reason had told him one starlit night. He still seemed to have a kind of integrity – like a useful plant, a cabbage for example, trying to assert itself amid a tangle of chickweed and dandelions. But how did he, how did anyone, ever become so muddled?

I said: 'Walsingham will be happy to learn how very willingly you will work for him. You should have mentioned all this at your trial.'

'It was too public. I feared reprisals. I sail in Spanish waters, and Spain has sympathizers here. Such testimony might have got to Spanish ears.'

'Master Frost, I repeat: I will keep your counsel. Walsingham will never know how Hunt bought your co-operation.' He flinched at the word 'bought'. 'Nor will I tell him of your loss of faith. You are right to be reticent about that. It is better not to think too much about matters of belief. I conform, I pray sometimes, I go to church. I even enjoy attending St Mary's in Hawkswood. But at heart I have seen too much of the world. I can't believe it was deliberately made as it is. There is so much cruelty, so much sickness, so much grief and death . . .'

I thought of my first husband – Gerald, Meg's father – dying young of smallpox. Of a hideous description that Uncle Herbert and Aunt Tabitha, my guardians, had given me of a burning they had witnessed. Of Dale's stark terror when we were in France and she was arrested for heresy. 'I think I lost my own faith, long ago,' I said. 'But I make no show of it.'

And I never would. I had held my peace and conformed. It was safer. For Dr Joynings, I was and would remain the respectable Mistress Stannard who had made St Mary's a gift of benches and a hitching rail. I wondered how many others there were like Giles Frost and me; and whether some day the word 'heresy' would no longer exist, and we would be free to be ourselves. That was one more opinion I would never express aloud.

I was invited to stay at court until the new year, but I convinced the queen that I could not. The Frost girls were at Hawkswood

in Sybil's care, and until I returned she could not leave for
Scotland. Christopher Spelton had been at court and went
home just ahead of me. By him, I let my household know
when to expect me.

I returned to Hawkswood two weeks before Christmas. I
caught sight of Hawkswood with feelings of relief, as I had
done a good many times before. Its chimneys always came
into view first and they meant home. They meant peace and
quiet and safety, and the end of what was often a tiring journey.
It had now turned very cold, but although Brockley and I
were both on horseback, we could not travel fast because
we were keeping pace with the coach, which contained Dale
and our luggage.

We therefore came into the courtyard at a dignified
pace. Hawthorn, Flood and Phoebe all came out to greet
us, accompanied by the twins. But whereas the others were
beaming, and Hawthorn welcomed us by announcing that
he already had a chicken on the spit and would make his
special white-wine sauce for our supper, Joyce and Jane
simply curtsied and then stood with folded hands, watching
us dismount.

I slid out of Jaunty's saddle and greeted them carefully,
with tactful restraint, expressing the hope that they were both
well and saying I looked forward to taking supper with them
presently. They made suitable rejoinders, in polite voices.
Trying to ease matters by talking of something that might
interest them, I said: 'Have you gone on with the parterre
pattern? Will it make a wall-hanging?'

'Yes, we have. It is finished.' I was pleased to see Joyce's
face brighten. She looked round and saw Sybil coming out of
the house and said: 'Mistress Jester, may we show Mistress
Stannard the parterre wall-hanging?'

'Of course,' said Sybil, and then said to me: 'It is in my
baggage, the twins have given it to me as a parting gift. It
is a credit to our teaching and their determination to learn.
But . . .' Her voice became serious. 'It is in my baggage,
because I am packed, ready to leave for Edinburgh. And it
is time I set off.'

'I expected that,' I said and managed to sound matter of

fact about it, though I felt as if a knife had been driven into me.

Harry came out then to join us. He was too grown-up now to rush into my embrace, but he bowed and said: 'Welcome home, Mother!' and the gladness in his smile was balm after the chilly formality of the twins. We all began to move towards the door into the hall, and I found to my surprise that Jane was gently tugging at my cloak. I turned to her quickly. 'Yes, Jane?'

Jane was smiling. It was the first time I had seen her smile since she came to Hawkswood. 'We have a guest. Master Taverner is here and is in the great hall.'

Tossing my cloak and hat to Phoebe, I made haste into the hall ahead of the others and found Martin Taverner sitting by the fire.

'I thought your household should have the pleasure of greeting you before I did,' he said, rising to his feet to bow.

'You are welcome, Master Taverner. Did you know I would be coming home today?'

'Yes. I have been staying with Dr Joynings, awaiting your return, and Mistress Jester has kept me informed.'

'I have been to Greenwich, and have also visited Master Frost in the Tower. I have brought a letter from him for his daughters.'

Taverner said: 'The day after that disgraceful scene in the church, I went to see Daniel Johns and Eleanor. I wanted to . . . apologize, I suppose. To set things right between them and myself as far as I could, though I also wished to make it finally clear that my betrothal to Eleanor was over and to wish her well for the future. Johns received me pleasantly enough. He let me see Eleanor because I wanted to, but warned me what I would find. Oh, lord, I did feel sorry for her! Poor girl, she was in bed, lying face down, attended by a dragon of a maid who glared at me as if it was all my fault. Perhaps it was. I didn't see enough of her during our betrothal. If I had, I might have had a chance to warn her away from her uncle's dreadful plot. The betrothal was very much an arranged business between myself and Master Stagg, and occasionally Master Johns. He left most of it to

Stagg – or Hunt, I should say. He just looked for someone in some branch of the glass trade. I tried to say I was sorry for everything and wished her well but she just moaned and cursed me. At least she isn't likely to become involved in any more questionable schemes . . .'

'I daresay. But poor girl, all the same!' I said, in heartfelt tones. 'The aunt and uncle who brought me up were harsh sometimes. I know what Eleanor has experienced.'

'I wanted you to be sure,' said Taverner, 'that there is no longer any entanglement between myself and Eleanor. I am now a free man, Mistress Stannard. I got here early today and have been talking to your wards, and most especially to Jane. From the first moment that I set eyes on her . . .'

'I know,' I said. 'I saw it.'

His eyes widened. I nodded. He said: 'For the moment, you are her guardian. I ask your permission to pay court to her.'

'I feel,' I said, 'that Jane should have the final say. She has been reared as a Catholic, but her father would like her to have a husband who may steer her into safer waters. How do you feel about that?'

'I know about her upbringing, and naturally hope to smooth that away in time. Will you call her?'

This was just what Frost had wanted. 'Of course,' I said.

I smiled, but my heart was heavy. I was going to miss Sybil very much. I had hoped that the Frost girls would warm to me in time and could be company for a while, but I clearly wouldn't keep Jane for long and Joyce would no doubt follow shortly. Indeed, it would be my task to see that she found a good husband. It would be better so. The twins wouldn't want to stay too long beneath my roof. I approved of Martin Taverner, and Jane would be safe with him. When both the twins were gone, I wondered, would I feel very lonely?

No, I would not! I had the Brockleys and I had Harry. Watching him mature into manhood was a pleasure that stretched ahead for me. And anyone who was blessed with such companions as my son and the Brockleys – and Gladys – could never justifiably call themselves lonely.

Sybil would not forget me. She had a memento of our time together in Knoll House in the shape of the parterre wall-hanging. And I would have a memento of her. Her ideas were enshrined in the new window that was soon to be installed in St Mary's church in Hawkswood village. Every time I looked at it, I would be reminded of her.